stab wound

A novel

by

James Gottesman

ACKNOWLEDGMENTS

Thanks go to many. Gloria Brown Gottesman, my longtime co-conspirator, like always, was brutally and painfully honest.

I need to thank the initial readers of the book, all friends, particularly Kim Boestam, Leslie Bauman, Susan Tapper, Greg Gottesman, Chuck Caplan and Ruth Bunin. If I forgot someone – oops.

I used Reba Hilbert as my editor for the first time. Where has she been? Best yet and great advice.

I always thank Diane Mackay Richie, the first person to teach me how to write. She may not remember, but I do.

Although I listened to everything and everyone, I didn't always follow all their suggestions. Alas.

I hope you enjoy Stab Wound.

DEDICATED

To no one else but Mrs. Brown's Lovely Daughter

Mrs. Brown, You've Got a Lovely Daughter, sung by Herman's Hermits, #1 on the U.S. Billboard Hot 100, May 1965

Chapter 1

Lopez Island, Washington, Thursday, May 8th, 2002

Nicole Marrone skip-scurried out the east gate of Lopez School and bounded onto Bus #2. She had no reason to think her life would change by the end of the next day. None at all.

Despite a sunny San Juan Islands afternoon, clouds of exhaust from just departed Buses #1 and #3 obscured Center Road like a tagger armed only with gray paint.

Mr. Harrington, the #2 bus driver, looked at his watch. *3:31 p.m.* "I'd never guess who's late again," he mumbled.

"Sorry, Mr. H," Nicole said with her biggest smile.

Harrington smiled back. He adored Nicole, the most upbeat teenager he'd ever met. He gave the eighth grader his customary eye-roll and pointed his right thumb backward over his shoulder. "Take a seat, Miss Blue Eyes."

Nicole quickly viewed the empty aisle seat next to her older brother, Tony, who smiled while he patted the well-worn black Naugahyde. Nicole's bus-mates had long given up any notion that she would sit anywhere else. Tony, three years the elder, had been held back, now twice, into the ninth-grade and she couldn't let anyone sit next to him, lest the teasing would commence.

Bus #2's large diesel engine sputtered, as if it had a bad mid-winter cough, then found its rhythm and started towards Center Road.

Nicole, head whirling, thought about the catapult she planned to create for her school project. She had seen the movie *Gladiator* two nights earlier and had been fascinated by, then dreamt about, a Roman catapult used in a battle scene. The next morning she woke up thinking, *I can make that.*

As the bus rumbled east along Vista Road, Nicole finished her preliminary drawing of her fire-and-stone-hurling machine.

Tony turned away from his customary window-trance and espied his sister's plans. "Whatcha doin'?"

"Designing a catapult," Nicole said.

"A 'what-a-pulled'?"

Nicole said, "Cat – a – pult. It's a weapon used centuries ago to throw huge stones or fireballs at castles. They don't make 'em anymore."

Tony turned back to the window. "Catapult, catapult, catapult, catapult..."

Buddy Szalwinski turned around from the seat in front of Tony and glared at the annoying perseverations. Szalwinski needed little excuse to start taunting Tony, or anyone. "Catapult, pull a cat, Tony's a cat, Tony's dumb as a cat..."

Nicole immediately leaned forward and snarled, "One more word and I'll punch your lights out." She continued glaring until Szalwinski turned away. Nicole hit the back of his seat with the heel of her hand and waited. Szalwinski knew enough to not turn around. Facing her brother, Nicole took his hand and gently squeezed it.

"That's enough, Tony," Nicole whispered. "We'll talk about catapults at home tonight. Okay?"

"What castle are you going to attack?" Tony asked softly. "I want to attack with you."

Tony didn't wait for an answer and turned his gaze back to the road.

"None. No castles, last I looked on Lopez," Nicole said, returning to her drawing.

Tony watched the pine trees zip by, lined up in soldier's formation standing guard over Vista Road. Tony saluted a minute later, after three battalions of trees had been inspected. Tony turned back to his sister. "Nic, you're so smart," he said. "I know it and everyone in school knows it. You're the smartest person I know."

"You're plenty smart. Just different," Nicole said. "Nobody on this bus could have taken Mom's old clock apart and repaired it. You think anyone on the bus knows the capitals of every country in the world like you do? I'm okay smart but I don't have your good heart or common sense. You care about everyone else first. I couldn't ask for a better brother."

"Well, maybe a smarter one," Tony said. "I try. It just doesn't come easy for me."

"Yeah."

Tony turned back to the window and softly mumbled, "Catapult, catapult..."

The bus stopped at the entrance to Dusty Road, a narrow, quarter-mile rutted dirt road, to let Nicole and Tony off. The intersection was as close as they'd get to home.

As Tony and Nicole walked together, she eyed the large madrona tree root that rose out of the road near Jane Redlim's house. The same root that caused Nicole to trip and break her wrist four years earlier. *They'll never fix it.* She kicked the root confidently to establish the indisputable truth that she now ruled Dusty Road.

Eyes forward, Nicole thought back to the catapult and whether her father could break away from his fledgling restaurant business to help her. Tony and her mom would be no help. *Maybe I'll do it myself.*

"Tony, listen carefully," Nicole said. "Tomorrow is Thursday and I won't be coming home on the bus. I've got a soccer game and Jodie's mom will drive me home. Make sure you sit next to Sarah Schneider and nowhere near any of the Szalwinski brothers. I'll remind you again at lunch tomorrow and I'll talk to Sarah."

Tony nodded.

Nicole made no note of a black sedan facing them, parked on a side road to Mr. Fadder's shed.

* * *

The next afternoon, Tony exited the bus alone and headed happily down Dusty Road. The Szalwinskis hadn't bothered him. He had not seen the black sedan the day before nor did he notice it this day. He didn't hear the car's engine running or see its dark-tinted glass. As he walked past the side road, he didn't hear or see a man exiting the car's back door just behind him.

* * *

Susan Marrone returned home at 5:45 p.m. to an empty house. By six-thirty, hyperventilation had turned her lips and fingertips prickly-numb. Her hands shook so badly she had trouble dialing the next mother on her school list. But she persisted, finally with success.

"What's up, Sue?"

"Have you seen Tony?" she pleaded. She couldn't remember which mother she had just called.

"No, I haven't seen him. Slow down. Are you okay?"

"I can't slow down. I can't find him. I can't find Tony. Nicole is playing soccer and I'm afraid to leave the house in case somebody calls."

"I'm sure everything is okay. Was he supposed to be at our house?"

"No, not that I know of, but...but...he's not home," cried Susan. "You're the fifth mother I've called. Tony didn't tell me he was going anywhere. He knows the rules. The bus dropped him off at four. Sarah Schneider said she saw him get off the bus. But his backpack isn't here, so I don't think he ever came home. It's not like him."

"Hold on. I'll ask Billy if he's seen Tony or knows..."

Susan interrupted, "Oh. Oh. I've got a call coming in." The phone's LCD display said, *Stevens Cascade Hospital.* "I'll call..."

The words "you back" were chopped off once Susan pushed the phone's *FLASH* button.

"Hello. Hello," Susan yelled into the receiver.

"Is this the home of Anthony Marrone?" a calm voice answered.

"Yes, yes. I'm Tony's mother. Has something happened?"

"This is Nurse Tanya Hetlinger calling from Stevens Cascade Hospital. First, your son is okay. He's stable."

"He's stable? What happened? Where is he?"

"As I said I am calling from Stevens Cascade Hospital. We're located in Index, Washington, on Highway 2. Your son was brought here seventy-five minutes ago. He was unconscious and appeared as if had been assaulted. He suffered a stab wound to his left back along with bruises to his face, legs, and arms."

"Index? I know where that is. What was he doing in Index? That's impossible. He couldn't be in Index. Are you sure it's my son? Is this some kind of prank?"

"He's about fifteen or sixteen," Hetlinger said, "black, curly hair, brown eyes, a small curved scar on his chin and..."

"That's him. That's him. Oh, my God. Is he okay? Is he okay? Oh, please God. Is he...."

"Mrs. Marrone, he's doing fine now," Hetlinger interrupted. "We found his name and phone number inside a hidden pocket in his jacket. His left kidney had been severely lacerated and he was bleeding internally."

"Oh God. Tell me he's okay again."

"Your son is stable and he's very lucky," Hetlinger said.

"What do you mean, lucky? He disappeared and was stabbed," Susan cried.

"I meant he's fortunate because Stevens Cascade is a small hospital with limited services. We're not usually staffed or equipped to handle major trauma. Luckily, a surgeon, Dr. Charles McNeil from Everett, owns a summer cottage in town and happened to be nearby when your son presented. Dr. McNeil felt your son's situation was critical and did not think he could be transferred to a major trauma hospital safely. He operated emergently here at Stevens and stopped the bleeding but needed to remove your son's left kidney."

"Oh my God. That's terrible."

"Dr. McNeil said he'd be fine with one kidney. Like nothing ever happened," Hetlinger said. "He'll be in recovery for thirty or forty minutes, but we're not staffed to handle this level of post-op care night. As soon as he is stable we'll transfer him to Everett General by ambulance. I expect he'll be in Everett within one and a half to two hours. Again, he's doing fine."

Chapter 2

Henry, Susan and Nicole Marrone rode the 11:00 p.m. ferry to Anacortes, the next and last eastbound boat leaving Lopez Island to the mainland on a weekday night.

Henry Marrone said nothing, holding a near death grip on their 1975 Datsun 710 steering wheel as Susan repeated her wailing. "Why?" "Why, Tony?" "He's so innocent." "Who could do such a terrible thing?" "Why?"

Henry would not answer other than, "I don't know."

Nicole finally echoed her mother. "Dad, why did this happen to Tony? You need to answer Mom."

Henry Marrone's jaw tightened until the veins coursing above his temples bulged deep blue. He didn't turn, didn't speak, and didn't blink as he headed east off the ferry toward I-5. He remained mute for the entire and painful forty minutes from the ferry terminal to Everett General Hospital.

Nicole sat in the backseat, still not fully comprehending the day's events but upset at herself for not being on the bus to protect her brother. Anger percolated slowly as her temples ached from clenching her jaw. Finally, she unsnapped her seat belt, leaned over the front seat, put her arms around her mother's heaving upper chest, and hugged her. Nicole repeated a short comfort in her mother's ear until they reached Everett: "Everything will be all right. Everything will be..."

* * *

The Marrones arrived at Everett General at 1:00 a.m. and rushed to the surgical intensive care unit to be met by a senior nurse. Her blue plastic nametag read, Pam Chase, R.N.

"Anthony will be fine in time," Chase said.

Nicole interrupted. "He likes to be called Tony.""

"Okay. Tony's lost some blood but has not needed a transfusion. Dr. MacNeil, who practices here at Everett General, miraculously happened to be in Index when Tony arrived at Stevens Cascade. Dr. McNeil took him directly to the OR. It could have been worse."

"What time was that? When did he arrive at Emergency?" asked Henry Marrone.

"About five thirty p.m. according to the nursing notes and..." Chase said.

"That's impossible," Susan interrupted. "You can't get to Index, or even Everett, from Lopez in two hours, and we know he got off the bus in front of our road at four. There aren't any ferries until eleven p.m. after three thirty. It's impossible."

"Honestly, I don't know the particulars," Chase said, clearly perplexed. "That's for the police, I guess. I heard he was left on the hospital driveway in front of the ER. As for why, that's for police too. I'm just one of the nurses caring for him here."

"I'm so sorry," Susan said. "I'm upset and confused. Can we see Tony now?"

"Sure, of course," Chase said. "He's still pretty groggy. Give me a minute to make sure everything is okay."

Henry mumbled as the nurse walked away, "Who could have possibly done this? It makes no sense." He wiped tears off his wife's face and then wrapped his large arms around her as he softly kissed her forehead. Henry

Marrone already knew the situation would likely change everything about their family, but said nothing.

The three Marrones walked into Tony's room to find him asleep and uncovered from the waist up. Bandages surrounded his forehead and upper right arm. Bruises and swelling had closed his left eye. Gauze and tape covered a left flank incision, and a suction drain exited below the bandages.

Susan started sobbing immediately and turned to Henry, who enveloped her in his arms.

"Everything will be okay. Tony's going to be fine," Henry said, unconvincingly.

Nicole looked at her parents, then her brother and then back to her parents. She bolted from the room.

Sitting on a nearby hallway couch outside the ICU, Nicole had just watched her father and mother disintegrate, knowing they could have lost their son, her harmless and loving brother. Her boiling anger finally reached liquid stage, although she didn't know yet that the family's situation was in the proverbial toilet.

Someday, somehow, I will find out who did this. I will. They'll pay. I swear.

     * * *

The next morning, Susan Marrone's eyes opened widely at her husband's declaration.

"You what?" she asked. "Please, with all that's happening, tell me you're kidding."

Henry Marrone repeated, "I haven't been paying for health insurance for seven months. We needed the money

14

for the restaurant. I meant to send a check in last week but forgot to mail it. It's in the glove compartment. We have no coverage."

"What does that mean?"

"I've been down to the hospital accounting office twice. The head lady down there said we'd probably owe the emergency doctors, the surgeons, the anesthesia doctor, the ambulance, and both hospitals."

"What are we talking about?" Susan asked, already starting to hyperventilate. "I mean, money wise. How much?"

"The hospital bills alone will be forty-five thousand, maybe more. The doctors about seven. They said we could pay them back over time."

"Can we borrow money from the bank?"

"No," Henry lamented, shaking his head. "I asked the bank last month for another five thousand for the restaurant. They said absolutely not. If we tell them we've got outside bills for fifty to sixty thousand, they'll shut us down."

* * *

For the next two weeks on Lopez Island, everyone's conversation centered on Tony's kidnapping and surgery.

Tony returned to school four weeks later, still listing to his left from the flank incision. Uncomfortably, he was the center of attention despite Nicole's attempt to shield him.

At lunch, Buddy Szalwinski joined the crowd around Tony and Nicole. Buddy, used to being the center of any conversation, felt compelled to add his two cents.

"You gotta be the stupidest person in the world," Szalwinski shouted. "Anyone that would let himself get kidnapped and then lose a kidney probably deserved it for being so dumb. Never would have happened to me."

Nicole exploded and forty-five minutes later found herself, with her mother, in the principal's office trying to explain the shiner surrounding Buddy's left eye.

She was suspended from school for four days after refusing to apologize to Buddy and his father.

"I'll do it again if he opens his trap. I swear," Nicole told her mom on the ride home.

Four weeks later, Henry Marrone declared bankruptcy and closed his restaurant. Lopez National Bank foreclosed on their home three months later.

Susan, Nicole, and Tony moved into the basement of Susan's sister's house in Arlington, Washington, while Henry took a job in Marysville driving a delivery truck.

Susan and Henry fought often in the beginning, but in time they accepted the hand dealt them. Henry became sullen and regarded himself a loser. He started driving long-haul semis and would come home only for short stays.

Susan hated the fact that she was relegated to the basement of her younger sister's home. In time, she pulled herself together and started working as a clerk in a nearby Home Depot.

16

Tony never understood the reasons for the family's move and actually enjoyed the cramped two-family living situation.

Nicole changed schools and lost dear friends, and despite her parents absolving her for Tony's kidnapping, she blamed herself for the woes of the family. Worse yet, she found little joy in life.

Susan and Henry would not move back to Lopez Island until both children had graduated high school.

Of course, the imaginary castles of Lopez Island were safe from Nicole's planned but now forgotten catapult. She would often cry herself to sleep. *Someday, somehow, I will find out who did this. I will. They'll pay. I swear. Someday...*

Chapter 3

Ten years later.... 2012

Seattle Medical Center

Urology and Transplantation -11 Southwest

Lucy Port, RN, sat at the nurse's station, ear to phone, while simultaneously intaking data from two computer screens.

"Dr. Roberts, glad I got hold of you. One of the new nurse's aides, Nicole, wants to speak to you," Port said. "We're two RNs short and I put her on Dr. Flanagan's patient, Mrs. Clemons, in 1147. We're swamped and I haven't had the time to check it out."

"I'm swamped too. We've got a kidney coming in at seven. Can it wait until later tonight?" asked Paul Roberts, M.D., senior resident in Urology and Transplantation.

"The aide goes off at six; probably better you talk to her before she leaves," said Port.

"Okay, okay," said Roberts. "Be there in five minutes. I'll take a quick peek. I hope it's not a waste of my time."

Paul, in his fifth year of a six-year residency program, had not been caring for the seventy-four-year-old Mrs. Clemons, the private patient of an outside urologist.

As Paul reviewed Clemons' history and hospital course on his iPad, the elevator rose to the eleventh floor.

Five days earlier, Clemons' urologist had removed, with great difficulty, a chronically infected left kidney. Post-surgery, Clemons' hospitalization had been unremarkable, and her chart contained no doctor or nurse's notes of alarm. Her discharge had been slated for the following morning

Paul closed his iPad as the elevator door opened and he looked at his watch. Walking quickly, he bypassed the nurse's station and entered Room #1147.

Applying a bandage over an elderly woman's left flank incision, two gloved hands moved effortlessly, while ponytailed, shoulder-length, auburn hair peeked outside a hair bonnet. Mrs. Clemons, on her side, faced the doorway.

"Hello, Mrs. Clemons. I'm Dr. Paul Roberts," he said, ignoring the hands and auburn hair.

Clemons, squinting, scanned the doorway, attempting to make eye contact with the voice. She closed her eyes, remained quiet, and made no effort to respond.

Realizing that Mrs. Clemons would be no help, Paul said to the hands and auburn hair, "Hey, are you the nurse's aide looking for me? I'm really busy and have to be somewhere."

The auburn ponytail stayed down and ignored the question. "There you are, Mrs. Clemons. All taped up." Nicole Marrone looked up briefly, then back to Mrs. Clemons' flank as she removed her latex gloves and lastly her hair bonnet.

Paul hadn't been prepared. His neck popped back an imperceptible fraction of an inch as his eyebrows arched. All he'd seen in two seconds were youthful, large eyes, swimming in blue, squarish shoulders, straight back posture and a soft, but resolute, physical aura. She had a warm smile, aimed only at Mrs. Clemons.

Turning Mrs. Clemons and then propping her head on a pillow were the hands attached to the warm smile. Paul remained transfixed and watched.

Nicole finally stood erect and was taller than Paul would have guessed. She looked at him, sans smile, and parroted his question with, "Hey, are you the resident that the head nurse said would answer my questions?"

Paul, unused to being made small by anyone other than his mother and the chairman of the Urology and Transplant service, said, "Uh. Yeah. Hello. Who exactly are you?"

"I'm Nicole Marrone, a nurse's aide."

"Nurse Port said you wanted to talk to me."

"I've been taking care of Mrs. Clemons this afternoon, and Nurse Port said you're covering. Mrs. Clemons told me she hoped to go home tomorrow. She's developed a little fever this afternoon, one hundred point five, and didn't eat any of her lunch."

"It's probably nothing," Roberts said. "She's done pretty well up to now. Tell me that's not why you asked to see me?"

"Well, no," said Nicole. "Something's bothering me and I was hoping you could explain it. Her urine has a funny color. She's still on IVs and taking fluids by mouth, so she's making lots of urine. I expected her urine to be pretty clear and..."

"She could have bleeding from the ureteral stump," Paul interrupted. "Maybe a little scab came off and caused some bleeding and..." He hesitated. *This girl has no idea what I'm talking about.* "Excuse me. I'm really

20

busy and don't have time for teaching right now. Is that why you dragged me up here?"

"Actually, yes. I was concerned that her urine had an unusual color," Nicole said.

"I'm guessing you didn't save a specimen for me to see?" Paul asked.

"That was a negative question, Doctor." Nicole, jaw set and lips pursed, walked toward the bathroom, passing Paul, who stood motionless. His eyes followed her into the bathroom.

Nicole's light olive skin, the quarter-sized scar on the right side of her neck, the hint of a small cleft in her chin, and the single crooked upper incisor didn't register with Paul. He saw only auburn and blue.

Exiting the bathroom, Nicole said, "And I did keep a sample for you to look at. I'd think that the urine would be reddish if that were true. I mean if there were bleeding."

Nicole held up a small plastic, sealed cup and handed it to Roberts. The fluid was yellowish, but a bright orangey-yellow, not the usual dull, straw color of urine.

Paul spun the cup around after holding it up to the light. "Hmm. Do you know if Mrs. Clemons has ever had any liver problems?"

"No, I don't know," said Nicole. "I didn't know to ask her."

"Actually, you're not supposed to ask. We are and maybe the RNs. Not the aides."

Nicole's jaw tightened at the apparent reprimand.

21

Paul hesitated and said, "I'm sorry, I didn't need to say that. Anyway, this urine looks jaundiced. I need to look at her chart again."

Paul spun his iPad into view and exited the room followed by Nicole. Nicole stopped and then backed into the doorway of Mrs. Clemons' room as Paul kept walking away, turning in to the nursing station.

"You're welcome," Nicole said loudly to the empty hallway, then added softly to herself, "asshole."

Forty-five minutes later Paul Roberts found Nicole in another hospital room bent over an empty bed changing sheets. An elderly male patient, who Roberts did not know, sat in a chair near the window. Paul stood in the hallway and said, "Miss...uh. Can I talk to you?"

Nicole looked up and dropped the sheets on the bed. "Excuse me for a moment," she said to the man in the chair and exited the room. The two seas of blue eyes returned as she faced Dr. Roberts.

"Nicole, my name is Nicole," she said, pointing to her name badge. Not sure if the doctor intended to reprimand her again, she crossed her arms tightly across her chest but didn't look away. She was clearly not intimidated.

"Nicole, then," Paul said. "I thought you'd like to know that we drew some stat liver function tests on Mrs. Clemons and she has cholestatic jaundice, a reversible form of hepatitis, probably caused by a couple of drugs she's been given here in the hospital."

Nicole's head swayed right and left, confused, trying to understand the meaning of Paul's comments.

"Acetaminophen and an antibiotic called Oxychloromycin. Both can cause the liver to malfunction, so I've stopped both. She'll need to stay in the hospital for a few more days, but should make a full recovery. That was a good pickup on your part. I just wanted to thank you."

Nicole's arms relaxed to her sides. "Thank you, back," she said. "I didn't understand much or most of what you just said. I guess I'll have to read up on it. I'm not sure why her liver problem made her urine orangey."

Paul, switching into teaching mode, said, "Oh, it's simple. Hepatic dysfunction. It's the excess bilirubin in her blood from liver dysfunction that spills over into the urine that causes the orangey..." Paul stopped when Nicole's arched eyes told him she still didn't understand a word. "Tell you what, it's not too complicated, but you may have saved her from a much worse outcome. Read up on hepatic insufficiency and cholestatic jaundice and we'll talk."

Nicole's eyes arched again at the unfamiliar terminology.

Paul took out his tablet and asked, "What's your tablet ID."

Nicole said, "NAM5188. You doctors and some of the nurses can take their hospital tablets with them. But aides can't take their tablet out of the hospital. I have to check it when I leave."

"Oh, yeah. I forgot about the rules for aides." Paul knew the coding system for tablets. *5188, born 1988, she's twenty-four.* "I just transmitted to you the word 'cholestatic jaundice.' Google it at home. I'll send you some references later."

"I don't have a computer. Well, I do. An old one, but we don't have Internet access; it's too expensive."

23

"The library has computers," said Paul.

"Aides don't get privileges here and I have to get home after my shift. The public library nearest to me has free Internet but it's not close and not safe at night. Maybe my neighbor will allow me to use hers. Or, I can do it here during breaks, if the nurses let me."

"I'll tell Lucy, uh, Nurse Port, to let you use the nurse's computer," Paul said.

Over Paul's shoulder, Nicole could see one of the senior nurses eyeing her conversation. "Thank you. I...I've got to get back to work now."

Nicole turned quickly and walked back into the hospital room to finish making the bed. She missed Paul's attempt to shake her hand. Paul turned and headed back to the nurse's station.

Three hours later Paul ducked into the doctor's lounge and ran into Art Brown, a chief resident in thoracic surgery. They had done internships together at the University of Chicago and both came to Seattle Medical Center to continue training in their respective specialties. Brown, married for five years with two small children, had little in common with Paul, other than an obsession with medicine and mutual respect as surgeons.

"I've got a little problem. Well, not really a problem but an issue," said Paul.

"Shoot," said Brown.

"Don't laugh."

"Jesus, what'd you do already?"

"Nothing. I met a girl I'd like to ask out for a cup of coffee."

"Why you talking to me, dufus?" asked Brown. "You haven't liked any of the girls Joan and I have set you up with. Please tell me you didn't pay one of those dating websites."

"No. She's a nurse's aide here. I met her on the ward today."

"A what? A nurse's aide," Brown said, then immediately rolled into a litany of putdowns. "You gotta be kidding. She probably hasn't finished high school. She speak English? What's she got that you want? Wait, don't answer that, I don't want to know. Little Paul is speaking to Big Paul. You know, you're never too old to learn or do something stupid."

"You are such an asshole," Paul said, smiling.

"That's Doctor Asshole to you. How young is she?"

"Twenty-four."

"At least she's legal."

"I know it's crazy," said Paul. "She seemed different. She picked up on a drug reaction causing cholestatic jaundice when everyone else missed it. I was acting a bit holier than I should and she gave me some shit. Most aides won't even talk to me. She wasn't intimidated at all and seemed way too smart and inquisitive to be a nurse's aide. So what's the protocol on asking out aides?"

"Red flag and against hospital policy," Brown said. "You're the one who's in harm's way. If anything happens, she accuses a doctor, a senior resident, at that, has forced her into something. She hires a lawyer and sues the medical center. Never goes well for the doc. That's why rules are in place."

"Nothing's going to happen," said Paul.

"Something happened if the aide says it happened, even if it didn't," Brown said.

"You're such a downer."

Brown, now laughing, said, "I'm trying to keep you above water. Find another girl. Trust me. This had B-A-D written all over it."

"Okay. Okay. I don't know what I was thinking."

Paul's mind flitted on and off Nicole until the following morning.

Four days later, he received a message on his tablet while making morning rounds. *Thanks 4 references on cholestatic jaundice. BTW, her anti-depression drugs could have caused it 2. NAM5188.*

Paul texted back, *Glad 2 discuss liver issues with u. Can I buy u a cup of joe?*

The response was immediate. *No, 4 obvious reasons. I can't afford to get fired. Maybe in another life. Thx tho. NAM5188.*

Chapter 4

Three months later Art Brown entered OR #4 to needle his friend. "Dr. Roberts, you were late this morning."

"Yeah, dead battery and the alternator is shot," Paul said, pushing himself away from the robot's control panel. "I tried to wait for Triple A, but they didn't show up. Some bullshit excuse. I called Uber and yadda yadda. I'll deal with it later this week, if I ever get home early enough. Needs to be towed to the BMW dealer."

"I get it," said Brown. "I'm headed home now but I'll pick you up tomorrow morning. Five forty-five?"

"Great, thanks. I'll Uber home tonight, whenever I'm done."

Paul exited Seattle Medical Center at 8:30 p.m. through the Arnold Pavilion to Madison Street at Summit to wait for the bus. Paul had been at Seattle Med for four and one-half years and this represented his first foray into the realm of public transportation. A list of five bus routes and two hundred times sat posted on a dimly lit telephone pole. He turned on his cell phone's flashlight app, but the numbers, now clearly visible, continued to make no sense.

"This is crazy. I'm a surgeon," Paul said loudly to the telephone pole. "I should be able to figure this out."

The pole remained emotionless, but a soft voice behind him broke the silence. "Excuse me. You look lost."

"I'm fine," Paul replied, without looking for the source of the voice. "Just trying to figure out all these numbers. How do you tell which one of these routes heads towards First Avenue in Belltown?" When he turned around to correct the intrusive interloper as to how lost he wasn't, two blue eyes greeted him. "Oh... It's you. Hi."

"Yep, just me," Nicole said.

"My car's in the shop and..."

"You're slumming it with us peons," Nicole interrupted.

"I guess," Paul said. "I could have called a cab, but there were none in front of the hospital and Uber wanted thirty bucks. I figured what the heck."

"Well, you need to take the 'what the heck' Number Twenty-two to the Jackson Street bus station and then the Thirty-eight, north along First Avenue."

The confidence in Nicole's easy manner and the pride without arrogance in her easy conversation mesmerized Paul in a nanosecond, as it had a few months earlier. He just stared for what seemed the longest moment the spoke.

"When's the Twenty-two come?" he asked.

"Soon. I take it too, but then head south on the light rail. You'll be home finishing dinner before I get close to my apartment. I've got to go all the way to SeaTac, then walk. Fortunately, I don't have to be back tomorrow."

The Twenty-two came as Nicole finished her sentence.

She flashed a transit card and sat in the third row of a near-empty bus as Paul pulled out his wallet.

"How much to go to the Belltown?" he questioned the driver.

"Two fifty. Take the Thirty-eight north from the bus station at Jackson."

"I knew that," Paul announced, trying to show he wasn't totally helpless. He then pulled a twenty-dollar bill from his wallet. "Change, please."

The driver looked at the twenty, then back to the road, shaking his head. "What rock you been sleeping under, bub? We don't give no change on city buses. If you wanna put the twenty in, fine with me, but you ain't getting no change or credit."

Nicole came around Paul and dropped ten quarters into the coin collector. "You owe me."

"You be one lucky man," the driver said.

Paul disregarded the bus driver's comment and returned to the seat next to Nicole. "Better you should owe me," he said. "Here's the twenty. You owe me seventeen fifty."

Without hesitation, Nicole took the twenty and put it in her purse.

I was kidding. Who takes the twenty? Paul thought better of the situation and remained quiet.

"Thanks again for the references on cholestatic jaundice," Nicole said. "I didn't understand everything, but most. Nurse Port gave me time on the computer in her office. She said the other nurses and aides wouldn't have understood if she let me use the computers in the nurse's lounge." Nicole, sitting by the window, stared out at the dark street. "Anyway, someone must have said something because they transferred me away from Urology."

"Our loss," Paul said. "You really did help that woman."

"Nurse Port told me that I'm too smart to be an aide and that I'd make a great nurse."

"I'd agree. You are too smart to be an aide."

"Thanks."

"By the way," Paul said, "I'm sorry how I acted when you asked me to see that patient on the ward. I was rude and didn't need to be."

"You were rude...but apology accepted," Nicole said.

"Is there any chance I can buy you dinner near the bus station?" Paul asked. "I haven't eaten yet. Or at least join me. There's a ton of good restaurants downtown."

"Not going to happen and I don't think it's a good idea," Nicole said immediately. "If anyone were to see us, I'd likely lose my job. The supervisor in charge of nurse's aides told us 'Day One' that we were not to fraternize with the doctors, or even male nurses."

"Really, what are the chances of someone knowing you at Il Terrazzo Carmine at nine p.m. on a weekday?"

"My brother and I need the money, so I can't lose this job. Even if the chance was one in a ba-zillion, I'd say no," Nicole said.

"First, you make a great pickup on the ward. Next you help me find a bus. I might have gone the wrong way and ended up in North Bend."

"Not likely," Nicole said, smiling.

"Plan B. Next time we're both free," Paul said, "I come down to SeaTac. You pick the restaurant. Some obscure, dark place. I'll come in disguise. You can't say no to that."

Nicole laughed for a moment then wrinkled her mouth and nose simultaneously. "Trust me, I could say no. But against my better judgment, there's a Mexican dive, Taqueria Vallarta, on International Boulevard, just north of South One Fifty-Fourth. It's in a large strip mall and no one you know, or ever will know, goes there."

"How do you know that?" asked Paul.

"Trust me, I know. Seven thirty, Saturday night. I'll meet you there."

"I can pick you up."

"No. I'll meet you. My way."

"Deal."

Nicole arrived home an hour later. The following morning she dialed a cell phone number in area code 442 north of San Diego and spoke for fifteen minutes. Then she called area code 862 in New Jersey followed by area code 248 outside Detroit.

Nicole knew all three numbers by heart.

* * * *

At half past seven, Paul walked into Taqueria Vallarta. His fair skin, broad shoulders, easy smile, and a height just over six two stood out against every other occupant.

Nicole's description of the restaurant did not disappoint. The Naugahyde chairs were probably from the fifties, and the peeling Italian motif wallpaper suggested a menu and owners from a different era. The cilantro-infused air reeked of refried beans and Spanish rice.

Paul, ski cap pulled down low over his forehead, had attempted to look the furtive bank robber. Not surprisingly, his fitted leather jacket, wool slacks, and loafers blew the cover. A few disinterested couples, clearly Hispanic, looked at Paul, then back to their Coronas, chips, and salsa. Paul was not one of them. Paul scanned the room looking for auburn and blue until he found Nicole sitting in a corner table, trying to withhold a laugh. She, now giggling, waved him over and he took a seat opposite her.

"Hi. What's so funny?" asked Paul.

"Your paste-on mustache is peeling off and the ski cap doesn't match anything you have on," Nicole said. "Nonetheless, thanks for trying. Trust me that no one you know would ever come in here, even to ask directions."

Nicole leaned over the table toward Paul. "This is going to hurt for a second," she said, and then quickly pulled his paste-on mustache off.

"Ouch." Paul massaged his lip for a second. "You could have met me in the city at someplace a bit nicer than this."

"No, I really don't want to jeopardize my job," Nicole said. "I need the money. I'm supposed to start school in the spring and I need to make enough to live on for a semester."

"You're different."

"Different than whom," Nicole said.

"The rest of the aides. Heck, any aides I've ever met. Not to mention you used 'whom' rather than 'who.' Honestly, nurse's aides seem intimidated by doctors, even intimidated by interns, nurses, or ward secretaries. You're not intimidated at all."

"Nope. I've seen worse," Nicole said.

"You've worked at other hospitals?" Paul asked.

"No. Afghanistan. Eight months."

"Really?" Paul asked. "The surprises keep on coming."

"You surgeons are nothing compared to a pissed-off Marine sergeant. Not even close."

"You were a US Marine medic?"

"Wish I had been; they'd pay me more at Seattle Med. I drove half-ton trucks, MRAPs, and Humvees attached to an infantry unit. I did a six-month medical assistant course at South Seattle after the Corps to get certified and land the job at Seattle Med."

"What the hell is an MRAP? Sounds like a fancy burrito." Paul picked up and scanned the one-page, refried-bean-stained menu, and said, "MRAP must be here somewhere."

Nicole laughed at the lame joke. "Sorry. It means 'Mine Resistant, Ambush Protected.' It's an assault transport that provides protection from IEDs. IEDs meaning 'Improvised Explosive Devices.'"

When Nicole stopped laughing, Paul saw her lip catch on the crooked upper incisor that she instinctively

33

cleared with her tongue. He said nothing but couldn't help staring at the whole package.

She's the most interesting person I've ever met.

"I knew what an IED was," Paul said, "but you're kidding me about the Marines. Really?"

"Not kidding." Nicole unfastened the top two buttons of her blouse, exposing bare chest above her left breast. The two-inch-high blue, bold-scripted "Semper Fi" tattoo lit up Paul's vision. The top of the US Marine eagle logo sat below the Corps' motto, suggesting that the rest of the bird extended well south of what Paul could see.

"I said you were different. But this is a whole different level of different. See action? I mean real fighting?"

"I was usually a few clicks behind most of the hot spots, but shit happens."

"A click. I've heard that used but it never registered."

"A click is a kilometer. And I did get into one real intense firefight. But that's another story."

"Shit. You carry a rifle?"

"That's a stupid question. Of course. But in the confines of a MRAP, my nine-millimeter Glock was more effective. I got shot in the leg and neck, but not bad. In the end, I did get a medal." Nicole pointed to the scar on her neck.

"You actually killed some people?" Paul asked.

"If you consider running over them in a MRAP, yes. I wounded one guy with my sidearm. The dude turned out to be some kind of important, so they made a big deal about it."

"Who are you? I'm just dumbfounded and I don't get it. How'd you end up in the Marines? You're smart. I expect you would have gone to college and done whatever."

"Let's put it this way," Nicole said, "life and situations don't always let you do what you want. Not to overuse my mom's favorite cliché—you've got to play the hand that's dealt you. The Marine Corps was part of a plea bargain."

"Oh..." Paul said.

"By the way, nobody's going to take our order if we just sit here," Nicole said. "We have to go up to the counter. The Burrito Grande Vallarta isn't bad."

They ordered two Burrito Grande Vallartas and returned with two Coronas to their table.

"I'm treating tonight. I'm flush with cash," Nicole said.

"No, you're not. I invited you."

"Yeah. But I've got seventeen fifty of your money from the Metro. I'm rich."

"I forgot about that."

"I assumed so," she opined.

"So where'd you grow up?" he asked.

"Lived in Bellevue until I was seven, then we moved to Lopez Island. We had to move back to the mainland to live with my aunt when I was twelve and I finished high school in Arlington, just north of Everett."

"That's a lot of information. Why would your family move to Lopez Island? I thought Lopez was for retired people and rich people with vacation homes."

"Not us. I liked Bellevue and my friends. We had to move."

"Who has to move to Lopez?" Paul asked.

"My dad's family owned a successful restaurant in downtown Bellevue called Antonio's. When my grandfather died after a heart attack, my dad took over. Antonio's seemed to be doing great, but the strip mall property was sold to a developer for a high rise, so the restaurant had to move or close. My parents said Bellevue was getting too crowded and it would be a good time to move. That's when we moved to Lopez."

"That doesn't make sense," Paul said.

"Didn't make sense to me either," Nicole said, "until later."

"Go on."

"Just from conversations I overheard between my mom and grandmother, I found out that my dad had starting gambling. My mom didn't like Dad's friends and I think my mom and my dad's mom, who was still alive, forced my dad to leave. Anyway, we moved to Lopez."

Nicole did not relate the story of Tony's kidnapping.

"You don't need to know any more, and I don't want to talk about my family," Nicole said. "It upsets me."

"Fine," Paul said, "I understand. But can't you tell me about the plea bargain? The only plea bargain I ever had was with my mother. I'd sneak off after dinner to my room to do homework." Switching into a high-pitched voice, he said, "'Paul, you want to help me with the dishes?' I'd respond, 'Mom, you want A's or clean dishes?' I always got As."

"My life has been just a tad more complicated, to say the least."

"Start somewhere. Plea bargain," Paul said.

"Carlo, my boyfriend at the end of high school, raced cars. I helped him work on the cars and during the races I was the pit crew. I worked my ass off. In turn, he showed me how to drive and got me a job in his uncle's auto shop."

"Plea bargain, where's that?" Paul asked.

"Getting there. Anyway, I got really good at driving. Carlo'd never let me race but I could take the car out if no one was using the track. I knew I was good."

"Plea bargain?"

"You need to hear the whole story," Nicole said. "The summer after I graduated high school, a course in Bremerton had a two-thousand-dollar competition time trial. Best time took a thousand bucks.

"Carlo was certain that the 'thou' was his. I asked him if I could enter. He told me, 'No, why would you want to embarrass yourself? Besides, what car are you going to use?'"

"Seems reasonable," Paul said.

"Not to me. He asked me who was going to pay for *his* car if I wrecked it. Emphasis on the 'his.' I said it was *our* car and I would pay for it. Emphasis on the 'our.' We got into a big fight and Carlo made me give him five hundred bucks as insurance or he wouldn't let me drive. The entrance fee was two hundred. So I was out seven hundred bucks, which represented every penny I had saved.

"The race was a week later. Carlo was already pissed that I'd wasted my money and could ruin his car. His time was four seconds faster than anyone else until I got on the track. He was already loading up on the high-fives with his buddies. Halfway through my run, one of the racing groupies yelled that I was only a half-second behind Carlo's time. The whole crowd was pulling for me and I ended up winning by one point four seconds, about four car lengths."

Paul said, "Every time you open your mouth, you amaze me further. Plea bargain?"

"When I got out of the car, a '66 Lotus Elan S3, everyone was there to congratulate me, except Carlo. I embarrassed him. I was a girl, his girl, and I beat him driving the same car. He had already gotten into a fight with one of his friends who had chided him that his dick wasn't as big as mine."

"Does this story end?" Paul asked.

"Shhh. I hadn't put a scratch on the car, but after the race Carlo said he was going to keep my five hundred as a fee for driving his car. He had five hundred for finishing second and I told him that wasn't fair. Actually, I used words worse than that. Things went downhill from there as we started screaming at each other. Everybody knew we'd worked on the car together, so I felt the Lotus was part mine. I did everything he asked and then some, on and off the track."

"This is sounding like a TV movie," Paul said.

"He called me a bitch and said, 'Get outta here. Find your own car. We're through,' turned and walked away. I hit him from behind with a twelve-inch tire iron and knocked him out. The cops and medics showed up and when he came to he told the cops he wanted me arrested for assault.

"I made bail with the thousand from winning the race. I was assigned an incompetent public defender, some lady who couldn't have cared less about me. After the judge heard both sides, he ruled that my assault with a potentially deadly weapon was careless and reckless."

"It was," Paul said. "You could have killed him."

"Yeah, maybe. I wasn't thinking I was so mad. Anyway, the judge then added insult to injury." Nicole lowered her voice an octave and a half. "Miss Marrone, you should have taken your ex-boyfriend to small claims court if you really wanted to recoup your five hundred dollars. You might have prevailed."

"So did you?" Paul asked.

"No, I was a smart-ass and told the judge, 'I did prevail.'"

"You're kidding me. You really said that?"

"I did and it didn't go well. He offered me three months at Washington Corrections for Women or join the armed forces and try to kill bad guys, not boyfriends. There you go, my plea bargain."

"Why the Marines?"

"I don't like boats."

stab wound

A voice from the counter said, "Señor, you burritos is ready."

Paul stood quickly and retrieved both meals, plastic utensils, and two more Coronas. Nicole sprinkled Cholula hot sauce over her entire meal as Paul observed.

"Want some," she said.

"No, I'm okay."

Nicole started on her burrito and Paul watched.

As they sat, Paul couldn't help staring at auburn and blue. Finally, Nicole realized Paul hadn't taken a bite.

"So, you going to eat?" she asked.

"Yeah but I was just watching you. I hate to be trite."

"So don't."

"No. It makes me feel better," Paul said. "You are fascinating. I've never met anyone like you."

"I don't know about the fascinating part. I know I have trust issues with men. Not all, but most want to take advantage of me."

"You know that's not me," Paul said.

"You might be right, but be aware that I'm always on guard. That's just me."

"I can wait," Paul said. "Do you know how beautiful you are?"

"That's what they tell me," Nicole said. "When I got out of the Marines, I tried modeling. Hard to get jobs with this tattoo," thumbing at her left chest. "Okay, Dr. Roberts, start eating and what about you?"

"Boring beyond belief after hearing your story," Paul said after starting on his refried beans. "I followed the script written out by my parents. Dad is an internist and my mother is a psychologist. I grew up in Bloomfield Hills, a suburb of Detroit. Went to Cranbrook, a fancy private school, then the University of Michigan. Played wide receiver for two years but never started and the football hours were crazy, so I quit. University of Chicago for med school and surgical internship. I'm here for the Urology and Transplant residency."

Nicole shook her head. "I would have loved boring. Didn't happen."

"You said the other day you're going to college in the spring."

"Hope to. I don't want to take out any loans but the GI Bill gives me some help. I'll start at a South Seattle Community College. I'd hope to transfer to the U-Dub at some point. My brother would like to go to community college and study programming."

"You can do anything you want. You're smart," Paul said. "No kidding."

"I did really well in school through eighth grade. I thought I'd be an English teacher. Then when our family went through the tough times, I gave up trying in school, although I've never stopped reading."

Paul listened, nodded, ate, but kept quiet.

"How do you like your burrito?" Nicole asked.

"Not bad. Will I be sorry later tonight?"

"Hope not. Hasn't killed me yet." Nicole then went to the counter, paid the bill, returned, and left twenty-five cents on the table.

"Big tipper."

"It's all I had left."

Paul threw another two dollars on the table

"Thanks," Nicole said.

"You want to go somewhere for dessert?" Paul asked. "Or go to a bar? Catch a late movie? I'll put my disguise back on, if you're worried about being spotted."

"No, but thank you. I have to be at work at six a.m., which means I leave home just before five."

"Can I drive you home?"

"No. I'm okay. It's not too far."

"Two things," Paul said. "First, I'd like to see you again. You're fascinating and..."

"You like me because I'm odd or different," Nicole interrupted. "You've never been out with anyone from my side of the tracks and..."

"Nicole, stop. You aren't odd and where you come from has nothing to do with it. Stop being so defensive. I like you because you are smart, intuitive, interesting, and pretty."

"What was number two?" Nicole asked.

"Two is there's no way I'm letting you walk home alone at night. I don't care how many times you've done it or where you live. And I'm not going to stalk you; it's not in my nature."

"Comforting."

"But if it were in my nature, I could definitely see stalking you," Paul said, trying his best to be funny.

"I'll walk. I can take care of myself."

"Nope. Then I'll drive alongside you."

Nicole grinned and nodded, as if she had Paul trapped. "You have a choice then," she said. "Take me out again, anywhere you want, or follow me home. You pick. One or the other."

"I'll follow you home, even though I believe that you can take care of yourself."

"You're different too," Nicole said. "Most would have gone for another date. I'm only six blocks away on Military Road."

Paul dropped Nicole off in front of an apartment complex that was likely in need of repair the day it opened. "May I walk you in?" he asked.

"No," Nicole said. "And don't even think of driving your car onto the driveway. There's a unlit pothole bigger than your car and I'd hate to see you lose your transmission."

"You live here with your mom?" Paul asked.

"No, I'm living with my brother. There were no jobs for us on Lopez. Tony's washing dishes six days a week and taking daytime programming courses. I have the nurse's aide job. Mom is on Lopez and Dad's off somewhere driving a truck."

"I enjoyed myself tonight. Can I get your number?" Paul asked.

"Me, too. Thanks."

"Can I get your number?" Paul repeated.

"No. It's not going to work." Nicole exited the car before Paul could ask again for a phone number or set up another date. She didn't look back and walked up the potholed asphalt driveway into the apartment complex.

On Monday night, Paul received a text message. "Saturday. 7 pm. U pick me up in front of my apartment. NAM"

"Sushi?" Paul texted back, but received no confirmation.

      * * *

Nicole spotted Paul's car across from her complex and ran across the street. She wore baggy silk pants bound tightly at the ankles and a loose yellow cotton shirt and a black Pashmina shawl doubled around her neck and hanging loosely on her back. Paul exited the car to open the door for her.

"That wasn't necessary," she chided.

"Not for you, maybe. For me." Paul closed the door and returned to the driver's side. My mom wouldn't consider entering or exiting a car until my dad opened the door."

"Your mom is like that?" Nicole asked.

"No, it's my dad. He demanded it."

"Misjudged that one. Different."

44

"Good different. On another note, it's nice to see you," Paul said.

"Back at you. Where we going?" Nicole asked, still thinking about having the door opened for her.

"Sushi Joe on First Avenue South, west of the airport. Southgate has some better places, but I guessed you'd be uncomfortable with all the people around."

"Thank you. That's nice. I mean it."

"You're welcome."

"I know the place," she said. "Never been there. Too expensive for my blood."

Paul drove slowly as the BMW's GPS spewed out data.

"Nice wheels," Nicole said. "This have the single-turbo 3-liter engine?

"Actually, I don't know. It's the engine that came with the car."

Nicole nodded and knew better to keep asking car questions or give directions to someone she hardly knew. They spent the next few minutes talking about the staff from the Urology wing until they arrived at the restaurant

Sitting in a corner table at Sushi Joe, Paul said, "I didn't get it until this past week. Why I am so fascinated by you."

"Great opening line," Nicole said. "Okay, why?"

"I hope this comes out right. I believe that I might intimidate most women that I've dated recently with my education, intellectual background, family, money, and

45

the doctor-surgeon stuff. They try too hard. That's not bad for me in the short run, but it's not a great chemistry builder. They agree with everything I say. It's tiring. You're the first person since eleventh grade and Diane Friedman who's intimidated me."

"Right. Like I believe that. Where's she now, Diane?"

"Not sure. But I think about her once in a while. First person I thought I loved. She had an older boyfriend in the Navy who was stationed somewhere in the Atlantic. In the end, I felt like I was an afterthought. Actually, she admitted to me, in so many words, that I was an afterthought. She just wanted to have fun until Navy-boy returned."

"Ouch," said Nicole. "The Marines taught me not to be intimidated. If you show signs of weakness, people take advantage of you."

"I know, you've been perfectly clear that I'm not as intimidating as you put it, 'a pissed-off Marine sergeant.'"

"Well, I am jealous. How can I not be?"

"Of what?" Paul asked.

"Please. You're a surgeon."

"We've taken different roads, but I believe that you're really smart. You could be as smart as I am."

As Nicole twirled the water in her glass with her finger, she said, "If I agreed with you, we'd both be wrong. You believe that shit, but no one else would, including me. Maybe in another life or time. You're smooth, I have to admit, but you're just playing on my ego. I don't have the education or background to be most anyone's equal, least enough you."

46

Paul said, "You have experiences that few people ever have. That counts. You picked up that lady's jaundice. The RNs and docs missed it."

"Few people want the experiences I've had. Trust me. I told my parents about you briefly. Short conversation that ended poorly when they found out I could get fired if we're discovered by anyone from Seattle Med. I really need the money right now so my brother and I can go to school."

"Can't your folks help a little?"

"My family has been underwater for more than ten years. I blame myself."

"How so?"

"Medical expenses. My dad and mom had a restaurant on Lopez Island. They put all our family money into it. Everything. They took out loans on the house, sold one of the cars, borrowed from friends. Anyway, they couldn't afford health insurance."

"Who got sick?" Paul asked.

"The proverbial shit hit the fan when my brother was kidnapped, stabbed, and lost a kidney."

"Oh, Jesus. Your family must have been devastated."

"It's worse than that," Nicole said. "The hospital and doctor bills were too much. My parents had to declare bankruptcy, and lost the restaurant and our house. My mom, Tony, and I had to live with my aunt. I can't help blaming myself."

"Why your fault? You were only, what, fourteen?"

"Can't explain it exactly. Tony was kidnapped just outside my house after getting off the school bus. Nine times out of ten, we'd take the bus together. That afternoon I had a soccer practice and Tony was alone. As if someone knew he'd be alone. That's all he remembers. I guess he was drugged. Anyway, he was beaten, stabbed in the back and dumped in the emergency room in Index, Washington."

"Who had your brother pissed off?"

"Nobody. He had some learning issues and difficulty dealing with others. But he had no real enemies."

"That doesn't make sense."

"It's stranger than that. He was found in Index less than ninety minutes after he got off the bus. Using the ferry system, which is the only way I've ever gotten off Lopez Island, you can't make it to Index, which is inland in the foothills of the Cascade Mountains, in under two hours. So they must have used a speedboat or helicopter. There were no witnesses."

"Your brother couldn't recollect anything?" asked Paul.

"Nothing. They put cloth over his face and injected something in his leg. That's all he remembers."

"That, in a way, makes it even stranger," Paul said. "Why would someone kidnap a young person, sedate him, and then stab him in the back? Makes not one bit of sense."

"My dad always believed someone didn't want to see the restaurant succeed or maybe it was someone who was still upset from my dad's gambling days," said Nicole. "Somehow they must have known we didn't have insurance. Nothing else fits, but the police couldn't prove a thing. They had no clues. It just happened. But, although I know it wasn't my fault, I still feel responsible for not being there."

"If you had been there, you might not have been able to prevent it. Worse yet, they could have taken you as well and done something really..." Paul hesitated. "Just done something."

"I'm strong but Tony is helpless in so many ways. I promised myself that someday, somehow, I'd get back at whoever did this."

"That's a heavy burden to carry. You still feel that way?"

"Yeah. My family hasn't stopped suffering. On the other hand, we'll probably never find out who did it. It's been ten years. Let's talk about something else. I'm just going to get agitated."

"Okay," Paul said. "How about you and me?" "I didn't think I'd hear from you. Pleasant surprise."

"I didn't think so either but I thought about you. You'd been nice and I didn't feel like I ended if fairly," she said. "My mom is really upset that I'm seeing you. She's afraid that someone will see us, say something, and I'll get fired. I told her the rules. I can't see you after tonight. Maybe when I'm in school next year, just maybe, but not now. I hope you understand."

"I do understand, but we can be real careful," Paul said.

"You don't get it. My mother is afraid. I've hurt her enough already. I can't do that anymore. Plus, I don't want to be looking over my shoulder twenty-four/seven."

Dinner ended quietly and Paul drove Nicole back to her apartment complex.

He parked across the street from the complex entrance. "Can I walk you to the door?"

"No. I know you mean well. But you have to leave me alone. That goes for the hospital as well. If you see me, pretend we don't know each other. Please." Nicole leaned over and kissed Paul gently on the lips. "Thanks for understanding." She exited the car quickly, walked across the street, and disappeared.

Once in her apartment, Nicole dialed numbers in area codes 442, 862, and, lastly, 248.

Chapter 5

Four years earlier

Camp Leatherneck, Helmand Province, Afghanistan

2008

Major Lester Bauman, USMC, entered the motor pool hut and barked, "Private Marrone."

Nicole rolled out from under a two-and-a-half-ton truck, or "deuce and a half," and wiped oil from her hands.

She stood quickly to attention, approached Bauman, saluted, and said, "Yes, Major, sir. Private Marrone here."

Bauman first, then Nicole looked down at her chest.

The temperature had hovered around 105 degrees all afternoon, and although the humidity was no more that fifteen percent, she had been sweating like the last living pig in Somalia for six hours. Only her olive, USMC regulation T-shirt covered her chest. The men in the motor pool were all shirtless and down to their skivvies in the un-air-conditioned tent. It was just too damn hot to wear anything else.

"You might want to cover up, Private."

Nicole turned and grabbed the only semi-clean oil rag for a thousand miles and covered her chest. "Sorry 'bout that, sir."

"Sarge said you were young," Bauman said.

"Sir. Old enough to be a Marine. Sir," Nicole said.

"Right. How long you been here in *Go to Hell-mand?*"

"Two months, sir." Nicole didn't smile at the over-used, lame description of Helmand Province.

"You like driving trucks, Private?" Bauman asked.

"Love trucks, sir. More than life. Love fixing 'em too."

"'Yes' would have been *suffish*, Private."

"Yes, sir. Then, yes."

"Sergeant Ross tells me you can drive deuce-and-a-halves, MRAPs, and Humvees better than anyone else in the pool. Wouldn't have guessed that."

"Don't know about that, sir. We all try hard."

"Listen up, Private, First Battalion needs three deuce-and-a-half drivers outside Musa Qala ASAP. The last three we sent out there couldn't drive my grandmother to church. Last thing they need is a non-hacker, and there'll be no skating out there."

"Yes, sir," Nicole said. "I can drive."

"We're not supposed to send WMs"—*Women Marines*—"to Musa Qala, but things are quiet up there now, and they need drivers," Bauman said, "so you shouldn't see any action. I know for a fact that there are no other WMs up there now. I'll get you replaced as soon as some of the new drivers arrive."

"Sir, beggin' your pardon, I'm a United States Marine, not a WM. You don't need to replace me. Sir."

"Private, like it or not, you are a WM. You ever driven a water buffalo?" Bauman asked.

"Sir. You mean the water tankers. I can drive anything. Better than most. Sir."

"Sarge said you'd say that. You sure you're okay with going up there?"

"Yes, sir."

"Against my better judgment, there's a chopper leaving at sixteen hundred," Bauman said. "Get your shit together. You, Lazzari, and Karson. Report to Master Sergeant Allen Rogers at the motor pool as soon as you land. Understood?"

"Oorah, sir. Every word."

"One more thing, Private."

"Yes, sir."

"Most of the men up in Musa haven't seen a female, other than sheep or goats, for three months. Just watch yourself."

"Yes, sir. Thank you, sir."

* * * *

The one-hour nighttime ride to Musa Qala in the Huey style UH-1Y 'Yankee' helicopter went smoothly other than the continuous whop-whop sounds that all Hueys emitted. The whop-whop would stay in Nicole's head for seventy-two hours. The cloudy skies and barren Afghan landscape, devoid of light, gave an eerie quality of disorientation. Nicole wouldn't have been surprised if chopper had returned to Camp Leatherneck except the temperature was twenty degrees cooler. The three

Marines hoisted their duffels, exited the swirling dust from the chopper blades and asked directions to the motor pool.

"Private Cary Karson reporting for duty, Sarge. This here's Private Rico Lazzari and Private Nicole Marrone," Karson said. Karson and Lazzari were bookended Marines, both just over six feet, grizzled and a head taller than Nicole.

Master Sergeant Allen "Roy" Rogers quickly eyeballed his three new drivers and fixated on Nicole. Rogers, an African-American, was horizontally challenged like the stump of a large redwood, only a few inches taller than Nicole, but looked wider than Karson and Lazzari together. He appeared to have no neck. "Sheeeit," Rogers said loudly. "I didn't believe Ross when he said he was sending me a half-pint. This a joke?"

Nicole stood motionless, at attention.

"Private. You gonna answer my question? Is this a joke?" Rogers demanded again.

"Marrone can drive," Rico Lazzari answered.

Rogers swiveled quickly to Lazzari and went nose to nose. "Private, if I want your goddamn opinion, I'll ask. Otherwise, you keep your trap shut."

Lazzari backed off and Rogers swiveled back to Nicole. "Last time, Marine. Is this a joke?"

"NO, Sergeant. No joke," Nicole said.

"We'll see. If you can't cut it, I swear I'll butt-fuck you all the way back to Helmand. Got it?"

"Cut what, Sergeant?" Nicole snapped back, then smiled. "The driving or the butt-fucking? I'm good with the driving. If you wanna teach me butt-fucking, you may have a problem."

"Okay, little lady." Rogers laughed. "I like your answer. But where the hell am I gonna billet you? Ain't got no lady's suites like Helmand."

"I can stay with Lazzari and Karson," Nicole said.

"Ain't got no wookie's latrine. You okay with that?"

"Fine with me. I shit and moon floss the same. Just piss a little different."

"Now you're talking like a Marine, but we'll see how tough you are." Rogers then backed away two steps to address the group. "Motor pool has their own tent just behind you. Throw your duffs in there. Pick any rack, 'cept mine. Mess is behind me. Should be someone around if you're hungry. Tell Cookie I said to feed you 'cause you just flew in. I'd double-time everything and get some shut-eye. We're on the road at 0400 to Kandahar with the deuce and a halves to pick up shit."

Rogers rousted Nicole, Karson and Lazzari from their bunks at 2:30 a.m. As the trucks headed east into the cool Afghan dawn, the desert resembled burnt pizza crust dotted with gnarly wormwood and camel thorn.

* * * *

"Marrone."

"Yeah, Sarge," Nicole said, sitting by an APC after changing out an alternator.

"You've been here a month and I gotta admit you're doing okay. I misjudged you. Where'd you learn to fix motors and drive?" Rogers asked.

"Bit of a story." Nicole then told the story of living with her boyfriend, Carlo, who taught her how to drive racecars and got her a job at his uncle's service station. She did not mention trying to kill Carlo with a tire iron and the subsequent plea bargain.

"Maybe we should get Carlo into the Corps," Rogers said.

"No way. Guy was an asshole. That's another story."

"I've been thinking that things are quiet 'round here, so I asked the major if you could stay. Not easy to find good drivers who are good mechanics. If things get hot, he says I'll need to send you back to Helmand."

"I'm glad to stay no matter what," said Nicole.

"I bet you are, but command doesn't feel the same way. Thanks for helping Lazzari fix the wiring on the half-ton yesterday."

"No problem, Sarge."

"Where's Karson and Lazzari?" asked Rogers.

"Just me here. Major Greavy from the 45th Armed Cav came by, not nice, and asked them to help his men load some equipment. He told me not to come, the boxes were too heavy. I didn't say anything because I had stuff to do here."

"He's not supposed to use my men. I'll find out what's what," Rogers said.

Nicole looked over her shoulder to see Greavy walking into the motor pool. "Major's behind you," she mumbled.

Rogers and Nicole turned and saluted.

"At ease. Sergeant," Greavy said, "I need a ride back to the 45th to pick up some topographic maps for the colonel. Can the private here take me?"

Greavy looked the prototypical Marine officer, with crew-cut blond hair under a non-reg crimson baseball cap that read "BAMA," ice-blue eyes, a head taller than Rogers and a neck bigger than Nicole's waist. Rogers remembered hearing that Greavy had been a three-year all-conference linebacker for Alabama and also the SEC Conference light-heavyweight wrestling champion.

"Major, sir, we always run a pair of MRAPs from here to the 45th. Just in case," Rogers replied.

"Not necessary, Sergeant. It's only twenty clicks away and there's been no activity in months. I gotta get there and back, quickly. Is this private the only driver?"

"Yeah. You should know, Major. You commandeered the rest of my team for loading duty."

"Stand down, Sergeant. You're out of line," Greavy barked angrily.

"Sorry, Major. I'm not comfortable sending y'all out alone. At least, you should have someone manning the fifty as a lookout."

"Not necessary. I need a ride now, so don't screw with me, Sergeant. That's an order. Back in less than an hour."

Rogers turned to Nicole. "You okay goin' alone?"

57

"Sure, Sarge."

"Take number three," Rogers said. "It's gassed. Be careful, Private. Eyes everywhere."

"Let's move it, Private, I don't have all day," Greavy demanded.

"Yes, sir."

* * * *

For fourteen minutes, the banter between Nicole and Greavy remained harmless.

Fifteen minutes out of Musa Qala, Greavy asked Nicole, "Pull over there for a moment," pointing to an abandoned, shell-pocked hut. "I gotta take a leak."

"Yes, sir," Nicole said.

* * *

Nicole returned alone to the motor pool seventy-five minutes later. Head down and her collar upturned, she walked silently past Rogers into their tent. Her hair, always tight, was in disarray and almost hid the small bruise under her right eye and swollen cheeks. A torn button from the top of her fatigues told Rogers everything he needed to know.

Rogers didn't have to ask. Nicole didn't need to say a word. Rogers mumbled to himself as she closed the tent flap, "Dammit, I should have known."

Certain that he had no idea what to do, Rogers closed and secured the tent flaps and then posted a hastily written "Do Not Enter" sign over the flaps. He knew that reporting the unsubstantiated event would likely be fruitless. Major Greavy wore a fruit salad full of pins and ribbons on his chest to prove his worth to the entire brigade. *I open my mouth and I'll be re-deployed to some shithole in Greenland.*

When Lazzari and Karson returned, Rogers told them they'd all spend the night somewhere else.

"Why's that, Sarge?" asked Lazzari.

"Marrone needs a little time alone," Rogers said. "Don't ask why now and maybe not tomorrow. She'll tell you, if and when she's ready. She's a good Marine. Let's keep it at that."

The next morning, Lazzari and Karson returned to the motor pool tent to find Nicole lying in the fetal position on her cot.

Rogers walked into the tent a few seconds later and told Lazee and Karso, their adopted nicknames, to shower, dress, and get out of the tent.

Rogers sat in Karson's cot next to Nicole and asked, "Anything I can do?"

Nicole heaved a few tearful sighs and said, "What could you possibly do? I'm a good Marine. I did my job. I was doing my job. I didn't deserve this."

Rogers sat quietly, not knowing what to say next.

"This is the third time in my life that I feel like I could kill someone," Nicole said.

"That wouldn't be a good idea. In fact, a really bad idea," Rogers said.

"My life was great 'til I was thirteen. Someone kidnapped my brother and he ended up needing emergency surgery. The cops never found out who did it.

Cost my family all their money, and all our lives ended up in the toilet. I swore I'd find out one day who was responsible and get even."

"That actually sounds like a good idea," Rogers said.

"Next, my boyfriend turned on me," Nicole whined. "He's the shithead that taught me cars and engines. When I finally did something right, he turned on me. I already got even with him. And now this. Why me? Why always me, Sarge?"

Rogers thought of putting his enormous hand on Nicole's shoulder but pulled back thinking that any touch could be taken the wrong way. "Private. As much as I hate to admit it, telling anyone what happened isn't going to get you anywhere but back stateside, or worse. Getting even will just put you in the brig forever."

"Yeah." Nicole nodded agreement.

"I'm sorry I sent you out alone. I'll do whatever I can to make sure that doesn't happen again. Yes, you are a good Marine. A damn good one. Don't let this one prick change your feelings about the whole Corps."

Nicole heaved a few more deep breaths and said softly, "Thanks."

"Here's what I guess'll happen. Greavy's waiting for you to go higher and file a complaint. You'll have no witnesses and he's a decorated Marine. Guess who wins? Not you."

"What should I do?"

"I s'pose best thing is to get up out of your bunk, do your job, act like nothing happened, and be careful. Let *him* say something stupid, not you."

"Is that what you'd do?" Nicole asked.

"Can't answer that exactly. If you were my daughter, I would have already killed the sonofabitch."

Nicole curled tighter.

"Private, I'll give you ten minutes; then I'll expect you to get your ass outta bed and start working on new alternators for the MRAPs."

Nicole nodded as Rogers left the tent.

Sixteen minutes later Nicole opened the engine compartment on MRAP number 6540-1, unbolted the old alternator, and starting replacing it with the newer, twenty-eight-volt, high-efficiency, three-phase, six-hundred-amp unit. She then showed Karson and Lazzari the same maneuver.

Rogers watched Nicole and mumbled, "I should have known."

      * * *

They waited for Nicole to storm out of the motor pool for the third time that day. Karson and Sergeant Rogers listened to the empty oil barrel at the gate get kicked for the umpteenth time. Lazzari said, "What happened? She ain't been the same for four days now. Never know when she's gonna bite my head off. I didn't do shit. I know you know, Sarge, so I think you need to bring Karso and me up to speed."

Karson added, "Lazee's right. Something happened. She was one of us and then all of sudden, she's the wicked witch."

Rogers nodded acknowledgment, then softly shook his head. "You guys are right. She's not the same, but I was hoping she'd work it out herself. I'll ask how she wants me to handle it. I'll tell you one thing, she ain't wrong and you guys did nothing to cause it."

Twenty minutes later, Rogers stood over Nicole, who had propped herself up against a motor pool fence pole. "So what's it gonna be? Can't have you acting like this."

Rogers watched Nicole gnaw on the situation with clenched jaw and tightly folded arms.

"Sarge," Nicole said. "Why? Why me? I was liking it here. All the guys would give me shit and I'd give it back. Anybody looks at me now, it's like they know what happened and I've lost any respect I might have had. I don't want to leave, but I can't stay."

"First, nobody knows nothing," Rogers said, "or I would have heard. Second, Greavy tells anyone, he gets court-martialed. Third, you say anything, you'll be outta here faster than a turd with cholera."

"I'm screwed."

"Bad choice of words, Private. Way I look at it is you keep this tight-lipped except for Karson and Lazzari. I'm pretty sure you can trust them to keep their traps shut. They know something happened, just don't know what. You think on it. Best if you tell 'em."

Rogers returned to the motor pool and gathered Lazzari and Karson. "Marrone's gonna tell you what's what. Maybe today. Dunno. But I'm gonna add one thing. She talks, you listen. If you ever tell anyone what she tells you, I swear I'll beat the crap outta you. Got it?"

Both nodded.

That evening after mess, Rogers told his small squad, "We're on the road to Gereshk at 0400. Four deuces and a support convoy to bring supplies to the 38th. Six hours out, two to unload, and six back. We're gonna hit the rack in forty-five minutes."

Just before lights out, Nicole stood at her bunk. "Okay. Here goes."

Rogers interjected, "Want me to leave?"

"No, you can stay," Nicole answered.

"Here goes what?" Lazzari asked.

"Lazee, shut up," Karson said, before Rogers could say a word.

"A week ago, you remember Major Greavy from the 45th came by and asked you two to do some unloading for him? He specifically asked me not to go."

As Karson nodded yes, Lazzari said, "Yeah. I thought that was strange."

"Anyway, soon as you two left, he asked Sarge who could take him back to the 45th HQ. Sarge said he'd like to send two vehicles, in case, or at least a gunner on the fifty, but the major said he didn't have time to wait for one of you, and he ordered Sarge to have me drive him."

"Uh oh," Lazzari said.

"Yeah, uh oh. Sending you two away was a setup. A click from their camp, I'm driving and he asks to see my non-reg nine-millimeter. I pull it out of my holster and as he's looking at it, he asks me to pull behind some shelled-out hut just off the road so he can take a leak. He's still holding my sidearm. He gets out and walks around holding up my Glock and asks me to open the door. I figure he's gonna give me my gun back."

Lazzari and Karson's heads had already tilted toward their knees.

"Next thing I know, he's got this huge hand around my neck and pulls me from the MRAP onto the ground. I try to fight back and he backhands me across the face and tightens his grip on my neck. I couldn't breathe. All I remember him saying was, 'What the fuck did you expect coming out here.' I passed out and the next thing I know my pants are down, he's got my arms pinned to the ground, and his dick's hanging over me. Want me to go on?"

Rogers said, "I think we've got enough."

Lazzari and Karson nodded.

"When he's done, he tells me that if I'm smart, I'll keep my mouth shut. Then asks me to drive him back to his base. He gets out and says, 'Thanks, Private. Look forward to having you drive me again. I'll get my own ride back.' He threw my sidearm on the floorboard of the passenger side and walked away."

Karson and Lazzari mumbled, "Sheeeeiiitt" at the same time.

"Part of this is my fault," Rogers said. "We're not supposed to let drivers go out alone. I told Greavy so, but he got all pissy and said it was an order. I should have gone to the captain and had one of you trail him."

"I was there, Sarge," Nicole said. "I didn't suspect any problems. It wasn't your fault."

"Yeah," Rogers continued, "I heard he's not a nice guy. I just should have known."

After a moment of quiet, Rogers said, "Hey. We all gotta watch out for each other. We would anyway, but extra careful."

Nicole said, with little enthusiasm, "Oorah," which Karson and Lazzari echoed.

The next day, Karson was alone with Rogers and asked, "What if this Greavy, or some dude with chest candy, comes back and tries to pull the same stunt? What then? I don't wanna screw a buddy, but I don't see me blowing off a major or a bird colonel."

Rogers nodded agreement and hesitated. "I dunno. I dunno what to tell you."

"Sarge. I like Nicole," Karson said. "Really do. So does Lazzari. Like most everybody out here, I wasn't so sure about her. But she carries her weight and knows a shitload more about engines than I do. But I'm not willing to put myself in the brig for insubordination. Just so you know."

Rogers nodded.

* * *

Three weeks and all quiet. No rumors circulated about Greavy, and he hadn't been seen anywhere near Musa Qala. Captain Evans, Roger's senior officer, told the motor pool he had been lauded by the Musa Qala's CO, Colonel Jimmy Hughes, on a few occasions at staff meetings.

After evening mess, Lazzari walked with Nicole back to the motor pool tent.

"Nico, I gotta tell you something."

"Yeah. I'm listening," Nicole said. "Full moon out and it's Friday. Better be good."

"Karson, Sarge, me, and a few gun bunnies"—*artillery soldiers*—"from the 4th were invited into Musa Qala by one of the ANA officers." *ANA stood for the Afghani National Army.* "Apparently he's got some family there and he thought it couldn't hurt community relationships. Yadda yadda."

"Right. Like they give a shit," said Nicole.

"Anyway, we're gonna borrow a couple of APCs"—*armored personnel carriers*—"and motor over there. Rogers checked it with the OD" *Officer of the Day.*

"Sure. I'll go," Nicole said. "Got nothing else to do."

"Yeah, well, I guess you're not invited."

"And why's that?"

"The ANA guy said it ain't the thing to do culturally, unless you wanna wear a burka, which you don't have and, if you did, you wouldn't wear it."

"You got that right," Nicole said. "No way I'm putting on even a head scarf or acting subservient to any of you assholes."

"Anyway, we were all fine with you coming, but the ANA guy was pretty definite that you were a no-go. We leave at 1900 and should be back by 2200."

"Fine," Nicole said. "I'll watch the fort. I've got to write a letter to my mom. She likes stuff handwritten rather than emailed."

"Cool," Lazzari said. But he might have well said, "Give a shit" as he ran ahead into the tent and exited before Nicole made it past the flap entrance.

Nicole walked to her bunk, propped up a couple of bedrolls, and took out a sheath of writing papers.

She had gotten only to "Dear Mom" when Karson rushed into the tent, mumbled "Hi," and went into his footlocker. He checked to see if Nicole was watching, then furtively rummaged through his belongings. Nicole, pretending not to spy, couldn't help seeing him put American dollars and a handful of Trojan condoms into his shirt pocket. Karson slammed the footlocker shut and scurried out of the tent, oblivious.

Nicole smiled and went back to her letter writing. *Good-bye to you too. Good thing I'm not going. Dumb-ass men.*

Chapter 6

At just past 8:00 p.m., letter written, Nicole decided to turn in. As she sat on the edge of her bed to unlace her boots, the motor pool walkie-talkie scratched for a second and then erupted, "Marrone, Marrone. We're in trouble. Marrone." The voice belonged to Sergeant Rogers and the tone differed from anything Nicole had heard. Pure, unadulterated fear.

Nicole grabbed her unit. "Marrone here."

"We were set up!" Rogers screamed. "Six of us in a small hut, third of a click southwest of the town. Two guys from the 4th have already been hit. We're surrounded by Taliban with AK-47s and RPGs. All we have are sidearms, and we're almost out of ammo. The APCs are fifty yards away and surrounded. We need backup now or we're dead. Marrone, do you..."

The radio scratched for a second and went dead silent.

Nicole pressed transmit. "Sarge. Sarge. You there?"

Nothing.

Nicole knew that going up the chain of command would take fifteen to twenty minutes. She remembered the MRAP she had worked on just before dinner was armed and gassed. Without hesitating she ran forty yards to the parked vehicle, spun rubber, and blew through the security gate at forty miles an hour as the guards, all facing the wrong way, screamed unintelligibly.

Nicole used the emergency radio channel to the OD desk as the speedometer hit fifty-five and screamed, "Marines in firefight southwest of Musa Qala. Need help!" She repeated the message once and threw down the mic.

Twenty yards past the gate the ambient light from the camp disappeared, leaving a huge half-moon low off the horizon and a blanket of stars to light the sky. But Nicole saw only black, the black of a witch's heart. She had never been this scared.

Nicole knew about the weatherworn perimeter track that bypassed the village to the southwest side and took it, keeping a death grip on the steering wheel with both hands as she hit one rut after another. She reached over to the passenger side and donned her helmet, almost losing control of the speeding vehicle. Intermittent firing could be seen from a mile away as the moon provided just enough light to outline a small collection of huts in the midst of the flashing. Sixty-five miles per hour. Less than eight hundred yards to go. She could see that the road headed directly for the huts. She turned off headlights. Seventy-one miles per hour. Peripheral gunfire lit up the hut and no flashes were coming back.

They're out of ammo.

The unit's two APCs were parked to the side, away from the cluster of huts and surrounded by Taliban. Forty yards to the north, three Taliban surrounded the windowless main hut's door. All three looked back, unaware that Nicole's MRAP approached at inconceivable speed. Nicole realized that she couldn't drive and shoot at the same time. She aimed the truck to the left side of the hut and jammed on the brakes as she turned hard to the left spinning the back end of the MRAP into the front door of the hut. Two of the Taliban were crushed instantaneously and a third was trapped against the mud wall. The rear of the MRAP had blown in the front door of the hut, leaving the vehicle's rear imbedded in the entrance, blocking any possible exit. Nicole hit the accelerator hard to free the MRAP, moved ten feet, then braked and took the MRAP out of gear.

Immediately, automatic gunfire staccato-slapped the front of her MRAP. She could see the starbursts of muzzle flashes from the Taliban that had surrounded the Marines' APCs thirty yards away. Nicole knew she was relatively safe as long as she stayed inside the bulletproof confines. She then looked into the passenger side mirror.

Freed by the MRAP's forward move from the hut's door, the third Taliban fighter, with AK-47 raised, moved slowly forward along the side of the hut on the passenger side of the MRAP. Ignoring bullets snapping off her bulletproof windows, Nicole grabbed her Glock nine-millimeter, opened the driver side door, and rolled out of the vehicle onto the ground. Scanning under the MRAP to the other side, she quickly saw the outline of the feet and ankles of the freed Taliban and fired four rounds into his lower legs, bringing him to the ground.

As gunfire continued to pepper the MRAP's open front door, at least two enemy bullets ricocheted off the armor plating of the MRAP, clanking off Nicole's helmet. She kneeled to jump back into the MRAP and felt a piercing pain in her left calf. Ignoring the pain she sprang back into the driver's seat and slammed the door. Bullets continued to bounce off the windshield as she looked down at a hole in her pants and could feel the blood slowly dripping down into her boot. She tested the strength in her left foot, which seemed normal, and made a quick decision to ignore the wound.

Looking back and right, Nicole could see Rogers, followed by Lazzari, both weaponless, running forward between the MRAP and the hut, hurdling the two dead and one injured Taliban. The remaining Taliban intruders continued firing at Nicole's MRAP with automatic gunfire. She unlocked the opposite door and moved quickly to the turret and the fifty-caliber machine gun. She started peppering the two Taliban-surrounded Marine APCs,

70

aiming at nothing in particular but providing cover for the Marines exiting the hut. Bodies started to fall and most of the Taliban took cover behind the parked APCs. A few Taliban, protected by the nearby huts, returned fire with automatic weapons. A bullet ricocheted off the housing of the fifty-cal and stung her neck briefly. Other than the slow dripping of blood onto her shoulder, she felt nothing.

Rogers entered the MRAP and yelled at Nicole, "Get down to the wheel! I'll take the fifty. You're the only one who knows how to get out of this piss hole—and put something on your neck. You're bleeding." Rogers looked at Nicole's leg as they switched positions. "Shit. You took one in the leg too. You okay?"

"I'm fine. I'm fine," Nicole yelled back. "Keep strafing our APCs. That's where the fuckers are."

Rogers took over the machine gun and continued randomly strafing as Lazzari entered the MRAP. Nicole grabbed a couple of dirty towels from behind her seat, stuffed one on her neck under the collar of her shirt and then knotted the other tightly around her leg at the hole in her pants leg.

As Rogers peppered their own APCs, Taliban starting running right and left and disappeared behind neighboring huts into the night. Once relocated, the Taliban resumed shooting at Nicole's MRAP. Lazzari replaced Rogers on the fifty-caliber and kept peppering the area around the APCs and nearby huts. Rogers exited the MRAP and helped Karson, apparently in shock, bleeding from his left shoulder, into the MRAP.

Nicole yelled, "He okay?"

"Not sure. Lost a fair amount of blood. Took a chunk of muscle. Two other guys hurt in the hut."

Rogers then jumped back out of MRAP, returned to the hut, and emerged twenty seconds later with two 4th Squad Marines carrying two injured squad members. Rogers, about to enter the MRAP, saw the writhing but very much alive Taliban Nicole had shot in the legs. The wounded enemy attempted to raise his rifle as Rogers kicked him in the face, rolled him over, removed his AK-47, and hurled it back into the hut. Rogers grabbed the injured enemy by his collar and waist, lifted him like a loaf of bread, and threw him into the MRAP.

Rogers secured the door and yelled to Nicole, "Get outta here!"

Nicole floored the accelerator and turned back along her entrance path. Lazzari, thrown against the back of the turret by the sudden acceleration, regained his footing and returned fire. Gunfire continued to pepper the MRAP but did nothing to stop the speeding Marine vehicle.

The gunfire from both sides stopped, and the only night sounds came from the speeding MRAP and the intermittent thuds from hitting potholes.

A quarter mile up the road, Nicole could see a small armada of MRAPs and APCs coming from the camp toward them. She turned on her lights, flashing them as a signal that they were friendlies as Rogers raised them on the MRAP radio.

Nicole came to a stop when the first vehicle arrived, and Rogers jumped out and yelled, "Get back to the base! Nothing more to do here. Get back. I don't know what's out there."

Rogers reentered the MRAP, and Nicole led the way back to the camp.

When they entered the base and exited their MRAP, Rogers turned to Nicole. "What were you thinking, Private? That was the stupidest thing you could have done. You certainly didn't get permission to leave the base," he said, then grinned widely and gave a stunned, open-mouthed Nicole a huge hug.

"But if you hadn't come," Rogers continued, "we'd have all been toast in another thirty seconds. We were all out of ammo. Thank you."

"I only came 'cause I thought you had run out of condoms, you dumb ass," Nicole replied. "Couldn't have you getting the clap out here in the middle of nowhere."

"God bless you," Rogers said. "Get Doc to look at your leg and neck."

As the two 4th squad Marines took their injured men out of the MRAP to arms of waiting medics, both stopped to face Nicole.

One, a corporal named Jennings, spoke. "Thank you, Private. You got balls. That's all I gotta say. You saved our bacon."

Karson then emerged from the MRAP with Lazzari's help. He stopped in front of Nicole. "Nico. I knew we were going to die." He wiped tears from his eyes with the filthy sleeve from his uninjured arm, composed himself, and stood straight. "We were out of ammo, and the walkie-talkie had been shot out of Rogers' hands. He wasn't even sure you got the message. We were dead meat. I'll never forget what you just did for us."

"Get your arm fixed, Karson. You're delusional," Nicole said, smiling broadly.

* * *

Helicopters, blades whirling in the night air, stood ready to accept the wounded, including Karson, and transport them to the surgical facility at Helmand.

Nicole limped over to the Medical tent and was aided onto an exam table. She removed her shirt and kept pressure on her neck with a clean towel. The medic removed the dirty towels on her leg and cut away Nicole's pants to above the knee.

"You're lucky, Private," the medic said. "The neck wound is superficial. Just a bit of skin. The leg bullet took off a chunk of skin and some fat. I don't see any muscle. I'll clean it up and leave it open. Both should heal quickly. Could have been lots worse. Just keep them clean and I'll give you some antibiotics to take for a week." The medic then irrigated the wounds with an iodine solution.

"Shit, that burns," Nicole cried.

"Must have hurt worse when you were shot," the medic said.

"Funny. It didn't. I was kind of occupied if you know what I mean," Nicole quipped.

"I heard you did good. But, you'll need to come in twice a day for a while to change bandages. Don't get it wet."

"How the hell am I going to shower. I must smell like a dog's ass," Nicole said.

"The cook'll have some plastic wrap they use for food. Seal the areas with wrap and tape before you shower. As to dog's asses, you must be the expert."

"Shut up and get me out of here. I need to get to the CO's tent," Nicole said.

The medic wrapped Nicole's leg with a soft gauze and applied a large bandage over her neck wound. "Keep the leg up as much as you can for a few days," he said. "You can get outta here."

Nicole covered her chest with her jacket and limped over to the motor pool tent to retrieve a clean shirt and pants. She then hobbled to the commanding officers tent.

The interrogations commenced immediately. Sergeant Rogers, Nicole, Lazzari, and the two healthy Marines from 4th Squad had been ordered into the large tent of Col. Harold "Howie" Hughes, the CO of the Musa Qala base. Hughes and Major Jamie Gaspar, second in command, had known of, and approved, the "goodwill" attempt from the ANA officer earlier that day.

The trip's origins began with an ANA lieutenant, known to both Marine officers. Not surprisingly, the lieutenant had excused himself fifteen minutes after arriving at the hut saying that he needed to check the security of the ANA jeeps and the Marine APCs. The attack of Sergeant Rogers' group started three minutes later. The lieutenant had not been seen since the attack started.

Hughes and Gaspar interviewed Rogers, the highest-ranking Marine, first. An hour later, the four privates were ordered into Hughes' office. Nicole sat on a chair with her injured leg up on another chair. Hughes walked into the room and the four stood quickly.

After saluting, Hughes asked the four to sit. He stood, walked around his desk and stood in front of Nicole.

"Private. Stand up."

Nicole stood slowly using Lazzari's shoulder as a crutch.

"Yes, sir." Nicole stood, saluted, and remained at attention.

"At ease, soldier," the colonel said. "Can you stand?"

Nicole, teeth chattering like an electric typewriter, remained at attention. "Yes, sir."

"Relax, soldier. I'm not going to bite you. Go ahead and sit back down and get your leg up." Hughes replaced the empty chair in front of Nicole.

Nicole sat, left leg up, but the chattering continued.

"I've heard from Sergeant Rogers, but that's only part of the story. In your own words, Private, what just happened?"

"Uh... Ummm..." Nicole stammered.

"Try and relax, soldier," Hughes said. "I need to know what happened while it's fresh in your mind."

"Yes, sir."

"Go on, please. Take your time."

"Yes, sir. I was on my bunk and just finished a letter to my mom when Rogers, uh Sergeant Rogers, got me on the motor pool walkie-talkie. He said they were ambushed in a hut, were out of ammo, couldn't reach their APCs, and were going to die. Then Sarge stopped talking. I thought maybe he was shot."

"Why didn't you contact the CO?"

"Didn't sound like Sarge would last that long going through channels. I jumped into a loaded MRAP and radioed the CO desk after I cleared the base gate."

"Private, you didn't 'clear' the gate, you drove through it."

"Yeah. Uh, yes, sir."

"You think you're the Lone Ranger, or Superman, uh, Super Girl?" asked Hughes.

"No, sir. I could make up what I think you want to hear, but I didn't really think about it. I just responded. The Marines in my squad were in trouble and I thought I could help. That's it."

"Private, you confiscated an MRAP, then ran through a security point at high speed, destroyed a gate, and ran the risk of injuring guards on duty, not to mention getting yourself shot by a guard."

"Yes, sir. Did all those."

"Did Rogers ask you to come?"

"No, sir. Never got that far in the conversation."

"How did you know where you were going?"

"Didn't exactly. Sarge said they were half a click southwest of the village. I've been driving the roads around Musa, so I thought I knew where they were. Half a click out I could see gun flashes. When I got close I could see rapid fire going into a large hut and none coming out. I figured that had to be where they were."

"Un-fucking-believable. How did you decide to spin the MRAP into the hut?" Hughes asked.

"Reflex, sir. When I got close, maybe a hundred yards, I thought I could see a few towel-heads trying to break into the front of the hut. I only had my sidearm, so I didn't want to exit the MRAP. If I had buried the front end I might not have been able to back out, plus the fifty might not be usable front end in. Thought the rear was a better choice."

"You spun the speeding MRAP one-eighty, perfectly, into the front door of the hut? Kind of lucky, aren't you?"

"A little lucky. I've spun them before. Well, not MRAPs, but APCs."

"And where the hell was that?"

"At Helmand, before I was posted here. My sergeant bet a captain fifty bucks that I could do it. He'd seen me do it."

"And?"

"He gave me twenty of the bet after he won."

"Where'd you learn to do that?"

"Used to race cars."

"Sheeeeiiiit. Okay, then what?"

"I think I crushed two of the Taliban after the spin. A third was freed when I moved the MRAP forward to free it from the hut. That guy started moving slowly forward, so

I exited the MRAP and shot out his legs from under the vehicle."

"With what?"

"My Glock. I like it better than the M9."

Hughes shook his head. "Go on."

"I took a bullet to my leg getting back in the MRAP, but it wasn't bleeding too bad. So I manned the fifty and started spraying the area where the fire was coming from. Mostly around our parked APCs. Killed a few I think. A ricochet hit my neck, but again not bad. Just some blood. By that time, Sarge and Lazzari exited the hut. Sarge told me to get back in the driver's seat and he manned the fifty and started peppering the area around our surrounded APCs. After Karson and the wounded Marines were loaded, Sarge exited and threw the wounded towel-head into the MRAP. Lazzari and the two guys from the 4th scattered the Taliban that surrounded the APCs with the fifty and M27s. Then I got the hell out of Dodge, so to speak. That's it, pretty much."

Hughes turned to Lazzari and the two other Marines. "That about it?"

All three nodded and said, "Yes, sir."

Hughes turned back to Nicole. "Private, I could have you court-martialed on three different counts. You know that?"

"Yes, sir. If you say so," Nicole responded.

"Knowing that, would you do it again, under the same circumstances?"

"Uh...yes, sir. I think I would. At least, I hope so."

"Thank you, Private. Just so you know, I am not going to court-martial you."

"Thank you, sir."

"You have any idea who the guy you brought in is?"

"No, sir. Just some dude trying to shoot up the hut that Rogers and Lazzari were in."

"Well, Private. He's actually a pretty big deal. His name is Mohammed al Farook. That ring a bell?"

"No, sir."

"He's the number two guy in the Helmand Province Taliban and he's responsible for the attack on Sengin last year. Twelve British Pathfinders were lost. He's a big deal. The Brits are sending over a team to take him. I suspect they're going to thank you personally."

"Wow. I mean, thank you, sir."

* * *

A day later, Captain Geoffrey Vernon from the 4th Squad entered the motor pool area and approached Nicole, who was sitting in a chair with her wounded leg up.

Nicole, Rogers, and Lazzari stood to attention.

"How can we help you, sir?" asked Rogers.

"I'm here to talk to Private Marrone, Sergeant." Vernon then took two steps sideways to stand in front of Nicole.

"Private, I just wanted to come by and personally thank you for helping the men in my squad. I've read the

80

reports and talked to the two privates that weren't sent to Helmand on choppers last night. None of them would be here had it not been for your bravery, skill, and ingenuity. I am proud to call you a Marine, Private."

"Thank you, sir," Nicole said. "I'd hope any Marine would have done the same."

"Hopefully you're right, Private. But it doesn't always work like that. Maybe someday the 4th will be able to repay you for your bravery."

"No need, sir. Your thanks are enough," said Nicole. She, then Rogers and Lazzari saluted. Vernon saluted back, turned and left.

"Well said, Nicole. Well said," Rogers said. "Now get your inflated head out of your ass, sit down, and get your leg up while Lazzari and I get back to work."

"Yes, Sergeant."

Lazzari laughed and said, "Hey, Nico. When you pass that head-sized turd, you'll show me. Right?"

"Oorah, Lazzari. Do you mind getting me a soda?" Nicole said, laughingly, as she sat and put her left leg up onto a free chair.

* * *

Karson returned to Musa Qala two days later, arm in a sling. Rogers, Lazzari, and Nicole met him at the helipad.

Lazzari spoke first after fist pumping his friend. "Sheeeiiit. Your arm's no good like that. Like tits on a snake."

"Great comparison, with a lady present, asshole," Rogers said.

Karson smiled. "Thanks. I forgot how much I missed you guys." He then turned to Nicole. "You know we're all dead if it wasn't for you."

Rogers added, "Nuff said. If we keep complimenting Nico, it'll go to her head, as if it isn't swollen enough already. I think she knows by now she saved our bacon. Every soldier in the 4th has come by to thank her."

Ten days later, Nicole returned to Col. Hughes' command tent.

"Private, just so you know, I submitted your name for a Silver Star. You deserved it. Captain Vernon agreed and also wrote a letter of commendation. Your heroism and initiative saved the lives of seven Marines, including your squad at the motor pool. You never wavered and you put yourself at great risk. Unfortunately, Marine Command downgraded the star to Bronze. Not sure why but I suspect they were scared it'll make the papers back home. As of now, women aren't supposed to be stationed at Musa Qala. Anyway, we'll have a ceremony tomorrow after mess at ten hundred."

* * *

Musa Qala remained quiet for the next three months, too quiet. Col. Hughes decided to move Major Greavy's 45th armed cavalry battalion encamped east of Now Zad, across the Musa Qala River, closer to the Kajaki Dam after ANA intel hinted that the Taliban planned to dynamite the structure.

Every heavy truck in the brigade mobilized for the move, likely to take two to three days and multiple runs between the old and new camps.

Rogers approached Nicole when the orders came through. "I know you don't want to be anywhere near the 45ᵗʰ, but we need all hands in on this move. You gonna be okay?"

"Absolutely, Sarge."

On the side, Rogers, without need to explain, told Karson and Lazzari to keep eyes on Nicole and Greavy.

By the middle of day three of the move, most of the men and equipment had been relocated when a lieutenant from the 45ᵗʰ approached Rogers.

"Sarge," the lieutenant said, "an APC has broken down after overheating five clicks east of the new Kajaki camp. My guys left two soldiers with the disabled vehicle. My motor pool men are all busy loading gear in Musa, and all the repair gear is still unpacked in Kajaki. Can you send someone out there to get the damn thing moving, or towed, before dark?"

"Yes, sir. We'll get on it," Rogers replied.

"Thank you, Sergeant."

"Uh, Lieutenant, sir, one more question, if that's okay?"

"That is?"

"Do you have any idea where Major Greavy might be at this moment?"

"What for, Sergeant."

"It's not important, sorry I asked," said Rogers, ending the conversation.

He immediately went to the communications tent and asked the lieutenant in charge to see whether he could locate Major Greavy.

"I saw the major forty minutes ago," the communications officer said. "As far as I know, he's still in a command meeting with the colonel."

Rogers found Karson and Lazzari, both still loading gear onto trucks for the last part of the move.

"Listen up," Rogers said. "I'm going to have to send Nico out to fix a stranded APC outside of Kajaki. She'll have an escort, and Greavy's supposed to be in a meeting with the colonel. But you two need to keep eyes out for Greavy heading back to Kajaki. I don't want to see him running into Nicole without one of us there."

"Got it," said both Karson and Lazzari in unison. Rogers returned to the motor pool with an uneasy sense about sending Nicole out, but he had little choice.

Rogers found Nicole changing out a carburetor on an APC. He asked her to take tools and an RG-33 tow truck to see if she could fix the stranded APC. If not, she was to tow it to Kajaki and drive the tow truck back to Musa Qala immediately.

"You are not to spend the night in Kajaki under any circumstances," Rogers said. "I'll send a chopper for you, if need be. I don't need to tell you why."

Nicole nodded, understanding. She departed in the tow truck immediately, joined by three infantrymen from the 45th and an extra driver in a heavily armed MRAP.

* * *

Lazzari was sitting against the wheel of a two-ton truck to catch a second wind. He pulled an already half-eaten Snickers bar from his vest pocket, peeled down another inch of wrapper, when he saw Major Greavy leave the command tent, jump into a Humvee with a driver, and head out of camp with another Humvee following. He was headed for Kajaki.

Lazzari chucked the Snickers and headed off, double-time, to find Rogers.

* * *

"Captain Vernon, sir, begging your pardon," Rogers said, out of breath after running three-quarters of a mile around the camp looking for the captain of 4th.

"What can I do for you, Sergeant?" Vernon said.

"Sir. I need a payback favor."

* * *

Nicole, with the three Marines and the MRAP, arrived at the site of the lone APC, sitting next to an abandoned hut, thirty minutes later. The sun was just above the low-ranging hills to the west and a chill wind had dropped the temperature fifteen degrees in the thirty minutes.

As the infantrymen stood guard, Nicole slid under the APC with pliers and wrench and quickly found one of the radiator hoses leaking fluid. She shimmied out from under the APC a moment later holding the damaged hose.

"Looks like someone cut this hose with a knife," Nicole spit at the infantryman. "This isn't a blown hose, that's for sure."

The infantryman, showing no interest, shrugged and said, "Beats me."

Nicole went into the back of her tow truck, grabbed a replacement hose and three jugs of radiator fluid, and slid back under the APC. She heard two vehicles approaching and yelled out, "Who's coming?"

One of the infantrymen yelled back, "Dunno. Two Humvees from the 45th, maybe. Dunno for sure."

Nicole kept working, unconcerned. Minutes later, after some muted conversations, Nicole heard the Humvees and MRAP engine start.

"Almost done here," Nicole yelled. "Five minutes." She heard no answer and then heard the MRAP and Humvees drive away.

"I'm almost done. What's happening?" she yelled, but again got no response.

Finished with the hose replacement, Nicole came out from under the APC and prepared to refill the radiators with fluid. She saw no soldiers, and only her tow truck and the just repaired APC remained.

"Hey. What's goin' on? Anybody here?" Nicole yelled.

As Nicole walked toward her truck to retrieve her sidearm and rifle, Major Greavy walked around the truck. "Just me," he said. He held her Glock, her rifle, and the keys to the truck.

Nicole spun 360 degrees hoping that she'd see someone else. She didn't. Facing Greavy, she yelled, "No fuckin' way you're touching me again. Asshole."

Greavy smiled as he approached. "That's *sir* to you, Private."

Nicole turned to run, but took no more than half a step before Greavy had grabbed her by the collar.

"Let go of..." Nicole tried to turn toward Greavy, intending to knee him in the groin.

Greavy swept Nicole's legs with his right foot and she went down to the dirt, face down, hard, hard enough to stun her senseless. He put a knee between her shoulder blades with enough pressure that Nicole couldn't breathe. He grabbed both of her arms, brought them together behind her back, and bound them with a plastic locking cable tie. He then bound her feet with another tie.

"Let me go, you fucking asshole. Let me go. You're hurting me!"

"Give a shit," Greavy said. He picked Nicole up by the collar and belt, like a small rolled bathroom rug, and carried her into the abandoned hut. Her legs kicked at air but did nothing to slow Greavy's pace. Stooping to enter into the semi-lit hut, Greavy hurled Nicole onto a dirty carpet, face down, then kick-rolled her over onto her bound hands and feet.

Nicole spit a mouthful of blood and dirt at Greavy, who smiled. "I swear, I'm going to kill you," she yelled.

"You can make this easy," Greavy said, unbuttoning his pants, "or you can make this hard. Either way you're fucked."

"You can't do this to me. I'll report you this time. I swear! Let me go."

"You have no business being a Marine and certainly no business being out here with real men. What did you expect? Respect? Nobody's going to believe a shit-ass private over me. I'm too fucking important."

Greavy took out a sheathed Marine knife and put it between his teeth. He unbuttoned and slid down his pants and underwear to his knees in one move. His full erection sprang to attention. He put a knee between Nicole's legs and let go of the knife in his teeth, catching it effortlessly in his right hand.

"Let me go. Let me go!"

Greavy flicked off the scabbard, freeing the serrated blade, grabbed Nicole's belt, and cut it in half. He then cut the cable tie binding her legs and put the knife back in his mouth.

"Let me go."

Greavy placed both knees between Nicole's legs, forcing them apart. He picked her up by the waistband and slid her pants down to her knees. Taking the knife from his mouth, he slid a hand into her panties and cut them free. He threw the knife to the side and leaned into Nicole's face.

"Let me go. Goddamn it. Let me go. Please."

Nicole looked into Greavy's eyes. He didn't care. With a mouth dry from yelling but half full of blood, she spit in his face. He backhanded Nicole across the right cheek, then wiped his face with sleeve. Dazed for a second, she tried to spit again but had nothing in her mouth. He clamped a hand over Nicole's neck as his knees spread, moving her legs further apart.

As she tried to mouth, "I can't breathe. Let go, please. Let me go..." she felt her consciousness drifting. She thought she heard voices, strange voices, then visions, strange visions. Everything turned gray, then black, then quiet.

Chapter 7

Rogers, first into the hut, hurled himself at Greavy's back, pushing him off Nicole. Greavy, about the same weight as Rogers, totally outmatched the sergeant. Greavy spin-rolled himself over Rogers' back and put the sergeant in a chokehold.

Lazzari, four steps behind Rogers, jumped onto Greavy's back, rolling the three entangled men to the side of the hut. Karson, following, grabbed Greavy's arms, trying to free Rogers from the chokehold.

Greavy yelled, "Okay. Okay," as he let go of Rogers. In turn, Lazzari, then Karson, released Greavy, who rolled away. The three motor pool men then stood around the major, now on his knees. Greavy looked up with a venomous sneer, then rolled quickly to the side and picked up his Marine knife. Rogers, Lazzari, and Karson quickly backed up as Greavy stood, knife waving back and forth.

"I'm going to kill you three pieces of shit," Greavy yelled.

Greavy took one step toward Rogers, who looked right and left for help.

"Major, if you take one more step, I'll kill you," shouted Captain Vernon, now just inside the door of the hut. "Put the knife down. NOW." Vernon had his pistol aimed at Greavy's right temple.

"You won't kill me," Greavy said, taking another step forward.

Vernon had already cocked his M9 pistol, moved his aim no more than a millimeter, and shot a round just over Greavy's head into the hut's dirt wall. "I will kill you," Vernon yelled, "if you don't put the knife down now. Get your pants on and get out of here. We've got to attend to a fellow Marine."

The hut became quiet as Greavy dropped the knife and pulled up his pants. Rogers moved to the side to let him pass. Vernon followed Greavy out to the Humvee just driven in by Rogers, Karson, Lazzari, and Vernon.

"I didn't mean any harm," Greavy said with little contrition.

Vernon shook his head. "Right. That remains to be seen. You'd better go now."

"What are you going to tell Colonel Hughes?" Greavy asked.

"Go. Go now. Take this Humvee back to the base."

"I'm essential to this mission. I don't want you to say a thing; that's an order, Captain."

"Go," Vernon yelled.

Chapter 8

Nicole regained consciousness slowly. Perhaps, deep down, her mind didn't want to wake up.

Gagging on a mouth full of blood, Nicole cried feebly, "Let me go," then spit out, hoping she'd spit in Greavy's face. Finally sensing no one on top of her, she opened her eyes, trying to focus.

Still gray, still hazy.

Nicole realized she was now on her side looking at the dusty carpet on the hut's floor. Someone's coat or shirt covered her abdomen and upper legs. She spit again but the taste of salty blood remained.

"Nicole. Nicole. Are you okay?"

Who is talking? Who is asking?

"Nicole. Are you okay?" Rogers repeated.

The gray faded.

"Nicole, it's me, Karson."

"Who is it?" Nicole rolled onto back, face up. Her hands went immediately to her swollen cheek and eye. *My hands are free.* Her head swayed right and left. "Let me go. Please."

"Private Marrone, you're safe now," Vernon said. "You're okay. We're here. No one is going to hurt you."

"I want to go home. Please, can I go home?" Nicole said softly, as the weeping began.

Chapter 9

Captain Vernon and Sergeant Rogers sat in the command tent in front of Colonel Hughes. Hughes paced the floor, mulling the predicament. He stopped, exhaled deeply, and then smashed the side of his fist on the wall of the tin Quonset hut. Dust showered the room.

"Son of a bitch. Who knows about this other than you two?" Hughes asked.

"Privates Lazzari and Karson from the motor pool and Doc. Marrone's getting some stiches on her lip, eye, and cheek," Vernon said. "I didn't tell them to not say anything, but I'm guessing they won't."

"Captain's right, sir. They won't say a thing," Rogers added.

"I need Greavy," Hughes said, then banged the wall again as the four men watched the picture of Barack Obama fall off the wall, shattering the glass and frame on the floor.

Hughes ignored the mishap and kept talking. "The whole goddamn operation needs Greavy. Shit, I just wrote a letter to General Eastwood recommending Greavy be promoted to lieutenant colonel and take my job when I return stateside in three months. Shit. Now what do I do?"

Vernon and Rogers had enough sense not to answer the question.

"Sergeant," Hughes said, "go find your men, pronto, and tell them to keep their traps shut, then get your ass back here. Move."

"Aye, aye, Colonel," Rogers said. He stood, saluted, turned, and ran out of the office to look for Lazzari and Karson.

"One mistake by the best commander in the unit and everything's gonna turn to shit," Hughes said.

"Apparently, it's not the first time, Colonel," Vernon said.

"What? What are you talking about?"

"On the ride back, Rogers told me Greavy had raped Private Marrone before. I think right after she arrived. Greavy had ordered the two other motor pool men to do some grunt work, then said he needed a ride back to the 45th. That made only Marrone available."

"How come this wasn't reported?" Hughes asked. "I should have known."

"Sir," Vernon said, "there were no witnesses and Marrone had no proof. Rogers talked her into forgetting about it and hoped he could protect her. Marrone stewed on it for a couple of days, then shrugged it off and went back to work."

"I should have been told. That makes my decision even tougher. What the fuck am I supposed to do?"

"I don't think you have much choice, sir," Vernon said. "You might want to go over to the medical tent and have a look at Marrone. She's pretty beat up."

"What the hell difference does that make?"

"I'm sure that I'm not telling you anything you don't know, Colonel, but you know by Corps regulations you have to report this to the NCIS"—*the Naval Criminal*

Investigative Service—"and also to General Eastwood's office within twenty-four hours."

"No way. The last thing I need in my life is the NCIS," Hughes said, ready to pound the wall of the hut again, but he thought better of it. "You think I have time to write up reports on a daily, weekly, and monthly basis on how we've handled this and what we're gonna to do to see that it doesn't happen again? Not to mention the shit hitting the fan if Private Marrone takes this viral."

"Marrone's a good Marine," Vernon said with conviction. "From what Rogers told me, I don't think she'd go outside the Corps, if the Corps backs her up."

"I need Greavy," Hughes said.

"Sarge said she's the best driver and best mechanic he's ever worked with," Vernon continued. "She loves being a Marine. She also saved the lives of her entire squad and a few of my men from the 4th. Go take a look at her, then make up your mind. She didn't deserve what happened."

Hughes and Vernon entered the medical tent to find Nicole heavily sedated and asleep in the fetal position. Hughes took one look at Nicole's swollen face, thought of his own daughter, turned, wiped the tears from his eyes, and exited the tent.

Hughes, along with Vernon and Sergeant Rogers, returned to his command office. Hughes thanked Vernon and Rogers and then dismissed them. Hughes then called CENCOM *(USMC Central Command)* and talked to General Eastwood. Twenty minutes later Hughes relieved Greavy of his command.

Five days later, Hughes had the entire motor pool squad in his office. The four were not asked to sit.

"I'll get to the point," Hughes said. "First, Greavy's JAG lawyer got him to agree to all charges. The weight of evidence was overwhelming. I'm guessing there will not be an official court-martial."

Rogers, Lazzari, and Karson nodded acceptance. Nicole, left eye swollen shut, remained stone-faced.

"However, there are, and will be, some bad feelings towards you guys and Captain Vernon from the men of Greavy's unit, the 45th," continued Hughes. "Right or wrong, I don't give a shit. But I can't have any discord in my unit, and CENCOM agrees with me. We're going to find a replacement motor pool ASAP and then ship all of you back stateside to finish your tours. I'm guessing it'll take a couple of weeks. This mess is not your fault and your records will reflect the outstanding service you've provided here. I just think it's best that you leave. Vernon is going to be reassigned as well. The decisions have already been made, but if you have any questions, ask."

"Sir, we'd like to stay together if possible," Rogers said.

"Really? Private Marrone, you okay with that?"

"Absolutely," Nicole responded.

Lazzari and Karson's heads bobbed in agreement.

"I'll see what I can do," Hughes said. "You're all dismissed, except Rogers. You stay."

After Lazzari, Karson, and Nicole exited, "How's she doing?" Hughes asked Rogers.

96

"Hard to tell, Colonel," Rogers said. "She seems sullen some of the time and I know she's not sleeping well. But she gets her work done."

"Doc told me she'll need some therapy stateside. Whether she wants it or not, she's gotta talk to someone. You make sure she doesn't talk herself out of seeing someone."

"Roger that."

"Also, I talked to the JAG officer in charge of Greavy. He's not going to fight the charges. Looks like he'll serve some brig-time, pay a fine, and be discharged from the Corps. You, your team, and Vernon won't have to testify at a court-martial."

"Seems fair, Colonel."

"I suppose. He was a good Marine, otherwise. You can tell Marrone about it if you think it will help. It's up to you."

* * *

Ten days later, Rogers walked into the motor pool holding up a piece of paper and yelled, "Orders came."

The three privates gathered around Rogers quickly. His head was down.

"Well?" said Karson.

"I'm going to Pendleton," Rogers said, "and you three are sentenced to Marine Corps Logistics in Barstow."

"What?" Lazzari said. "That's in the middle of the goddamn desert. I thought we were going to stay together."

"We will, sort of," Rogers said. "Pendleton and Barstow are only three hours apart by car. You guys can come visit and enjoy San Diego when you get leave. That's the best Hughes could do."

"I'm happy to leave here," said Nicole, softly. "I don't care where it is, as long as it's far away."

"Am I supposed to be happy?" Karson asked.

"You three are Marines," Rogers said, shaking his head. "You take any assignment with enthusiasm. It's the Corps way."

Karson and Lazzari said, "Oorah," together, half-heartedly.

"Now get your asses back to work," Rogers said. "We leave Thursday at 0600. The replacements are here tomorrow and we've got two days to get them up to speed."

Lazzari, Karson, and Nicole turned and headed back to work.

"Hey, dumbos. I'm just shitting you three. We're all going to Pendleton," Rogers yelled.

A small wrench and two oily rags whistled by Rogers' head, followed by laughter and high-fives.

Chapter 10

Camp Pendleton, California

Colonel Jon Brandler, Chief of Psychiatry, Medical Corp, Camp Pendleton, sat confidently behind his desk looking at Nicole.

"I've finished reading your record in Afghanistan. Impressive," he said.

"Thank you, sir."

"Rather than me ask you a bunch of questions, why don't you tell me your story. I won't say much until you're finished. We'll meet weekly for an hour. Sound okay?"

"Oorah."

Nicole spent the next six weeks talking about her time in Afghanistan, the rape and attempted rape, her experience with Carlo, two deadbeat, overaggressive boyfriends before Carlo, and her brother's kidnapping.

"That's about it," Nicole said.

"There's a ton of 'it' there," Brandler said.

"Actually, I'm pretty much over Afghanistan. Greavy got what was coming to him and I didn't end up in the brig. So that's good."

"It's not that easy and you're likely to have flashbacks to some of these negative events," Brandler said.

"I suspect so," Nicole said. "Other than my three friends from the motor pool, most men that I've been close to have caused me more harm than good. I don't know when or how I can trust them—men. I guess I'm not a good judge of character."

"We're not all bad. Men, I mean," Brandler said, "but..."

"I still can't figure how my brother got kidnapped," Nicole interrupted and changed the subject, "and how my family's life turned to shit after that. I blame that for everything, I guess."

"Not really the Corps' problem."

"I realize that, but it sticks in my craw, and one day I'm going to find the son of a bitch that caused it and get even."

"Nicole, maybe you need to let the anger go and get on with your life."

"You're not the first to tell me that, and I suppose you won't be the last, 'cause I'm not going to forget."

* * *

Thirteen months later, the four Marines closed in on the end of their Marine commitments.

Lazzari, Karson, and Nicole decided not to re-up. Rogers received a well-deserved promotion to master sergeant, re-enlisted, and switched careers to the military police. Lazzari joined his uncle's security protection firm in New Jersey. Karson found an auto mechanic's job with a Ford dealer in Southfield, Michigan. Nicole returned to the Northwest and, with Uncle Sam's help, enrolled in a medical assistant accreditation course at South Seattle Community College.

Chapter 11

Seattle Medical Center 2012

Paul Roberts exited the elevator on 11 Southwest and sat at the computer terminal at the nurse's station. The head nurse, Lucy Port, nodded hello to Paul as she dispatched nurse's aides, LPNs, and nurses to various tasks. She then sat next to Paul with that "something's on my mind" look.

"What's up, Luce?" Paul asked. "Seems like a quiet day."

"Yeah. I'd tell you there's been no catastrophes," Port said, "but that's like asking the hospital gods to create one just to be spiteful."

Paul nodded agreement. "Amen."

"Do you remember that nurse's aide, Nicole, who was up here a few months ago?" Port asked.

Auburn and Blue. Paul, wary of where the conversation might lead, said, "I think so. She's the one that picked up on that drug-induced hepatitis."

"That's her. Nursing transferred her to Ortho for some reason, but I liked her and we talked in the cafeteria once in a while. Anyway, so I hear, she exited an elevator this morning in the main lobby and punched Dr. Hendriks. All hell broke loose. She had to be restrained. Hendriks said he'd done nothing. End result, she was fired. Too bad. She was too smart to be an aide. Could have been a great RN."

"That's terrible. You and I both know Hendriks is a jerk," Paul said. "Good surgeon, but a total jerk.

Remember that time he cornered Louise what's-her-name in the med supply room?"

"Yeah, of course I do," Port said, shaking her head. "Nothing came of it and Louise quit two weeks later. I heard she's been selling real estate in Issaquah. Someday, Hendriks will get what's coming to him. He knows how I feel about him. Worse yet, he doesn't care."

* * *

The next afternoon, Paul finished his surgical cases by four. He surveyed the TV screens outside the main OR desk and saw that Dr. Fred Hendriks, chief resident in ENT, was performing a thyroidectomy. Paul went down the hallway and peered into OR #9 and could see Hendriks and a junior resident closing the neck incision. Paul then perused the surgical board to see that Hendriks had no other cases scheduled. He went into the surgical dressing room and sat by his locker and waited. The locker belonging to Hendriks sat two stalls away. Paul checked to see if the note-recording function on his iPhone was working. Every time someone entered the locker room, Paul would start the recorder and place it in his top pocket, lighted side inward. He would stop and erase the recording if that someone wasn't Hendriks. Fifteen minutes later, Fred Hendriks entered the locker room and opened his locker. Paul pretended to be busy straightening out his own locker, waiting on Hendriks to start the conversation.

"Hey, Paul. How are things?" Hendriks asked.

"Hey, Fred. Great," Paul responded. "Easy day for me. Two stone cases and a hydrocele. Say, I heard about some brouhaha from yesterday morning in the lobby. What was that about?"

"Shit, I dunno. Some nurse's aide hauled off and kept hitting me," Hendriks said, "and then accused me of attacking her."

"Nurse's aide. God, they're usually such losers. Never seen a pretty one yet," Paul said.

Hendriks slid closer to Paul. "This one was a total fox. Just gorgeous, big blue eyes and a great set of jugs. Just the two of us in the elevator."

"How come I never meet cute ones? Shit. Urology gets such dogs. I guess they don't want to slosh around in piss." Both men smiled at the lame joke.

Hendriks came even closer and whispered, "Trust me, this one was not a dog. I'd seen her before, but there we were in the elevator alone. She gave me a big smile as I walked in so I thought she was interested. Hell, I put one arm around her from the back and just pinched her ass gently to see where it might go. I would have stopped the elevator between floors, if you know what I mean. She totally overreacted. What a bitch. Like she'd ever do better than me."

"Amazing. Who do they think they are?" Paul said, trying to shake his head in agreement.

"Exactly." Hendriks said, backing away. He then shut his locker and said, "Gotta go write some orders and make rounds. Have a great day."

"You too. See ya."

* * *

The next afternoon, Paul sat in the office of Donald Stevens, the hospital's in-house attorney.

"What can I do for you, Dr. Roberts?" Stevens asked.

"I'm here about that incident day before yesterday in the lobby with Dr. Hendriks and a nurse's aide."

"What about it?" asked Stevens. "It's a done deal. The aide had to be restrained by two security officers. Can't have that kind of person working here. Dr. Hendriks said he did nothing and there were no witnesses to whatever happened until they exited the elevator."

"A few things," Paul said. "First, I was approached by some staff members who knew this aide and thought she was a valuable asset to the hospital. I didn't really know her."

"Then why are you here?" Stevens interrupted.

"The nurses asked if I could help. They told me this aide apparently saved the life of an elderly woman by picking up a case of cholestatic jaundice when everyone else missed it."

"What's that? And what difference does that make?"

"Probably nothing other than the patient could have died from a drug reaction and the aide made an astute pickup. Second, Hendriks is a jerk. All of us on Urology know that. He groped a nurse on the Urology floor about six months ago. Good nurse too. She was too humiliated to file a complaint and ended up quitting. Our loss. Again, no witnesses. Third, I want you to listen to this tape." Paul hit the play button on his phone.

"Does anyone know about this recording?" Stevens asked, after listening to the tape.

"No. Just me, and now you," Paul said.

"I'd like you to erase it," Stevens said.

"No can do. The nurse's aide did nothing wrong. I do happen to recollect that she's a decorated U.S. Marine."

"I know about that. But you obtained the recording without Dr. Hendriks' permission. That's illegal," Stevens said.

"Perhaps, counselor. But it's all about finding the truth. Right?"

"I protect the hospital's interests, and those are my only interests."

"Then I think it's in the best interest of this hospital to see that this nurse's aide is compensated, her work record is cleared, and employment is found for her at another hospital. If that's done, the recording disappears," said Paul.

"That's extortion."

"I'm not a lawyer so I can't answer that. It's just the truth. You know if this gets out, legal or not, it would be a publicity nightmare. Also, I don't want anyone to know about this meeting. That goes for Dr. Hendriks, or my boss, the chief of Urology, Dr. Muller. I expect the CEO of the hospital will need to know a tape exists, but if he's smart, he'll leave it there. Simple deal. Some compensation, clean work record, and a job at another hospital. Make it happen."

Paul Roberts stood, turned around, and left before Stevens could offer any Plan B.

* * *

The following afternoon, a secretary escorted Nicole into Donald Stevens' office and told her to sit in front of a large executive desk. Nicole crossed her arms tightly across a wrinkled blouse. Auburn had not been combed for forty-eight hours, and swollen eyelids and red splotchiness from nonstop crying overshadowed the blue.

Donald Stevens entered his office and peered over his half-glasses at the mess staring back.

"I did nothing wrong except defend myself," Nicole said before Stevens could take a seat. "Why would nobody listen to my side of the story? Why shouldn't I be safe, alone, in an elevator?"

"You should be, but the hospital can't control everything."

"Do I need a lawyer?" asked Nicole.

"You are always entitled to an attorney. But I think you'll be satisfied after you hear what I have to say."

"We'll see." Nicole's arms tightened further.

"Unfortunately, no one witnessed the events two days ago other than you slapping Dr. Hendriks after you exited the elevator into the lobby."

"Right. But I was there. He grabbed me around the chest with one arm and my butt with the other hand. I protested but he only let go when the door opened."

"So it's 'he said, she said.' No one wins. But I have some information, obtained illegally, that your accusations may have some validity. I, or you, or a court of law cannot use or have that information."

Nicole uncrossed her arms and sat up straight. "Why not?"

"It was obtained illegally by someone on the hospital staff who trapped Dr. Hendriks."

"I'm confused," said Nicole.

"I can't go into the particulars but I'll try and make things simple. I will offer you a generous settlement if you agree that you will not press charges against the hospital or Dr. Hendriks. This whole mess can go away, right here, right now. You will be bound to tell no one, including your family, any news sources, an attorney, or the police. No one."

"I'm listening," Nicole replied, "but that's all I'm doing until I hear what you are offering."

"You agree that if the terms are satisfactory, you will tell no one?"

"I'm listening, but that's all. You're not taping this conversation, are you?" Nicole asked.

"No," said Stevens, "that would be illegal without your permission. There will be no records of this conversation."

He pulled out a piece of paper from his desk, turned it around, and slid it in front of Nicole.

"Okay, what's it say?" Nicole asked. "You tell me."

"This is what we are offering. First, your work record will be cleared of any negative comments. Second, you will start work at Highline Hospital next Monday at the same pay scale you have here at Seattle Med. Third, you will receive a severance check for five thousand dollars."

"How did this happen?" Nicole was stunned.

Disregarding Nicole's comment, Stevens asked, "Is that acceptable to you?"

"Yes. Yes. I believe it is," Nicole said, "but how...how did this happen?"

"I can't tell you, other than you have friends here on the staff. You may not even know who that person is. Something about 'Cooly Plastic' jaundice or some such. You probably don't even remember and I'm not telling you."

Paul. Nicole hesitated. "Uh, I haven't a clue who or what that could be."

Nicole left Stevens' office ten minutes later after signing the non-disclosure agreement and keeping a cashier's check made out to her for five thousand dollars. Before leaving, she turned at the door and said, "By the way, it's called cholestatic jaundice."

Stevens said, "Whatever. Close the door on the way out."

* * *

Back in her apartment, Nicole called her mother and then dialed numbers in area codes 442, 862, and 248.

* * *

Hank, the doorman at Belltown Tower Two on First Avenue, thought he knew every evening deliveryman from every pizza service in the area. Few worked after ten, even on Saturdays. An unknown, young, attractive woman in an open, long trench coat, carrying a pizza box and an empty paper grocery bag at 11:00 p.m. would raise suspicion to even the densest of security people.

"How can I help you, miss?" asked Hank.

"I have a pizza delivery for Dr. Roberts," Nicole said.

"Right. Do you have a suite number for Dr. Roberts? Was he expecting you? He didn't call me."

"No, but you know it. Call and ask if he's expecting a pizza."

"Sure. You stay here," Hank said as he walked into his cubbyhole office and closed the door.

"Dr. Roberts, Hank here from the front door. There's a lady down here trying to deliver a pizza. I don't think she's a delivery person."

"Hank, I didn't order a pizza. Not at this hour. I'm exhausted. What's her name?"

"She didn't say."

"Uh. What's she look like?"

"Pretty. Real pretty. Reddish brown hair and big blue eyes."

"Oh. I actually know who that is. Send her up."

"You can go up, miss," Hank said, exiting his cubbyhole. "Suite 509. Fifth floor, any elevator."

"Thanks. Is there a bathroom in the lobby?" Nicole asked.

"Yep. Against the back wall next to the elevators. Want me to hold the pizza?"

"No. I'll be okay. Thanks again."

Nicole walked into the bathroom and exited three minutes later with the grocery bag, now full, in one hand, the pizza box in the other, and wearing the trench coat, buttoned to the top. She exited the elevator on floor five and knocked on Apartment 509.

"This is a nice surprise. I didn't expect to see you," Paul said, barefoot and wearing an old T-shirt and scrub bottoms.

"Really," Nicole said. "Maybe you did, maybe you didn't. But I brought a pizza just in case. Thought it would help get me through the front door. Can you turn on the oven? The pizza's probably frozen by now."

"Sure. Give me the box."

Nicole handed Paul the box. As he turned to walk into his kitchen, she started to unbutton her trench coat.

"Pretty light box," Paul said, shaking the box up and down slowly. He opened it and stopped abruptly. "Hey, there's nothing in here."

Paul turned to face Nicole. The trench coat had dropped to the floor. She was naked and confirmed that her tattoo did, in fact, extend onto her left breast. Paul fumbled the pizza box but caught it before it hit the ground.

"Of course the pizza box is empty," Nicole said. "I didn't come here to eat. When was the last time you woke up and thought this could be the best day of your life?" She took three steps toward Paul. Only the empty pizza box now stood between them.

"I wasn't expecting you or this. I don't know what to say," Paul said.

"Put down the pizza box first. That'd be a start. I thought you surgical types knew how to handle the unexpected."

Paul dropped the box to his side, closed the gap between them, and put his arms around her. "I just needed to get my bearings and wait for my heart rate to fall below one-sixty. I know exactly what to do. Why are you doing this?"

"Really?" Nicole asked.

"Yeah, really. Why are you doing this? It's a simple question."

"I owe you. I'm here to pay you back."

Paul's arms went slack and he abruptly backed away and held his arms up. "Stop," he said. "You don't owe me shit. I didn't do what I did so you'd sleep with me, and I didn't force you to come here. I did it because it was the right thing to do."

Of the responses Nicole expected, Paul's was not on even the long list. "Oh...oh," she stammered as her face turned expressionless.

"Hendriks was and is a prick," Paul continued. "You didn't, nor anyone, deserve what happened."

Nicole, still stunned and caught completely off guard, crossed both arms over her exposed chest. "Do you want me to leave? I...I...can...go. I'll leave now."

"I just don't understand why you'd cheapen yourself," Paul demanded. "You have so much going for you."

"I'll...go...if...if...you want," Nicole said, close to tears.

"Maybe it's best," Paul responded, then hesitated. "Well, no. I don't want you to go. But I have to know how you feel about me. I would have hoped that's why you came."

Nicole put her head down for a second and then looked up. "I'm just not used to people doing things for me without demanding something in return."

"I didn't contact you and I didn't demand anything," Paul said firmly.

"I know," Nicole said, "it's just..." She stopped talking as she bent down to retrieve her trench coat. She turned away from Paul, slid on the coat, fumbled with the two top buttons, and then turned back. Tears mixed with mascara cascaded down both cheeks.

An uncomfortable moment of silence passed as both stood facing each other.

"I'll just go," Nicole said.

Paul continued to stand mute as Nicole picked up the shopping bag with her clothes and headed for the door.

"I'm sorry. I really am," Paul said as she walked away.

Nicole opened the door and, without looking back, closed it softly and headed toward the elevator.

"Why am I so stupid," Nicole said to the closed elevator door as she pressed the down button. The elevator came almost immediately, but when the door opened, she stood still, unwilling to enter. As the elevator closed she again said, "Why am I so stupid." She turned and went back to Paul's apartment and knocked.

Paul, thinking he should go after Nicole, had grabbed a sweater and was at his door to open it immediately. They stood motionless for a long moment, separated only by her shopping bag full of clothes

"I was coming to get you," Paul said, speaking first.

"Please. Please. Ask me again why I'm here. Please," Nicole said softly.

"Why are you here?"

"I missed you."

Paul waited for more.

She walked forward, pressing the shopping bag against his chest, then stood on tiptoes to kiss him softly on his lips. "I wouldn't have come unless I wanted to see you."

Paul didn't have to say, "Better answer," as he returned her gentle kiss. He stood back and said, "I wanted to see you too." He then pulled up the lowest edge of his T-shirt and wiped the mascara off Nicole's cheeks. "You want to talk some?"

"No," Nicole said, putting down the shopping bag. "I want you to hold me."

Paul closed the door and gave Nicole the hug she needed. Taking her hand, he walked her into the bedroom and dimmed the lights.

"Are you okay? I need to know," he asked.

"You've said a few times that I amaze you. But it's you that amazes me. I don't think I deserve you. Sometimes I feel like I don't deserve anyone. But, yes, I'm okay," Nicole said.

Paul sat on the edge of his bed. Nicole, still wearing the trench coat, grabbed his hands, straddled his knees, and sat on his lap, face-to-face, and put her arms around his chest and her face into the nape of his neck.

Paul said, "You've got to be freezing. You came all this way with just a trench coat?"

"No. I took off my clothes in the lobby. They're in the bag."

"Hank must have loved that."

"No. In the bathroom off the elevators."

"You're too much."

"I hope not. I'm guessing you risked a lot last week trying to help me. Why?"

"I'd bet you're not supposed to be talking about it," Paul said.

"You're right. I signed something that I'm not to tell anyone. I haven't—yet. But I'm about to. I need to talk to someone. That smug hospital attorney told me in so many words it was you."

"He mentioned me?" Paul asked.

"No. Didn't have to. He butchered pronouncing cholestatic jaundice. That's all."

"I can't say a word," Paul said, smiling, and faux zipped his lip.

"Funny," Nicole said. "I was thinking about you in the elevator before that creep grabbed me. From then, my world turned upside down. Déjà vu all over again. It happened so quick."

"Nicole, you are smart and caring. I realized that the first time I saw you. I haven't stop thinking about you. You didn't, nor does anyone, deserve a jerk like Hendriks making their lives miserable. I couldn't just stand by and let that happen. And I missed you."

"Am I forgiven?" Nicole asked.

"I forgave you at 'I missed you.'"

Nicole stood and took off Paul's T-shirt. Paul, still sitting on the bed's edge, stood and slid off his scrub bottoms, as they both looked down. His erection was complete.

Paul and Nicole stood facing each other again. He kissed her gently on the lips.

"God, how I missed you," Paul said.

Nicole released the two top buttons, and her trench coat fell to the floor for the second time. Instead of the pizza box, only his erection now separated them. She grabbed his firmness and pushed it to the side and again stood on her tiptoes and kissed him again on the lips.

Nicole said, "I missed you, too. Really."

Paul cupped Nicole's face and kissed her gently, sweetly, then softly bit and tugged at her lips. She responded by doing the same to him, alternating tugging with sucking. While she singsonged a gentle hum, Paul cupped her breasts, then slowly closed his fingers until he found her nipples, still soft. He twirled them delicately at first until they started to firm. Nicole's hum lowered in pitch as he increased the pressure.

Paul guided Nicole down onto the bed and placed a pillow under her head. He spread her legs and kneeled

115

between them. He caressed one nipple with his fingers as he circled the other with his tongue. Nicole took and held deep breaths. Paul alternated nipples between his lips and fingers, stopping only to look into her eyes, glazed with tears again, but this time like translucent icing on a birthday cake.

"I love the way your eyes tell a story," Paul said.

"I've got so much I want to tell you."

"First things first," Paul said as he moved lower. Deep, moist, coarse scents had already spilled onto the sheets. Paul lifted his head and inhaled deeply. "You are something special."

"I wish I were. I feel so nothing most of the time," Nicole whispered.

"Trust me. Under that tough granite shell of yours lies something incredible."

Nicole grabbed Paul's firmness and used it like an airplane's joystick, circling and massaging her excitement. She shut her eyes and inhaled and exhaled in double time, small murmurs of nothing intelligible.

Paul watched, as long as he could. "Slow down. I need you to catch up."

He moved down in the bed and Nicole lost her grip. He circled his arms around her legs and under her back and could feel the warm beads of sweat that rested in the curve of her spine and the small dimples on each side of her tailbone. He buried his head between her legs, using his tongue and lips to add dimensions, fervor, and depth that the joystick could not provide.

Nicole's "ohs" and "ahs" became deeper and throatier interspersed with inhaled semi-whistles as she shuddered once, then twice. "Please. Paul. Please."

Paul rose and pinned Nicole's arms above her head as he entered and exited, each time deeper to the core. Both, unblinking, looked at newfound joy, until both collapsed, finished.

As they lay side by side, each drenched in sweat and scents, he nibbled on her ear.

She turned toward him and said, "That was intense."

"Yeah. Amazing intense."

Twenty minutes later they stood face-to-face in the shower. Paul pulled Nicole's head onto his shoulder and sweetly kissed her forehead. Neither moved, or wanted to move, until the hot water tank emptied.

As they dried off, Nicole said, "It's late and you must be exhausted."

"Can you stay?"

"My brother's back on Lopez until tomorrow. Nobody will miss me 'til then."

"Good." Paul handed her a well-worn, frayed, Swiss-cheesed, blue and maize "Go Blue" T-shirt.

"What's this from?"

"You're now a Michigan fan. It's my favorite and I'll keep it until there's only the collar left. It's been everywhere with me."

"All the girls get to wear this?"

"Actually, no one but me has ever had that on. I swear."

"Why me?"

"Dunno. You look good in maize and blue. Maybe you'll break the spell and we'll beat Ohio State."

"Please."

"It felt right. And I am exhausted."

Nicole slipped on his threadbare, giveaway T-shirt and walked into the bedroom. Pillows of all kinds, sheets and blankets laced the floor. As she surveyed the cyclone remnants, Paul returned to the room with a fresh bottom sheet and together they started making the bed.

"What's going to happen to us?" Nicole softly asked.

"Dunno yet," Paul said. "Prediction is very difficult, especially about the future."

Nicole stopped tucking her side and stood. "That's the stupidest statement I've ever heard. Did you just make that up?"

Paul, nonplussed, smiled and kept tucking. "I'd agree, except it's supposed to be kind of a famous quote by Niels Bohr."

Nicole finished her side of the bed and giggled. "Like B-O-R-E?"

"Actually, it's B-O-H-R. He won a Nobel Prize in Physics by describing atomic structure and introducing quantum mechanics."

"I missed that chapter," Nicole said as they slipped under the covers facing each other. "Really, what's going to happen to us? I'm a big girl."

"I actually enjoy how you don't let me get off by saying anything I want. And you're blunt and to the point. I do know three things for certain."

"And that is?"

"I'm really happy right now, I'm exhausted, and I'm going to dream about pizzas." Paul buried his face in the nape of Nicole's neck, kissed it softly, then inhaled deeply through his nose. "God, you smell good. And this may have been the best day of my life."

Sleep came quickly to both.

Chapter 12

At nine, Nicole, wearing Paul's robe, walked out of the bedroom into the kitchen. Paul, sitting on a stool reading a medical journal, stood quickly. The kitchen sparkled with reflections of light everywhere as the southeast facing kitchen window let in the rare full force of a clear Northwest morning sun.

"Good morning. Coffee?"

Nicole nodded. "Black."

Paul moved around the counter, poured coffee into a cup, and handed it to Nicole.

"Thanks."

Both smiled, waiting for the other to break the what-do-you-say-the-morning-after-that-first-night-together moment.

"I got up," Nicole caved, "and you were gone. I thought maybe you left, waiting for me to leave on my own."

"Where's the confidence, Miss U.S. Marine? Admittedly, I thought I'd wake up and find you gone. You were dead to the world an hour ago. I was about to wake you."

Nicole shook her head. "Better you didn't. I haven't slept much lately. First, depressed, then ecstatic. I heard you banging kitchen drawers, saw the PJ bottoms, robe, and a new toothbrush in the bathroom, so I took it as a good sign."

"I just love that you say exactly what you're thinking without the slightest hint of filter."

"It works for me. I'm not much of an actress."

Paul approached Nicole and put his arms around her. He gently kissed each eyelid. "Whatcha wanna do today?"

She circled her arms around his waist and said, "Didn't exactly know if I'd be here, so I hadn't given it much thought."

"We could drive up to Snoqualmie, have breakfast at the lodge, and maybe hike down to the falls?"

"That'd be great but I've got to meet my brother at Sea-Tac at two something."

"Why's that? He's a big boy," Paul said, a bit confused.

"Tony tends to get lost or distracted. My mom will have him walk onto the ten-thirty ferry from Lopez, which gets into Anacortes at eleven twenty-five. He'll take the airport shuttle at the dock and get to Sea-Tac at two-fifty. I need to meet him and we walk home. Mom makes me promise to be there. He's got to be at work at six tonight."

"Okay," Paul said. "Plan B. We can be at the Anacortes terminal in an hour or so. Let's toast a bagel, go pick up your brother, then lunch and I'll drive you both home."

"You'd do that?"

"Uh. I just offered."

"You did. Didn't see that coming. I'd have to call my mom and let her know. Why you being so nice?"

"Pizza."

Nicole raised her eyebrows.

Paul added, "Well, to be honest. I really enjoy being with you, pizza or not."

Nicole walked out of the room, called her mother, and returned to the kitchen minutes later. "Done. We'd have to leave here by ten, about forty-five minutes. Okay?"

"Sure. Perfect. I'll toast some bagels," Paul said.

Nicole dropped the robe and took Paul's hand and pulled him back toward the bedroom.

"Pizza it is. We'll eat bagels in the car."

* * *

Paul drove north down Ferry Terminal Drive toward the ferry dock. The line of cars heading south on Terminal Drive meant the ferry had already docked.

"Let me go to Tony first," Nicole said. "You stay in the car for a moment, then come. I don't want to weird him out."

"Sure."

Nicole exited the car twenty feet from her brother, who was perched on a bench near the ferry dock and engrossed in a video game on a small tablet. Paul could see Nicole wave and say something, but Tony continued to concentrate on the tablet. She covered Tony's tablet with her hand to get his attention. Neither appeared upset with the other. Tony stood, hugged Nicole, and faced Paul's car. The fact that Tony was tall, dark-haired, slim, and distractingly good-looking juxtaposed the fact that Paul knew Tony had issues. When Nicole signaled, Paul exited the car and walked toward the sibs.

"Hi, Tony, I'm Paul. I'm a friend of your sister." Paul extended a hand.

Tony quickly moved both hands into his jacket pockets.

Nicole pulled her brother's sleeve and said, "You're supposed to shake hands when you meet someone for the first time. Remember?"

Tony looked to the ground as his right hand came out of his jacket, slowly. His hand extended limply toward Paul, then retracted quickly after the first shake and retreated to his pocket.

Paul looked at Nicole and did a slight eye shrug. She shrugged back.

"What say we get some lunch," Paul said. "I'm starved. Tony, where'd you like to go?"

"McDonald's," Tony said without hesitation.

"Really. I'm saying we can go anywhere," Paul responded.

"McDonald's."

"Probably shouldn't have given him the option," Nicole said. "He likes their ads. My parents would never let him go there."

"Then McDonald's it is."

Tony smiled but said nothing. Paul opened the back right passenger side door for him, but he stood outside the door, refusing to enter.

"What now?" Paul queried.

"I can't sit on that side," Tony said. "Nic knows that."

Nicole watched Paul shake his head with a mild look of frustration. "The seat belts on the right side of the car rub on his left side, where his scar is," Nicole said. "He hates it. He says it makes it numb and tingly, whatever that means."

"Okay. At least there's a reason," Paul said.

Once in the car, on the correct side, Tony asked Paul, "Do you like programming computers?"

"No," Paul said. "Not really. I use computers for everything, but I've never written any code. Nicole tells me you're good at it."

"I'm really good at it," Tony said. "My teacher, Mr. Bligh, says I'm really good. No one has ever said I was good at anything, 'cept Nic and my mom. He thinks he can find me a job someday."

Forty minutes later, after a Big Mac, fries, and a vanilla shake, Paul was Tony's new best buddy.

As they were about to leave, Paul said, "Tony, stand up and let me look at your scar. I'm a doctor. Maybe I can help the numbness and tingling."

"Here, at McDonald's?" Tony looked at Nicole, who nodded approval.

Tony stood and pulled up his shirt to reveal a six-inch scar just under his rib cage in the left flank. Tony looked down over his shoulder and touched a spot just under the incision. "There. That's where it feels funny. Sometimes tingly. Sometimes numb, like at the dentist when the medicine wears off. The seat belt rubs here."

124

Paul palpated the scar. "Feels okay. Probably some nerves were cut or were trapped in the scar tissue. There's probably nothing that can be done." He kept looking at the incision and mumbled, "Hmmph." A second later he mumbled "Hmmph" again.

"We don't like to talk about his 'thing,'" Nicole added, holding up two hands and two wiggly fingers in V-signs denoting a quote. "Let's talk about something else."

"Okay," Paul said. "I get it, but I need to talk to you about Tony's scar..."

"Later," Nicole said, nodding a big NO.

An hour and thirty-five minutes passed quietly, and Paul pulled in front of Nicole and Tony's apartment.

"You go on ahead," Nicole said to Tony. "I'll be up in a minute. Remember that you've got to be at work at six. Okay?"

Tony nodded, exited the car, and walked straight into his complex without saying good-bye to Paul.

"Tony's Tony," Nicole said. "He should have thanked you for lunch and said good-bye, but that's the way he is. It's not you. In fact, he's going to ask me as soon as I walk in when the three of us can go to McDonald's again. That's the closest to 'Thanks' you'll ever get."

"I didn't say anything. But I did think it was odd," Paul said.

"He's actually quite smart, just not practical. The docs and teachers on Lopez said he was slow, so he never got the right education. He's loving the programming class and apparently he's really good at it."

"I've had a great weekend," Paul said, switching subjects. "I'm on call all next week through Monday, so I need to be around the hospital. But I want to see you."

"I dunno." Nicole giggled. "Tony would be really upset if I see you."

"Why? You've gone out before without him."

"Yeah, but he'll think we're going to McDonald's. You acted like it was the greatest meal in history. Thanks for being so sweet." Nicole leaned over and kissed him. "I'm off Saturday and Sunday. I can tell Tony I've got to work a night shift Saturday and won't be home until Sunday morning. He'll be fine."

"If I have sick patients or emergencies, I may not make it back to my apartment until late Saturday night," Paul said. "I'll leave an envelope with a key with Hank at the front desk. Hank leaves at ten on Saturdays, so you have to be there before he leaves or you can't get into the building. Let yourself into my apartment if I'm not there. Just be prepared that you might not see me."

Nicole leaned over and kissed Paul again.

He hesitated a moment, then said, "I've got something else to say. I don't want to upset you."

"Don't spoil a great weekend. What?"

"Promise you won't get freaked out when I tell you..."

"Jesus, tell me already."

"I don't think Tony was stabbed. In fact, I'm pretty sure he wasn't."

"What? Why would you say that? That's so mean. Do you think I'm making all that up?"

126

Paul tried to grab Nicole's left hand, but she pulled away, leaning hard against the passenger side door. As she searched for the door handle, Paul reached for her hand again, which she slapped.

Nicole, angry, raised her voice. "How would you know? You weren't there. The doctor, Dr. McNeil, said he was bleeding to death and they saved his life by removing his kidney. Why would the doctor say that if it weren't true?"

"Please stop and listen," Paul pleaded. "I know Tony had surgery and I believe he had his kidney removed. I just don't believe he was stabbed."

"The doctor that saved his life and the nurses all said he was stabbed. He was beaten around his face and arms and legs."

"I know what you were told," Paul said. "But the incision, it's wrong. Trauma one-oh-one. Any penetrating injury to the abdomen or flank is approached with a midline abdominal incision. Always, no exceptions."

"You're making me angry," Nicole said. "Why is that?"

"One never knows the depth of the stab wound, so the surgeon is obliged to inspect the inside of the abdomen as well. Also, the surgeon needs to first get control of the blood vessels before exploring the kidney. You can't do that with a flank incision. I'd flunk my boards if I answered that a flank incision was acceptable. Unless McNeil was trained on the moon, he doesn't make that incision for a stab wound to the kidney."

Nicole was staring straight out the window, biting her lower lip. "I don't get it. What does that mean? What happened?"

"Honestly, I'm not sure and I'm not going to speculate unless I can examine Tony's hospital records. I can't get the records without permission. Can you sign a record release for Tony?"

"Not me, but Mom can. C'mon, what do you think happened?" Nicole pleaded.

"I don't know yet."

"You are freaking me out. You know my mom is going to ask; then it's going to bring up issues and memories she's spent a decade trying to forget."

"Can Tony sign his name?"

"Sure. Not legally. Mom does all that."

"The hospital doesn't need to know that. We don't need to bring your mom into this. Tony's an adult; just let him sign."

"Please, Paul, what do you think is going on?"

"Let's see the records first, rather than jump to conclusions. I may be totally wrong."

"Yeah, but you have to have some idea what..."

"Let's wait. Please," Paul interrupted.

"You're making me so mad. You think Tony gets in your way and you're going to pick on him like everyone else. Why are you doing this? Why? I'm going to go crazy thinking about this."

"Stop it, goddamn it," Paul said. "I don't mind Tony. Let's work this out together. Call me this week when you have a standard record release form from Highline

Hospital. We'll just change the addresses and I'll walk you through it."

Nicole said nothing, turned, opened the door, exited the car, slammed the door, and headed toward her apartment. Paul put his window down and yelled, "Don't go away mad. I'm trying to help."

Nicole whirled around. "You're not helping. I'm confused."

"I'm confused too. Let me help you."

Nicole turned and walked away.

Back in her apartment, she dialed numbers in area codes 442, 862, and, lastly, 248. She started each call by saying, "It's over. He's like all the other guys I've trusted."

Once hearing the story, all three said, "You're wrong."

Two days later, Nicole called area codes 442, 862, and 248. Again, each caller ended with "You're wrong."

* * *

Paul entered his apartment two Saturdays later at 2:30 a.m., forty-five minutes after finishing his second emergency ureteral stone extraction and stenting. After unsuccessfully attempting to reach Nicole by phone or text more than twenty times in the past thirteen days, he had given up.

Throwing his jacket, keys, and wallet onto the kitchen table, he opened the refrigerator to see if, by chance, anything edible could be salvaged. He couldn't remember if any of the Chinese takeout from three nights earlier still remained. He laughed knowing he had looked for the Kung Pao chicken remains the night before, unsuccessfully, and was hoping he had just missed it. To his surprise, a Styrofoam container sat on the top shelf, filled with pad Thai and brown rice.

What? Oh.

He turned and walked directly into his bedroom. The ambient light from the living room was sufficient to see a body curled up on his bed, wearing a "Go Blue" T-shirt.

Twenty seconds later, wearing only his scrub top, he curled beside Nicole and kissed her gently on the ear.

She turned slowly toward him and whispered sleepily, "Hi. What time is it? I got here at nine and held out until one."

"Just after two thirty. Two stone cases, back to back."

"You must be exhausted."

"I was, not now. I didn't expect you to be here," Paul said.

"You left the key with Hank."

"Yeah. Wishful thinking when I left it. A few days ago I told him you probably wouldn't show up. He was supposed to put it back in my condo but I guess he forgot."

"My good luck. I showed," Nicole said.

"You didn't answer any texts or voicemails for two weeks. I thought you were angry. I finally gave up."

"Angry would be an understatement. I was really pissed. Not so much now. Stuff happened," Nicole, now fully awake, said.

130

"Like?"

"I talked it over with friends."

"Which friends?"

"Just friends. They said I was wrong about you."

"Smart friends."

"I don't know about smarter but less impulsive," Nicole said. "Anyway, I finally sent in the record release after forging Tony's signature. Apparently, Stevens Cascade Hospital was purchased by Everett General in 2005, then closed in 2006 when they couldn't get accreditation. All the records were supposedly transferred to Everett. A really nice nurse at Highline helped me. We faxed it to Everett and then I called later to make sure they received it. I talked to some lady named Thelma. She had the fax and told me Tony's records would be held in storage off campus, but they would have them within forty-eight hours."

"And."

"I called on Friday, three days later."

"And."

"Thelma said they couldn't find any records. None. Nothing."

"She have any ideas where they could be?" Paul asked.

"No. She had already called administration and registration to confirm the dates. Tony had been registered. She said in twelve years she'd never seen a file go missing—entirely—and no one had signed it out. She called pathology and radiology because they keep copies

131

of their own records. Nothing. She then called billing for anesthesia and radiology, which is also separate, and they had records of Tony but everything had gone to collection. She called pathology billing and they had no records at all. Thelma said, 'Like he was there, but wasn't there. This is very strange.'"

"Yes. Very strange," said Paul. "By law, even if the pathologists don't look at the kidney under the microscope, they're obliged to view and record it."

"I'm so confused," said Nicole.

"I know it sounds crazy, but I'd like you to come to the clinic tomorrow with Tony. No one is around on Sunday. I'm just wondering if they really took out his kidney. We have a portable ultrasound unit and I can take a look. If the kidney's gone, I'll know."

"You mean they said they took out the kidney and didn't? And why were his face and arms and legs cut and bruised? I saw that. It was real."

"I don't know anything for sure. I'm sorry I even brought it up. I missed you, you know."

"When you surprised me by saying Tony hadn't been stabbed, I thought you were being mean and insensitive. Like the creeps in school who made fun of him. I was mad at myself for liking you. Another bad choice by Nicole."

"And now?"

"How tired are you?"

"A little. Less than I was when I walked into the apartment. I have to make rounds with my team at seven, and..."

132

Nicole put her fingers on his lips to quiet him. "I figured so." She sat up and pulled off her T-shirt. Then she straddled Paul's legs, sat him up, and helped him remove his scrub top.

"God, how I love the U.S. Marine Corps," Paul said as he buried his face over her tattoo and caressed her nipple with his tongue.

Nicole backed away for a second, then pulled the bedcovers over her head. She forced her knees between his legs and bent down to an already throbbing hardness, praying for attention.

Paul moaned, "Are you sure you want to do... Ohhhh." He gently caressed her hair with both hands as her movement created one guttural moan after another. Finally, Paul held her head firmly. "No more. I can't take too much more."

Nicole surfaced from under the sheets, moved up and mounted his firmness then circled and rocked until Paul exploded two weeks' worth of wondering.

She kissed Paul deeply on the lips, her tongue tickling deep. "That's how mad I am now. I'm sorry I doubted you."

Paul rolled Nicole onto her back and returned the penetrating kiss. "Heck. The last thing I wanted to do was hurt you, or Tony, for that matter. I swear."

"I believe you, now. I'm sorry," Nicole said.

"I forgive you but I don't know how I'm going to handle your ups and downs. You're here, you're not here. You're angry, you're not angry," Paul said. "There's no end of surprises with you."

"I try," Nicole deadpanned.

"Anyway, I'm glad you're here."

"There's something else as long as I'm on a roll," Nicole said.

"Good or bad?"

"I'm pretty sure you're not going to like this one."

"Okay?"

"I applied for a handgun permit."

"You what?" Paul semi-shouted. "Why would you do that?"

"McNeil. I swore to myself the night we came to Everett that whoever did this to Tony, I'd get even."

"You're insane. Did you bring the gun here tonight?"

"No. I don't have it yet, but I will. My prior felony conviction for assault was after my eighteenth birthday, so it's still on record. My Marine record may clear that up but I have to wait. I'll never be able to live with myself if I just let him get away with hurting Tony and destroying my family. I'm going to confront him."

"That's more than insane," Paul said. "The only proof you have is the incision on Tony's side. That's it. Not to mention the chart is missing. There's nothing else."

"It makes sense to me. He and the hospital billed us for a big surgery and it destroyed my family."

"You're not listening. It's the same response you had when you hit that guy with a tire iron. That didn't go well for you."

134

"Yeah, but that didn't affect my whole family and..."

"Besides," Paul interrupted, "McNeil could be totally innocent."

"That's not possible. He told us the kidney had been stabbed."

"Okay. Maybe he's not totally innocent, but I doubt he drove around Lopez Island looking for someone to have one of his or her kidneys removed. Whoever took Tony took him specifically, and there's got to be a whole bunch of other people involved."

"So what do I do?" Nicole asked.

"First, you have to promise me you won't buy a gun or do anything to anybody. Even if McNeil is guilty, you can't use vigilante law. Promise."

"I dunno. Maybe," Nicole said. "No, I won't promise yet."

"That's not good enough. Let's say you actually do something really stupid like shooting him, or worse, killing him, whether he's guilty or not. You think spending the rest of your life in jail is going to make your parents happy? You need to promise me you won't do anything."

"Okay. I promise," Nicole said, grudgingly, "...but I could change my mind."

Paul rolled to Nicole's side. "How do you expect me to concentrate on anything this week?"

"Beats me."

* * *

Nicole's calls to area codes 442, 862, and, lastly, 248 all ended with "Nico, don't do anything stupid."

Tony and Nicole took the bus to Seattle Med and met Paul in the hospital foyer just before Sunday noon, and together they took the elevator up one floor to the Urology and Transplant Clinic. As Paul circled the main desk to switch on the lights throughout the clinic, Tony found a waiting room chair, sat down then stood immediately and announced to the room, "I don't like hospitals."

"I don't like this hospital and, in particular, one specific elevator," Nicole mumbled.

Paul, understanding but ignoring Nicole's commentary, said to Tony, "I bet so. I don't really know anyone who *likes* hospitals."

"And I don't like pain," Tony added.

"I promised you that this wouldn't hurt," Paul said, "even a little. Remember, we're just trying to see why your scar aches when you put on a seat belt. I probably won't find anything, but it can't hurt to look."

"Okay. You didn't promise Nicole it won't hurt me. Promise her too," Tony demanded.

"Nicole, I promise not to hurt Tony."

"Got it, Tony. It won't hurt a bit," Nicole said.

"Can Nicole watch?" Tony asked.

"Absolutely," said Paul.

The ultrasound took less than five minutes. Tony's left kidney was missing.

"I'm sorry, Tony," Paul said as he wiped the gel from Tony's flank. "I can't find any reason for your numbness. That didn't hurt, did it?"

"No. Just the jelly was cold."

"I have a little time," Paul said. "You guys wanna get lunch at the cafeteria? I can't leave the hospital."

"Oh, that's not necessary. We have to get back..." Nicole said.

Tony interrupted. "I'd love to. What do they have?"

"The best mac 'n cheese and lots of other stuff," Paul said.

"Tony has to be at work at six and the buses don't run as often on Sunday, so we can't really stay," Nicole said. "Not to mention, I don't want to run into you-know-who."

Paul pulled Nicole aside. "You're probably right about that, particularly if I'm with you. I can go with Tony to the cafeteria, pick up the food, and we can eat here in the clinic lunchroom."

Nicole nodded agreement. "Okay, we'll stay for lunch, but it has to be quick," she announced to Tony.

"We need to talk, in person," Paul said, "without Tony, and I can't leave the hospital. I have a ureteral stent to put in about four, two consultations to see, and a possible transplant late tonight. So, I'm probably not going home. How about I loan you my car so you drive Tony home and to work. You can pick me up here at the hospital tomorrow evening and I'll drive you home."

"You don't need your car?"

"No. I have to stay in the hospital tonight. Plus, you having my car guarantees that I see you tomorrow. I look at that as big positive."

"I can't stay tomorrow night. I have to work in the morning. Can't you just tell me what you think?"

"First, I need to do a little research into Dr. McNeil. Then I want to bounce this whole thing off a few other people, without using names. I need to make sure I'm not missing something."

"I can't believe this. Dr. McNeil was like a god to my parents. We felt blessed that he saved Tony's life. Will you call me tonight?"

"No. I want to be with you when I explain everything. Your reaction after I said Tony wasn't stabbed may be the tip of the iceberg. All of this, everything, is supposition."

"I've never made peace with myself about Tony, but it hasn't consumed me like it did for years. Now, I'm so confused and afraid that nothing good will come of this mess, and my parents and I will go back into a funk. Oh, God."

"Remember, no matter what," Paul said, "it's not going to put Tony's kidney back. We can stop looking into this anytime you say so."

As they walked to the car, forty-five minutes and three mac 'n cheeses later, Paul asked Tony, "So, how was lunch?"

Tony, hands in pockets, was miles away and didn't answer. Paul didn't ask again.

Nicole mumbled, "Told you so."

* * *

Nicole returned the next evening at seven thirty. She pulled Paul's car into the loading zone outside the Starbucks on Madison Street abutting the hospital. Paul got into the car on the passenger side.

"Hi. Glad you got here safely," he said.

"Where we going?"

"I thought you'd drive to your place and we can talk on the way."

"You wanna drive?" Nicole asked.

"Nah. I'm exhausted. Late last night and then a five-hour surgery this morning."

"Okay. On a lighter note, I'd like to tell you that once we left the parking lot last night, Tony said, 'Paul is really nice to me. I like him. Do you like him?'"

"What did you say?"

"I said I liked you okay."

"That's it?" Paul asked.

"And that you were nice," Nicole said.

"I'm on a roll. Both okay and nice."

"Yep. That's it. With Tony, things go really, really slow. But then he said, 'Well, don't do anything stupid, sis. Maybe we can get another McDonald's meal. I think you should kiss him. I won't tell Mom.'"

"And?"

"I said I'd give it some thought."

"You do that."

"I haven't stopped thinking about Tony and Dr. McNeil. Why would he say Tony's kidney was stabbed? Just so he could bill for some surgery?"

"It's possible. Anything is possible but I don't think so. Not for sure. Curiously, have you ever read the book *Coma* by Michael Crichton?"

"No. What's that got to do with it?"

"Maybe a similar story. I've talked to two other urologists without using Tony's or your name. I've got to ask if there is anything about Tony that would make him unique other than his autism-Asperger's?"

"No, not that I know of," Nicole said.

"No. You don't happen to know Tony's blood type?"

"Actually, I do. AB negative."

"How would you know that?"

"Tony and I and most of the Lopez School were tissue-typed when Janell Meric was diagnosed with leukemia. That must have been when I was in fourth grade. They finally found a donor in Colorado, but the Meric family made a push to have every Lopezian typed to support Janell. She died three months later. The science teachers at school made a big deal about teaching blood typing to everyone. It stuck with me. My dad is A-positive, Mom and I are B-negative, and Tony's AB-negative."

"AB-negative is the most rare, but that doesn't explain it."

"Curiously, six months later, the blood bank in Seattle contacted my mom and asked if they could run some more tests on Tony," Nicole said. "They said they'd come to Lopez to draw the blood. Apparently he had some unusual findings on some other blood tests."

"Probably HLA. Those are other tests used in tissue typing."

"Anyway, the people at the blood bank said Tony's AB negative and the other stuff was really unusual. One of the nurses told my mom that Tony better not need a transplant. They did a bunch of other blood work and then we never heard from them again."

"Okay, here goes," said Paul.

"Here goes what?"

"What I think happened, none of which I can prove." Paul then hesitated. "You understand that I can't prove anything?"

"Yeah."

"My guess is that someone needed a kidney transplant badly and couldn't find a match. Someone powerful and with a ton of money. Tony was kidnapped because he was the match. Today it might not have been so important because the anti-rejection medications and protocols are much better. But fifteen years ago, it was a big deal. If Tony had some really unusual tissue type, that would explain why they'd go to the trouble to come to Lopez. It's the only thing that makes sense."

Nicole said, "Oh. And what about the bruises and cuts on his face and arms and legs? Why would they do that if they only wanted his kidney."

141

"You're right. That doesn't make sense unless they wanted to deceive the doctors and police. They wanted everyone to believe Tony had been assaulted. The bruises were a subterfuge."

"A what?"

"A subterfuge. A deception used to achieve their goal to make you think this was an assault. He was kidnapped and shows up sixty miles away in less than an hour. Obviously something was very well planned out."

Nicole nodded, clenched her jaw tightly, and then mumbled, "Oh, shit."

"It's crazy because we can't prove a thing and we could be wrong. Just the fact that the incision is wrong doesn't make a case, even if it was bad judgment. And even if I'm right and could find the records, I'd guess they'd be doctored to make everything look reasonable."

"Now what?" Nicole, unusually sedate, asked.

"I did a little checking on McNeil. One of the chief residents from two years ago is working at Everett General and asked around. Apparently McNeil trained in Chicago and was hired in ninety-three to set up a transplant program. He wasn't busy enough, so he did general urology on the side. He and his wife lived very modestly and he complained often about not making enough money. He did own a cottage in Index. His wife was a surgical tech and apparently assisted him on most of his cases. Rumor was that he told Everett General he was going to move back to the Midwest. The hospital apparently continued to subsidize him. He and his wife started a restaurant in Everett that lasted six months and failed. They apparently lost a ton of money and declared bankruptcy."

"I'm listening," Nicole said.

"Then, out of the blue, ten years ago, give or take and apparently just after Tony's surgery, McNeil announced that he was quitting medicine. He and his wife had purchased a winery near Walla Walla. He worked another six months, sold their houses, and walked away from the practice. That's it. Apparently, the winery, called Reversement, has done really well. I Googled it. It's huge. My guess is that someone paid him a ton of money to remove Tony's kidney so that he could buy the winery."

"I want to kill him," said Nicole, no longer sedate.

The tone of Nicole's comment chilled Paul. "You can't. Despite all I've told you, we don't know for sure that I'm right."

"It's the first time anyone, and I mean anyone, has come up with an idea why Tony was kidnapped and stabbed. The police had no clues, and we weren't smart enough to even think that Tony wasn't stabbed."

"I'm sorry," said Paul.

"Sorry isn't close."

"You have to promise me you won't do anything unless we have some proof. Promise?"

"I promise...but my fingers are crossed." Nicole held up her right hand with her index and middle finger crossed. "So what could we do?"

"Tony can't help. Neither will McNeil or the kidnappers. You can't just knock on the door and ask, 'Did someone kidnap my brother and then steal his kidney?' and expect to get an honest answer. Plus, these might be very bad people who may not want you to talk to anyone...ever. Get it?"

"I get it. But I'm not such a nice person and I have friends too."

"I know you do, but it's like the Bad News Bears playing the New York Yankees, except the losing team disappears forever."

"Okay. What do we do?" asked Nicole.

"The only way we prove this is to find the person who might have received Tony's kidney."

"How do we do that?"

"Good question. I don't know."

"I have friends. Friends from the Corps. We could make McNeil talk."

"Please, for the love of God, don't do anything stupid. Remember, McNeil might not know where the kidney went, then what? Just keep your cool."

"Okay. But then I should probably mention that my license to buy a handgun was approved."

"Shit. You don't get it," said Paul. "I'm not going to help you unless you promise not to buy a gun."

"Okay. Okay. Okay. I get it. I'm not doing anything...yet."

"Hopefully I can get someone to look at the NMDP registry and see who might have matched Tony's tissue type. Then we can look at the SRTR and..."

"What's SRTR and NM whatever?" asked Nicole.

"The NMDP keeps track of all the tissue typing. The SRTR is a registry that keeps track of all the recipients of transplants in the US. We see who might have had a transplant within twenty-four hours of Tony's accident. It's a start. Maybe we'll get lucky."

"What happens if the kidney went out of the country?"

"We're screwed. Let's hope not."

"Can I tell anyone what we've been doing?" Nicole asked.

"Who would you possibly tell?" Paul asked back.

"Friends. Friends from the Corps. Friends that could help me straighten this out."

"There's nothing to straighten out yet."

"You've made that abundantly clear. But these guys saved my bacon in Afghanistan and I saved theirs. None of us would ever do anything to hurt the other. I trust them."

"The surprises keep on coming. You wanna talk about the 'friends'?"

"We'd need a whole day for that. But I tell them everything. They all know about you."

"What do they know?" asked Paul. "Are these guys?"

"All guys, just friends. They know enough."

Paul thought for a moment. "Don't tell anyone yet, please," he pleaded. "I think that'd be really dangerous. If for any reason what we're doing gets out, you're putting our lives and the lives of your friends, parents, and Tony in jeopardy. I get the feeling whomever we find will not be nice people. Plus, if I get linked to this, in any way, I could lose my job, license, and residency."

"For what? Looking for the truth?"

"I'm not a lawyer, but privacy laws trump smelling around, unless you get a court order. If you go to the police, trust me, everything will shut down and no one will be able to prove a thing. Let's look for clues while no one is expecting us to look. It's been years and I'd bet whoever did this is a bit more relaxed."

"I'm not a patient person," Nicole demanded.

"Really. You think so? What was your first clue?" Paul asked, not nicely.

"Hey, drop the sarcasm."

"Remember, I'm on your side as much as your friends. Let me do a little work first."

* * *

Nicole talked to Paul every night for the next three days and each time received the same response. He was working on 'it' in his limited free time and what he was doing went well over the line of being legal. He reiterated that he needed to explore the situation slowly so as not to arouse suspicion.

Despite admonitions from Rogers, Karsen and Lazzari to be patient, Nicole's tolerance for waiting had disintegrated to wafer-thin. Desperate, she surprised Paul on Friday night with a late night meal and intense sex, hoping for answers. She got none.

She then turned a one-eighty, guessing that refusing his calls and texts would spur him into action. "Don't call or text me until you have something, I won't answer."

Her impatience morphed into nervousness and then into frank agitation. She realized that contacting Paul wouldn't change a thing, so she didn't.

Finally, five days later she received a text from Paul at nine-thirty p.m. that he had information, was leaving the hospital, and would call her when he was outside her apartment. She flitted around, hummingbird-like, watching the clock. Even Tony, usually oblivious to Nicole's antics, asked if she was okay.

At 10:05 p.m., Paul called to say he was parked outside.

Nicole hustled out of her apartment wearing only a T-shirt and pajama bottoms into the cold and damp Seattle night, ran across Military Road and got into Paul's car.

"It's been ten days. So what did you learn?" she asked.

"Well, hello to you too. Nice outfit," he responded.

"Sorry. I'm anxious."

"Forgiven. Don't even ask how I got this information," Paul said. "If what I've done gets out, I've lied and committed enough HIPAA violation felonies to give up hope of practicing medicine anywhere in the Western world."

"I'm sorry. So...?"

"I been talking to the tissue registry in Minneapolis," said Paul.

"And?"

"You and your parents are on the tissue-typing databank but not Tony. I called and asked how that could happen and they said it couldn't. Once you're typed, you're there forever. Even if you die. And Tony's not there."

"How is that possible?"

"They said it's not possible but I gave them my number in case they could figure out what happened."

"And?"

"They couldn't figure it out and referred me to the data manager. Apparently there's a backup that's done every three days, and they have backups to 1994. I told the manager the same story and he said, 'Couldn't happen,' but he'd check. He called back thirty minutes later and said, 'Impossible but Tony was registered in 1999.' He couldn't explain it. In fact, he said the President of the United States couldn't change the registry. Anyway, they put Tony back on."

"I don't get it. How does that help us?"

"It doesn't. It just suggests someone really powerful or rich or both was able to get access to the database and delete persons they didn't want found. I then asked the data guy if he could check to see if anyone else registered before April 2002 was removed along with Tony. He asked why and I told him I'm doing a research project and have to be sure that everyone on the database is still there or else three years of research is worthless. I lied."

"And?"

"He said he'd need a couple of hours of programming time to run both sets of data and he'd also need to check with his boss. I asked if the boss was likely to say 'no' and he said, 'It's a definite possibility because we're busy.' I told him that I needed it badly for the research project and I'd be happy to pay him a hundred bucks on the side to run the numbers. He said he would, but made me promise not to tell anyone. I told him, 'Absolutely.' He said he'd like to be paid first."

"Now what?" Nicole asked.

"We wait again."

"I can't stand this."

"Me either. Be prepared that we've reached a dead end. I called the transplant registry to see if anyone had gotten a kidney in Washington State about the time Tony's kidney was removed."

"And?" Nicole asked.

"None were done for three days."

"So?"

"No one would wait three days to transplant a kidney. No way. So that leaves a few possibilities."

"And they are?"

"One, McNeil did nothing wrong. Two, the kidney was taken and sent out of the US. If so, we're done for. Three, and most likely, the kidney was sent out of Washington State but still in the US. If it's in the US, there were about three hundred transplants done in the days after Tony's surgery. There's no way in hell that we'll be able to check Tony against all three hundred without raising red flags everywhere."

"This is getting so complicated."

"Our best chance, maybe our only chance, is to see what the tissue typing data guy comes up with. If they took Tony off, they likely took the recipient off too. That might be the only mistake they made, taking the recipient off. So, we wait again."

"Shit. I hate this," Nicole said as she softly pounded the passenger side window.

"I'm doing the best I can," Paul said. "We just have to be patient. I've got to get back to the hospital but we should know more within a few days."

"Fine. Fine. Call me when you know."

"I've really got to go," Paul said.

"I'm sorry. I know you're trying. Go."

The visit ended on an uneasy note as Nicole shut the car door. A light rain had begun but Nicole was too anxious to head back into her apartment. She walked out onto Military Road, sans coat, and called Allen Rogers. A quarter of mile later, Rogers had calmed Nicole enough that she realized she was wet and freezing. She thanked him and hurried back to her apartment.

Tony, worried, was on the apartment complex driveway looking for her when she ran up the driveway.

"You scared me, Nic. I was worried when you weren't outside the door and didn't have a coat," he said

"I'm not a patient person," she said. She grabbed Tony's hand and together they reentered their apartment.

* * *

Paul fielded a call at home three nights later.

"Dr. Roberts. Frank Moss, here. From the NMDP."

"Hey. Frank. It must be after midnight in Minnesota. What's up? I assume you got the cashier's check."

"Yep. I'm calling from home. I wrote an Excel program to search the current database, comparing it to the database from the April 2002 backup, looking for registrants that don't show up currently. Technically the readout should have been a null set, now that your research patient has been re-registered. Much to my surprise we did find one other exception from Southern California about the same time, and I've reinstated her into the registry. Thank you again for finding the missing link. I'm guessing that the one exception isn't going to change your research findings."

Paul had prepared for the response. "Well, that's wonderful. I'm sure you're correct that the one deletion is not significant, but, in my case, it may be. I know that you cannot give me a name, nor do I want or need one."

"You're right about that. I've already done a private search that I wasn't supposed to do."

"I understand. But without giving me any personal information, I'd like to ask you a few details. Is that okay?"

"We'll see. It depends on what you need."

"I, of course, have no idea who this person might be, but I'd like to make an educated guess about their tissue type profile. All you have to do is tell me if I'm right or wrong."

"Uh. I don't know."

"I know you've got thousands and thousands of registrants. Giving me their blood and HLA typing isn't going to divulge anything. In fact, using my research, I'm going to guess what the typing revealed. All you have to do is tell me if I'm off base."

"Okay. What do think?" Moss asked.

"If my data collection and algorithm are working, I'd say the person is AB negative."

"That's right."

"I'd guess HLA-A star 02:110:03:02N."

"Right again. Wow. You gonna publish this?"

"Yep. Just need to rewrite the conclusion. I'm presenting the paper at the AUA meeting in San Diego, then submitting it to a journal, probably *Transplantation*."

"Cool," Moss said.

"HLA-B star 01-109-03-02J."

"Yep. Oh, wait, 02H."

"That's fine. Close enough." Paul went through four more major types—HLA-DP, HLA-DQ, HLA-DR, all close to perfect.

Paul, knowing no paper or algorithm existed, nor would one ever see the light of day, thanked Frank and said he'd let him know when and where the paper might appear.

After disconnecting, Paul realized that his lips and fingertips were numb from hyperventilating. He laughed at himself as he tried to slow down his breathing. Closing his eyes he couldn't stop himself from going through the physiology of hyperventilation.

I'm blowing off CO_2, which changes the ratio of CO_2 to bicarb levels, which causes the pH in the blood to rise. The body responds by constricting the blood vessels to the brain, which causes the numbness.

Within a minute, the numbness had dissipated.

Paul then called Nicole and quickly explained what he had just discovered.

Nicole asked, "But we still don't know who this person might be?"

"Well, no. But we're closer," Paul said. "The database guy said the registration occurred in Southern California, and he used the word 'her,' so I assume he's not mixing pronouns and it was a woman."

"Great. That's great," Nicole said emphatically, clenching her fist.

"That's as far as I've gotten so far. As of now I have no access to the databases in Southern California. Heck, I don't even have full access to the databases here in Seattle. I can't tell you how many lies I've told already and how many laws I've already broken. I'm sure enough that if someone catches wind of this, I won't be practicing medicine in the Western world. At least you've got a region for your kidney thieves, probably a female recipient, and Dr. McNeil removed Tony's kidney. We know a lot, but also don't know even more. I don't want you doing anything stupid. You have to promise me."

"Let me think on it for a day or two. Are you on this weekend? Hope not."

"I'm not off until a week from Friday evening after rounds. Maybe six, six-thirty. Then I'm free until Monday."

"You've been beyond amazing. I'm sorry I doubted you," Nicole said. "I've still got your key. I'll meet you at your place a week from Friday, if that's okay, and we'll see what'll happen next."

"Do you know what'll happen next?" Paul said.

"Pretty good idea. But I've got ten days to think on it."

"You won't make any decisions until we talk, right?"

"Right. By the way," Nicole said, "I finished my nurse's aide internship on Wednesday, and the proctor sent in my certification papers. That's good."

"Nice. Congrats. We should celebrate. You think I'll be able to concentrate on anything until then?"

"Probably not. But I'd try and get some rest the night before."

Nicole hung up, then dialed Allen Rogers and explained what she had just learned from Paul.

"There are still a shitload of *I dunnos*," Rogers said. "We don't know for sure that the kidney stayed in Southern California or the person who got the kidney hadn't moved. Could be anyone, anywhere."

"At least we have McNeil. He would know, wouldn't he?" Nicole asked.

"Maybe," Rogers said, "but probably not if these guys knew what they were doing. Shit, they accessed and modified an inaccessible and unmodifiable national database. If these guys were pros, then I'm guessing

154

McNeil might have been used without knowing where the kidney was going or to whom. He may have had one contact person, who may or may not exist or be reachable. McNeil could be a total dead end. If McNeil could ID them, I'm thinking he's dead meat. Then again, I could be wrong. But I'm never wrong."

Next, she called area code 862 and, forty minutes later, area code 248.

All three calls gave Nicole the same advice: *Don't make any decisions until we conference.*

Chapter 13

The next evening, Allen Rogers sat swiveling on his home office chair while he used his cell phone to set up a three-way conference call with Rico Lazzari and Cary Karson.

"What are we going to do with Nico?" Rogers asked.

"I'm not at all comfortable getting involved," Lazzari said. "She's jumping into a snake pit. These may be really bad people."

"Hell if I know," Karson added. "Rico's right."

"Hey, assholes," Rogers shouted, "when you guys left Pendleton, we all agreed that if one of us needs help, we'd help. Remember, this conversation wouldn't be happening if Nico hadn't saved all our sorry asses."

"I don't get it," Lazzari said. "This shit happened years ago to her brother. Can't put the kidney back, and her brother is okay. I say let sleeping dogs lie."

"I don't think she understands, or doesn't care, what she's stepping into, Sarge," Karson said. "You know how hot-headed she gets when she's got a burr up her ass. We gotta go slow and think this out real careful like."

"We don't know who kidnapped her brother," Rogers said, "but it's unlikely that whomever it was used government people. Even the CIA and FBI aren't stupid enough to get involved. These guys were pros and were not getting paid by Uncle Sam. Agreed?"

"Yep," Karson and Lazzari said together.

"So, how we gonna find them?" Karson asked.

"Don't know yet," Rogers said, "and I'm concerned big time. If the people behind all this find out Nicole knows about the kidney snatch, they're going to appear real quick. My guess is that they're so connected they can't afford to let this go public. Nicole, her family, and McNeil might just disappear. Nico's doctor friend too, if they figure out who tipped Nico off."

Lazzari and Karson echoed, "Sheeeit," together.

"I'm not sure where McNeil fits in," Rogers continued. "Nicole wants his ass, but he's probably way out of his league. I say let's wait a few weeks and see where Nico's head goes. Let's hope she cools off and doesn't do anything stupid."

"She's Nico. She can find trouble even when she's not looking," Lazzari added.

All three laughed and then said good-bye.

Chapter 14

Although Paul had talked to Nicole every day, when he entered his condo that Friday night, he hadn't seen her for twelve days.

The night before, Paul had ended his call to Nicole with, "Talking is talking. But I need contact. I need to feel you, touch you, and kiss you. You're addicting and I can't get enough. I'm thinking and dreaming of you twenty-four/seven."

"I'm sorry. See you tomorrow night. Sleep tight," Nicole said.

* * *

Paul entered his unit at nine thirty Friday evening, praying that some sense, smell, sound, or sight would live up to the week's dreamy diversions.

Please let her be here.

Sight came first—the unit was dark. He turned on the lights and listened—quiet.

She's not here. She's not here.

Overcome by a sense of sadness, Paul felt no urge to hang up his coat and threw it over the couch. He took a deep breath, resigned to his fate of longing. In doing so, he sensed a faint smell.

Different.

The smell rekindled hope. Paul inhaled again, this time through his nose—vanilla or lavender? He opened the door to his bedroom. Nicole's clothes lay strewn across the bed.

"Nicole?"

"Yep. I'm in the bathroom." The words came from the closed bathroom door. "Just got out of the shower and was combing my hair."

"When I walked in, I thought you might not have..."

The bathroom door swung in quickly, stopping Paul in mid-sentence. Nicole entered, towel-drying her hair, wearing only his Michigan T-shirt.

"Hi," she said. "I put a lasagna in the refrigerator and brought a bottle of wine. I thought that we could..."

Paul, listening to Nicole's melodious tone, felt all three senses sated as he wrapped his arm around her neck, drew wet hair into his face, and inhaled. Everything that he feared and everything he loved was there in his grasp. He interrupted her before she could finish her thought. "Oh my God, have I missed you. You can't even imagine. When I walked in, I thought for a moment you weren't here or, worse, not coming."

Nicole dismissed the comment. "You're not hungry?"

"Not now."

"I thought this might happen. The lasagna will have to wait. Do you want to take a shower? I'm game for another. The bathroom's still steamy and toasty."

"Sure."

Past the bedroom, past clothes strewn on the bed and floor, past sheets already turned down, into the bathroom, hyperventilation created numbness and tingling in Paul's fingers and lips. Nicole turned on the shower and removed her T-shirt. Paul saw her back, rosy from the hot shower minutes earlier, and gently touched her warm shoulders with his lips.

Turning, Nicole said, "My turn to undress you."

Heated by steam-overloaded senses, she walked Paul into the shower, deflecting the too-hot water. She turned him around until the water poured over his head like a thick knit cap, and began to wash his chest and abdomen, then kneeled to his thighs, moving left and right around the now-pole-like obstruction.

Nicole disregarded Paul's plea—"I can't promise I'm going to last very long"—as she gently scrubbed his body. He watched the water deflect from his chest to her head and shoulders as she knelt to wash his legs.

Paul's hands, resting on her shoulders, moved slowly upward to her temples and then he moved her head to center. Nicole swirled her tongue around his pulsating hardness.

Paul loosened his grip on Nicole's temples and grabbed the showerhead with his left hand to steady himself. "Enough. I'm going to lose it."

"It's okay if you do." Sliding his firmness between her breasts for a moment, she stood slowly and turned off the water. They toweled quickly and Nicole led him to bed.

"I missed you so much," Paul said. "I've not been processing reasonably for three weeks. I made love to you every night, or I wouldn't have slept."

Nicole kissed him softly on the lips, then straddled his chest and leaned forward to allow her still damp hair to cover his face like a tent.

Paul turned his head to inhale the sensual aroma of her auburn locks. "I missed you so much."

Nicole rotated over his chest with her knees above his shoulders. She placed the auburn tent atop his groin and massaged both thighs softly with the back of her hands as she swirled her tongue, softly, around the tip of his hardness.

"You're moving too fast," Paul said, separating her legs and pulling her moist muskiness up against his face, searching for that certain spot with his tongue.

When Nicole could take no more, she turned back and guided Paul into her warm and inviting depths. He erupted, a volcano with little sound other than deep and gratifying breathing.

He held her pelvis tightly against him as the hardness softened into a gentle ache. "I missed you so much."

"I know. I missed you too."

"You don't make it easy. I don't like wanting something so bad I can't think."

Nicole leaned forward and buried her face in Paul's neck. He moved his arms up and squeezed her chest into his.

"You know I love you," Paul said softly.

"I love you, too," Nicole said back.

The words came too quickly, without conviction, and felt small, too ordinary. Both knew her thoughts were elsewhere. She rose up and kissed Paul on the forehead.

Getting out of bed, Nicole donned the Michigan T-shirt, but said nothing else and walked back into the kitchen to heat the lasagna. Returning to the bedroom she found Paul's eyes closed. She nudged his shoulder gently, and his eyes popped open.

"Oh. Oh. I didn't realize how tired I was," he said, fluttering his eyes. "Let me close my eyes, think of you, and wake me up when the lasagna is ready. Is that okay? I need to get a second wind."

Nicole kissed his forehead once again, and his eyes closed.

* * *

Paul awoke at 4:20 a.m. He read the bedside clock, cleared his eyes, and refocused on the digital readout. Four twenty-one. Gathering his senses, he rolled over to ask Nicole why she hadn't rousted him for dinner.

Empty. The bed was empty.

Paul switched on the bed light and looked back to where Nicole should have been. The pillows and sheets lay flat, cold, and undisturbed.

The room had no answer for Paul's plaintive "What's going on?" He jumped out of bed, ran into the main living area, flipped on lights, and searched. Nothing. He doubled-timed back to the bedroom for his cell phone when he saw a folded letter on the table next to the charging phone with "PAUL" written clearly across the front.

> *Paul,*
>
> *Forgive me but I knew no other way.*
>
> *You can't be with me now. I have things to do.*
>
> *I can't, in good conscience, jeopardize your ability to practice medicine any more than I have already. You may or may not understand or agree, but it's for the best.*
>
> *Please don't try to reach me. Tony wouldn't understand and he won't know where I've gone, nor will my parents. I don't know when I'll be back. Tony can't manage without me, so he's going back to Lopez.*
>
> *Please don't contact my parents. They don't know about Tony's kidney and why I've disappeared.*
>
> *I did keep the Michigan T-shirt, to which I have grown quite attached. Maybe, just maybe, I'll be able to return it someday. I put the lasagna into the fridge. OK to reheat it if* you're hungry.
>
> Nicole

Paul called Nicole's cell phone activating an immediate machine response.

"This phone number does not exist or has been disconnected. Message 492."

The line self-disconnected. Paul sat hard on the edge of the bed and crumpled the note. "Shit. I hope she didn't buy a gun."

* * *

Paul's car clock said 6:02 a.m. when he pulled in front of Nicole's two-story apartment house, parked on the streeet and walking up a pitted driveway. He guessed twenty units, ten to a floor with single doors facing outward. Seven or eight automobiles, two up on jacks with tires missing, another with the passenger side windows duct-taped, were randomly parked against a rotted wooden fence across from the first-floor doors. A weather-worn, semi-legible directory of the tenants had been nailed to the wall just under the cement staircase to the second floor. Using his cell phone's flashlight app, Paul reviewed the entire list carefully. **M rr n , N** was stuck onto the Unit #204 slot. Most names were Hispanic, and no other name was close to Marrone. He climbed the stairs to the second floor. The first door had the number one written with a felt-tip marker. Paul counted three more units down the exterior walkway and rapped softly once, then twice.

A hesitant voice came through the door. "Uh. Who...who's there? Nicole, is it you? Did you forget your key?"

Paul put his mouth next to the door and said, "Tony. It's me, Paul. Nicole's friend."

"Who?"

"Paul. The one who took you and Nicole to McDonald's."

The sound of a slide lock disengaging preceded the door opening. Tony peeked outside. A chain lock allowed the door to open no more than four inches.

"It's me, Paul. I'm looking for Nicole."

"So am I. I thought she was with you. I was mad."

"I saw her last night," Paul said, "but she disappeared."

"Like magic? She was there and then wasn't?" Tony asked.

"No. She visited my apartment and I took a nap. When I woke up she had left."

"Oh."

"Can I come in so we can talk?" Paul asked.

"No. Nicole and my mom told me never to let anyone in."

"Okay then. Think carefully. Do you have any idea where she might have gone?"

"No. She left a note." Tony walked into a bedroom and returned with a piece of paper that he slid through the small door opening.

Standing outside, Paul read the note, twice.

> *Tony,*
>
> *I have something I need to do. I don't know when I'll be back. I didn't take my phone. If I'm not back by Tuesday, you'll have to move back to Lopez.*

> *Don't tell Mom until Tuesday. She'll pick you up at the ferry terminal.*
>
> *Nic*

"Do you have her cell phone?" Paul asked.

"No. I tried calling it, and it said the service was disconnected."

"That's what it said when I tried her number," Paul lamented.

"I'll have to go back to my mom's house if Nicole doesn't come back. I can't live by myself. That's what my mom and Nicole have told me."

"Who does Nicole talk to when she's on the phone?"

"I don't know," Tony said. "Nic usually goes out of the apartment to talk. She gets upset at me when she thinks I'm listening. I ask too many questions, I guess."

"Did she have a list of people to call if you needed help?"

"No. Just Mom and Dad. I know their numbers."

"You have no idea who she calls?"

"No. I'm hungry. Do you want to go to McDonald's?" Tony asked.

Paul shook his head. "Not yet. Do you have any of Nicole's phone bills? Maybe there's a clue."

"She keeps bills in a file in our bedroom closet. I'm not supposed to open it."

"She's gone," Paul said. "Maybe there's a clue in the box."

"Nicole will yell at me if I touch it."

"I'll do it. You just show me where it is," Paul said.

"I don't know. Nicole will still be mad at me."

"Two Egg-McMuffins and a large OJ if you show me."

"Okay. But you can't tell Nicole I showed you."

"Of course. My lips will be sealed forever," Paul said as he slid pinched fingers across his mouth.

Tony returned from the bedroom with a small box. "Here." The box wouldn't fit through the small door opening.

"You can open the door. I'm a friend," Paul said calmly.

Tony hesitantly nodded acquiescence, then unlatched and opened the door and handed Paul the box. Paul sat at a small kitchenette table and started rummaging through the box's contents.

Paul found a group of cell phone bills quickly and started scanning.

"What are the phone numbers of your mom and dad?"

"360-232-8288 and 360-290-0536," Tony said.

"Anybody in area codes 442, 862, or 248? Those numbers show up on every bill. I think 442 is near San Diego, but I have no idea where the others are."

167

"I don't know any of Nicole's friends," Tony said, "except from high school, but I don't think she talks to them. She'd tell if she did."

"She doesn't talk about anyone else?"

"No. Except about her friends from the Marines and sometimes from the hospital."

"I've got to leave now," Paul said, "and make some calls. Okay?"

Tony looked unsettled, shifting back and forth on both feet.

"What's wrong?" Paul asked.

"You said you'd take me to McDonald's."

"I did, didn't I?"

"Yes."

"A promise is a promise," Paul said, "and you're a friend of mine. I'll make the calls after McDonald's. Let's go."

I hope she didn't buy a gun.

* * *

Paul Roberts dialed the 442 number on his cell phone immediately after dropping Tony back at his apartment an hour later.

"Sergeant Rogers, here."

"Oh. Uh. Sergeant, you don't know me. My name is Paul Roberts. I'm a friend of Nicole Marrone."

"I know who you are. You're her doctor friend, eh? The one who found out about her brother's kidney."

"That'd be me."

"Is Nicole in trouble?" asked Rogers.

"I don't know. She's disappeared."

"Oh shit. I hope she didn't buy a gun."

Paul looked at the cell phone as if it had magical powers. "I thought the exact same thing," he replied. "That's a distinct possibility."

"Hey, how'd you find me? Nicole told me specifically she hadn't discussed us with you."

"Who is us? You and the ones who live in area codes 862 and 248?"

"You know more than I thought," Rogers said.

"I'll 'fess up. I got worried about Nicole and went to her apartment. Her brother found old phone bills. Your number kept showing up and I called. That's it."

"That's it?"

"Yep. Nicole has said she had friends that would help her out. I assumed she had called them."

"Nicole said she wanted to protect you," Rogers said. "You'd already risked a lot. She didn't think keeping you in the loop would be fair."

"I would have hoped that would have been a joint decision," Paul said. "I care for her. I guess she didn't care that much about me."

stab wound

"Listen, dickhead, before you get all weepy, if Nicole didn't care for you, she would have kept you around. We both knew you were an incredible asset. I told her so but she said she needed to protect you."

"So you know everything?"

"Yeah. Probably. So do Karson and Lazzari."

"I don't get it. Who are you guys?"

"My name is Allen Rogers. I was Nicole's sergeant. Cary Karson, Rico Lazzari, Nicole, and I ran a motor pool and bunked together in Afghanistan. Nicole risked her life to save ours and, in turn, we rescued her. I stayed in the Corps as an MP. Nicole, Karson, and Lazzari opted out. Nuff said. Any more you'll have to get from Nicole."

"So you're a cop?"

"Yeah."

"You know where she is now?" Paul asked.

"I have a pretty good idea. She wasn't listening to us when we gave her advice."

"She didn't listen to me either. I'm guessing she's on her way, alone, to confront Dr. McNeil," Paul said.

"Unless she's on her way to Southern California to look for the woman that got her brother's kidney," Rogers said. "But I don't think so. There wasn't enough to go on."

"You knew that too, about California?"

"Like I said, Nico told us everything," Rogers admitted.

"What did you think she should do?"

"I've got some connections and I thought I could get some intel on McNeil. We all told her to wait awhile, but Nico wasn't listening."

"She gets impatient quickly," Paul said.

Rogers laughed. "You have no idea. Anyway, I think her brother's kidney deal is a trigger. Once you told her about McNeil and then she couldn't find his medical records, she stopped reasoning. You think he's responsible? McNeil?"

"Absolutely, he's in on it. But he's only one small piece in the puzzle. Last I looked, kidnapping isn't taught in surgical residencies. Someone or somebodies had to approach McNeil. Then either pay him a ton of money or threaten him. My fear is that some really bad people are involved."

"You got that right. Had to be pros," Rogers said.

"I figure there's one more amateur who isn't used to doing these kinds of things," said Paul.

"And who might that be?"

"The transplant doctor in Southern California would have been the only one that could have found her brother as a match. Or, I suppose there is the possibility that the California doctor didn't even know the source of the kidney, and the whole thing was arranged by someone with a little knowledge about transplants and a lot of power or money or both."

"Shit. That just complicates things more. One more unapproachable asshole. I still think McNeil may be the best first step," said Rogers.

"I don't know that I agree with you. But I don't know what to think. To complicate things," Paul added, "Southern California is huge. LA, San Diego, Orange and Riverside Counties. All have multiple transplant programs."

"My biggest concern right now is that Nicole is gonna do something really stupid, with or without a gun," Rogers said.

"So what now?" asked Paul. "You're the cop."

"I work and so do Karson and Lazzari. None of us can just leave and play cowboy with Nicole."

"I don't have to be back to work until Tuesday," Paul said.

"Can you get to Walla Walla?"

"Sure. It's a five-hour drive or a fifty-minute flight. I checked and there's a flight tonight at eleven."

"Good," Rogers said. "I hope you don't own a gun?"

"No. Never."

"Good. Call me when you get there. Better yet, if you find Nicole have her call me."

* * *

Nicole left Seattle at noon on Saturday and arrived in Walla Walla at 10:25 p.m. The Greyhound bus from downtown Seattle went only as far as Pasco. From there, she switched to a Grape Line shuttle to Walla Walla. She had lightly packed a small suitcase. The only weight was a small metal box containing her new Glock G43 Single Stack nine-millimeter pistol and twenty-four rounds of ammunition.

172

Nine hours sitting in the back of the buses and empty terminals gave her ample time to visualize every scenario she could conjure up and her responses to each. None had her firing her pistol. She knew using her weapon would be calamitous, but she still felt better having it.

Nicole read and reread a downloaded brochure on tours of Reversement Vintners. The winery offered three tours on most days, but only one on Sunday at one o'clock. The Sunday tour, listed at 150 dollars, was the only one that would be led by Charles McNeil, and would accommodate only fifteen reserved guests. The tour included a three o'clock wine tasting followed by a visit to the McNeil's new mansion, supposedly the nicest in the region. The brochure strongly suggested reservations for the Sunday tour, as it usually booked full. Nicole had called on the prior Thursday to secure her single reservation, available only because of a cancellation earlier that day. The next available Sunday tour would be three months off. Nicole took her good luck as a positive omen, despite the warnings from Paul and her Marine compatriots to the contrary.

The tour required that each visitor be picked up and dropped off by a reserved bus because of the amount of alcohol likely to be imbibed. The pickups and drop-offs had to be one from a list of major Walla Walla hotels.

Nicole listed the Whitman Hotel, the oldest, largest, and most expensive property in Walla Walla. She had no intention of booking a room, nor could she afford the two-hundred-dollar rack rate. She secured a room at a Motel 6 for thirty-eight dollars, three blocks away, and would walk to the Whitman on Sunday morning.

* * *

173

Paul arrived in Walla Walla at eleven thirty Saturday night and booked a room in town at Red Lion Inn through the airport kiosk. The car rental facility had already closed for the evening, so he took a cab to the hotel. He had no idea where Nicole might be, if she was even in Walla Walla. He had done enough research while waiting for his flight at SeaTac to learn that the Reversement Winery had a strict no-guest policy and the only way to gain access to the grounds was on their daily tour. Paul assumed that Nicole would be on the tour.

Paul asked the nighttime concierge/desk clerk about access to the Reversement winery tour the next day. He told the clerk that he thought a friend of his might be on the Sunday tour and would have booked it in the last few days.

The clerk, shaking his head, responded immediately that the Sunday Reversement tours were always booked out months in advance and that Reversement never released a guest list. The Red Lion had no one booked onto the next day's tour. The clerk told Paul how he had tried earlier in the day to book a Sunday tour for a hotel guest and was told that the guest would need to wait until Monday and could pick any of the three times. The concierge said that Paul's friend would almost certainly be on one of the Monday tours.

"If my friend was on the Sunday tour, where might I go to find them?" Paul asked.

"Beats me," the clerk said. "Maybe you could check out the Whitman Hotel. The tour usually picks up guests there. Not always."

"What time will the tour bus be at the Whitman?"

"Dunno. S'pose about eight thirty in the morning. Their bus is usually here by eight forty if we have someone on the tour."

"Could you give me a wake-up call at seven thirty?"

Paul awoke at 7:10 a.m. of his own accord, dressed, and went down to the lobby to find a new clerk on duty.

"How might I rent a car?" he asked.

"No problem. The Hertz desk opens at ten a.m.," the clerk said.

"Oh no. That won't work, I have to be somewhere at eight fifteen."

"Can't help you. I have no access to the rental cars. You'd have to go back to the airport to find a rental car at this hour."

"Can you call me a cab, please?"

The same cab that brought Paul to the hotel showed up at 7:45. Paul drove out of the airport at 8:25 with his rental car, made two wrong turns, and arrived at the Whitman Hotel at 8:55.

The bellman, a white-shirted, somewhat portly gentleman in his fifties, stood under the portico at attention and smiled while Paul stopped in a clearly marked no-parking zone. Two young parking attendants stood behind the older man. Paul exited his car.

"Are you checking in?" the bellman asked.

"No. I'm looking for someone, a young woman, probably alone, who might have been on the bus for the Reversement winery."

"Can't help you there. The bus has already come and gone. I didn't see anyone other than two older couples from the hotel get on."

"You didn't see a young woman?"

"Nope. Just said I didn't, and I was standing right here."

"Would twenty bucks jog your memory?" Paul asked, putting his hand on his back pocket.

The bellman turned to look at the two parking attendants and then back to Paul. "Is this a trick? Are you trying to get me fired? No, twenty bucks won't jog anything. And get your car moved unless you want me to park it."

Paul said nothing as he watched the bellman turn and walk into the hotel. He returned to his car, fist pounded the window, and yelled, "Shit," at no one in particular.

As Paul searched for his car key, he heard, "I saw someone."

He turned to find one of the young parking attendants who had been standing behind the bellman. The attendant stood there with a quizzical look on his face and rolled his eyebrows.

"What did you see?" Paul repeated.

The young man looked skyward.

"Oh, I see," Paul mumbled, took out a folded twenty-dollar bill, and put it in the attendant's hand. "Okay?"

"A young girl, maybe twenty-one or twenty-two, real pretty, blue eyes, reddish-brown hair, walked in from off the street. She said something to the bus driver and pulled out ID. The guy looked on his clipboard and said something back. She had a backpack that looked full. She wasn't happy when the guy made her stow it in the luggage compartment. Anyway, she boarded the bus."

"That's it."

"Yeah. That's it. The bus took off and I went back to work."

"You saw all that and the bellman saw nothing?"

"Like I said, she was real pretty. I don't think Ben gives a shit about that. I do. I watched her until she got on the bus. You think she's who you're looking for?"

"Probably not," Paul lied, "but thanks anyway."

"Yeah." The attendant turned and walked into the hotel, twenty dollars richer.

Paul got into his car and headed east on Highway US12 toward Reversement.

     * * *

Paul's watch said 10:15 when he arrived at the Reversement Vintners entrance. An eight-foot stone wall fronted the property and appeared to continue indefinitely beyond the main gate along the highway. Glass shards were imbedded in cement at the top of the entire length of the wall to reinforce the notion that no one was welcome. A short driveway off the highway led to a guardhouse centering two huge wrought-iron gates. Paul drove up to the guardhouse and was greeted by signs proclaiming that no one could enter the property without permission. A uniformed man in his thirties exited the guardhouse and stood in front of Paul's car. He

177

wore the badge of a private security company. A holstered handgun and a walkie-talkie pinned to his chest with an earplug screamed "Listen up!"

"How may I help you? You lost?" the guard asked.

"I'm afraid I missed the tour bus, and my girlfriend is on it. Can I join the tour?" Paul asked.

"Your name?"

"Paul Roberts, but I'm not on the list. I'm not absolutely sure my girlfriend is either. Can you check for me?"

"I'm afraid we don't give out information like that. Even if we did and your friend is on the tour bus, the tour was full. The ticket instructions are quite clear. You miss the bus, you miss the tour. We don't allow private vehicles onto the property. The tour ends at four p.m., and our bus will drop the guests back at their hotels by four-thirty or five. You'll have to wait at your hotel. Sorry."

"I really need to see if she's on the tour."

"We instruct everyone to turn their phones to silent, but you could text her."

"Shit. She just changed phones and I don't know her new number. Please. Can't you just check the list?"

"I'm sorry. I can't do that. You're going to have to leave and wait at the hotel."

"I was surprising her and I don't even know which hotel she's staying at."

"For a boyfriend, you don't seem to know a damn thing. Best I can do, buddy, is suggest you wait for the

178

tour to end and follow the bus back to town. Sooner or later she'll have to get off the bus."

"Isn't there any way you could make an exception and..."

Just then the guard's walkie-talkie came to life; he quickly turned and re-entered his guardhouse.

Paul listened intently and all he could hear was the guard saying, "Okay. Okay. Shit."

The guard hit a button on his console and the exit opened. He turned to Paul and yelled, "There's been an emergency. Don't move your car until I say so."

"What happened?" Paul yelled.

The guard had already turned and walked out the exit side door of the guardhouse and stood.

Paul opened his door and walked in front of the guardhouse. "What's happening?"

"Get back in your car. Now. We've had an emergency, and a car is going to be coming through the exit at high speed. Get back in your car."

"I'll wait here," Paul said.

The guard unbuckled the safety strap over his holster and patted the top of his gun, "I said get back in your car and stay put."

"I'm a doctor, for God's sake. Maybe I can help. Will you tell me what happened?"

"Like I believe you. And I'm the President of the United States. There's been an emergency. That's all I know. Get back in your car."

"I need to know if my girlfriend has been hurt. That's all," Paul pleaded.

"Don't know who or what is hurt," the guard yelled. "All I know is there was an emergency of some kind. That's it. You get in the car and stay there until whoever's coming clears this gate."

Paul opened his car door and stood on the doorframe trying to get a look up the long driveway to the winery. A large black Mercedes, driving at extremely high speed, approached the gatehouse. Checking to see that Paul or his car hadn't moved, the guard looked back quickly.

The Mercedes slowed down to about forty miles per hour as it rumbled over the brick pavement, past Paul and the guard. The car fishtailed as it turned right onto Highway 12 and accelerated, heading toward Walla Walla. Through the tinted glass, Paul could make out the driver, a man perhaps in his fifties. The passenger seat was unoccupied, but a passenger with long hair, probably a woman, sat against the window of the back facing inside the car.

After the car cleared the property, the guard returned to Paul.

"You've got to be going now. And I mean NOW," he said, returning his hand to the top of the pistol.

"Shoot me if you want, but I'm not leaving until I find out if my friend was in the car."

"I'm gonna call the cops unless you move."

"Call. I'm being reasonable. I just want to know if my girlfriend was in that car. That's it."

"I'll try and find out what happened, but you've got to clear the property and park on the shoulder across the road."

"Okay. But you'll wave when you hear?"

"Yep. Soon as I know, you'll know. Might be a few minutes. I've got to make some calls," the guard said.

Paul drove across Highway 12, parked on the shoulder, and stood by his car. The guard returned to his guardhouse and picked up the phone.

Five minutes later a Walla Walla sheriff's patrol car made a U-turn in front of Paul's car and stopped.

Twenty minutes later, Paul, handcuffed, was booked at the Walla Walla Sheriff's Office. His rental car was towed back to the airport, courtesy of JoeBob's Towing service. Paul made bail and exited the sheriff's office on Alder Street at 4:00 p.m. He would need to return to Walla Walla for a trial or pay an exorbitant fine.

Having no car, he walked five blocks to the Whitman Hotel. He still had no idea who or what was in the Mercedes or even if Nicole had been on the tour.

As Paul walked, he called Allen Rogers in San Diego and explained the previous five hours of sheer aggravation.

Rogers could do nothing but laugh. He promised he would tell no one the story other than Lazzari and Karson. Paul said he'd call Rogers back as soon as he found Nicole, or if he didn't find her.

As soon as Paul disconnected, Rogers called the Walla Walla Sheriff's Office in an attempt to fix things for Paul—cop to cop. The sheriff was an ex-Marine and had been an MP before moving to Washington State. Two *semper fi*s later, Paul's aggravation was gone.

Paul arrived at the Whitman fifteen minutes before the tour bus. After two couples exited the bus, Paul jumped on to see if Nicole was aboard. She was not.

He exited and quickly caught up with one of the couples who had entered the hotel.

"Excuse me" he pleaded. "I am looking for my girlfriend. I thought she was on the bus. Could she have gotten off or didn't take the ride back?"

The woman was dismissive and walked away. The man, perhaps in his early sixties, said, "There was a young, pretty girl that started on the tour. After the accident, McNeil departed quickly to an emergency room."

"Was she or McNeil hurt?" Paul interrupted.

"No, silly. An empty oak wine barrel fell on McNeil's dog's front leg. I think it was broken. He left to take the dog to the veterinary hospital."

"Oh," Paul sighed.

"The tour guide offered everyone a refund because we didn't get to meet with the vintner. Bummer. He's supposed to give an extraordinary talk on Washington wines. Reversement offered us a total refund or one hundred ten dollars in credit at the wine shop at the end of the tour if we stayed. Only the young lady, who was visibly upset, chose the refund. She left the tour and was brought back to town immediately. That's the last I saw of her."

"Could you tell me what she looked like?"

The man looked to see if his wife was near. She wasn't. "Strikingly beautiful, with large blue eyes and auburn hair. If she's your girlfriend, you're one lucky SOB."

Paul lied again. "Nah. Doesn't sound like her. Thanks anyway."

He made a quick call to the bus station. The only bus to Seattle had departed at 9:00 a.m. Paul already held a reservation on the last flight to Seattle at 11:00 p.m.

No way she pays for a flight. She'll stay until tomorrow, so she's got to be in town. Somewhere.

Paul went in and out of bars and restaurants for almost an hour until he entered the Blue Hippo Bar on Colville Street. He found his Michigan T-shirt first. Nicole, back to the door, sat alone on the edge of a corner booth, staring into space, nursing a beer and a half-eaten hamburger.

Paul sidled up to the booth and broke Nicole's trance. "Go Blue. Did you go to Michigan?"

"No," Nicole said, as she turned, "I didn't but my... What the hell," she yelled, standing. "What...what are you doing here? How did you get here?" She poked Paul in the chest. "It is you."

"Yeah, it's me. No mustache disguises this time."

"I didn't want you to be here. I told you so. Why did you follow me?" Nicole demanded.

"Listen," Paul said, "I didn't want you to be here either. And finding you wasn't easy. I could so easily strangle you but I'm so happy to see you alive and not in jail that I'll forget everything."

"How did you find me?"

"Sit and I'll tell you what you put me through," Paul said.

"I can't believe you're here," Nicole said, as they both sat.

"I went to your place when I awoke, and Tony found an old phone bill, then..." Paul started the saga of his last thirty-six hours, including Rogers, the flight to Walla Walla, the parking attendant, the gate guard, the sheriff, jail, and the man in the hotel.

Every three sentences, Nicole would interrupt in disbelief. "You're shitting me."

As Paul was ending the saga, he speed-dialed Rogers and handed the phone to Nicole. "Here, someone wants to talk to you."

Nicole saw the number on the phone front. "You're shitting me." She put the phone to her ear. "Hello, Sarge. It's me."

Paul heard only Nicole's responses, but he had a good idea of the conversation.

"Yeah, I'm fine." ... "Well, fuck you too." ... "Tomorrow. I'll take the bus back to Seattle." ... "I dunno." ... "Really. Thanks." ... "I dunno." ... "I dunno, maybe LA. I'll call you tomorrow or the next day."

Five minutes later, Paul and Nicole sat quietly, not knowing what to say.

"Were you really thinking you'd shoot him?" Paul started.

"When I left Seattle I was so goddamn mad I could have done anything. But I had a whole bus ride and seven hours to sort things out and think about what you and Sarge had said to me. In the end I just wanted to see McNeil and maybe talk to him. I'm not even sure I would have told him who I was, and I had used a phony name to register. I'm positive that he didn't know who I was. Not surprising. I was only thirteen when he last saw me and then only for a few minutes here and there. My first impression was that he seemed nice. Then all of a sudden he left when his dog got hurt. So strange."

"Strange doesn't even cover the tip of this whole day and a half," Paul said. "I may still have to come back to Walla Walla for a trial."

"Nah. Sarge took care of it," Nicole said. "He told me so. Made a call to the sheriff, who's an old Marine. You'll get a letter saying it's all been taken care of."

"It's who you know, I guess. I'll call and thank him. More importantly, I have to be at work tomorrow. Alaska has a flight back to Seattle at 11:10 tonight. I'm going to book a seat for you, whatever it costs."

"Too expensive. Besides, I have a room rented and bus ticket for tomorrow already. Not to mention I can't check my gun through airport security without a locked case."

"You're not going to try to see McNeil again, are you?"

"No. I'll take the bus home. I can always come back here if I want. I think I need to go to Southern California and try to find the girl who got Tony's kidney. Maybe that'll make sense."

"There's a needle in a haystack if there ever was one. You want me to come..."

Nicole interrupted him. "No. I don't want you involved. I said that in my note. You've done enough and I'm not going to risk your medical license. You've got to stay out of this. Please."

"Isn't that my decision?" Paul asked.

"No. It's my decision. You've done enough."

"That's not fair. I don't want to lose you."

"When it's all done, I'll come back if I can."

"When might that be?"

"I don't know," Nicole said. "As long as it takes."

"Can't you keep me in the loop? I'll go crazy if you don't, and nobody needs to know."

"What part of 'no' don't you get?"

"I just don't want to lose you or my T-shirt."

Nicole laughed, looking down at her chest. "Yeah. I guess I don't want to lose you either. But I refuse to put you in jeopardy."

"What are you going to do next? Have you given it any thought?" Paul asked.

"I'm going to Southern California. That's all you need to know."

"Do you honestly think you can find out who took or got Tony's kidney?" Paul said.

Nicole disregarded the question and pushed her half-eaten hamburger toward Paul. "Hey, you hungry? You can have this half burger. I'm not going to eat it."

"I'm not hungry. I had a Big Mac four restaurants ago looking for you. I was going crazy. When McNeil drove out of the winery at ninety miles per hour, I was sure you were injured or worse."

Nicole shook her head and rolled her eyes in mock disbelief. "Oh. Thanks, I guess."

They sat for a second, silent. "What time is your flight?" Nicole asked.

"Just after eleven. The airport is close, so I could take a cab at ten and still have time."

"Just so you know," Nicole said, "I'm glad you're here. Really. I'm sorry I left so abruptly. I thought I had to."

"You didn't have to."

"Yes I did. You can't follow me to Southern California. I'll be okay. My Marine buddies will take care of me."

"They're not doctors. I can help you."

"You've already helped me. Rogers is an MP and I don't need a doctor helping me."

"Well..." Paul started.

"And you can't call me. Ever," Nicole demanded. "Once I leave Seattle, you need to let me go. And you can't call Sarge or any of my Corps friends. It's just too dangerous."

"It's hard."

"I'll never be at peace unless I do this. Let me go," Nicole pleaded.

Paul gently nodded. "I'll try."

"Thanks," Nicole said. "I'm not going to talk to you when I get back to Seattle."

"Why? That's not fair."

"Life's not fair. It'll just make it harder for both of us."

Paul had the look of a sad Bassett hound, said nothing, and slid his hands across the table and held Nicole's softly.

Nicole looked at their hands together for a moment. "Please let me go until my head is straight. Please."

Paul stared off into nowhere-land with hollow eyes and remained silent.

"Your flight doesn't leave for four hours," Nicole said a moment later. "Let's go back to my motel."

Paul awoke from him mini-trance and smiled. "You think that'll make losing you easier?"

"Nope," she said, smiling back. "Probably worse. But I owe you for stealing your T-shirt."

She slipped her right hand from Paul's grasp, spun her left hand to grab his right hand, slid to the end of the booth, pulled him up, and walked him to the door of the Blue Hippo Bar and then two blocks to the Grapevine Motel.

As Paul surveyed the missing "v" in *Grape_ine* and the potholed motel driveway, he mused, "This is worse than your apartment."

"You'll forget you said that in ten minutes," Nicole opined as she led him into her room.

Paul forgot in five.

* * *

Nicole returned to Seattle and helped Tony pack up their apartment. She rented a U-Haul truck and moved everything back to Lopez.

She could not answer her mother's repeated question: "Why are you moving? Tony and I need you. Why?"

"Mom, I can't explain it other than I need to get out of town."

Nicole did not telephone Paul and refused to take his repeated calls to her parents' house, even to say good-bye.

* * *

"Now what, Sarge?" Nicole asked.

"Good question," Rogers said. "You seem to do what you want to do. You ain't been listening to me for a while now."

"Sorry 'bout that. But I need your help. I promise to keep you in the loop."

"How much money you got?" Rogers asked. "You'll need money in LA."

"A little over four thousand bucks," Nicole said. "All that's left from the hospital settlement."

"It ain't gonna last you long in a motel. First get a place to live, hopefully cheap, maybe with some roommates. Check Craigslist. Then get a job. Doesn't make sense looking for whatever you're looking for until you get settled."

Three days later, Nicole departed Seattle for Southern California.

Chapter 15

Nicole found three women, looking for a fourth, renting a small house in West Los Angeles on Brockton between Wilshire and Santa Monica. She bought a new cell phone and purchased an inexpensive laptop computer. Next she applied for a job as a nursing assistant at four nearby hospitals.

Ten days later, Nicole started work on the surgical floor at Centinela Hospital in Inglewood. The bus ride from West LA to Inglewood was ninety minutes with three transfers each way. She quit after two weeks. A week later she landed a job on the graveyard shift on the Neurosurgical Service at UCLA Medical Center, making twelve dollars an hour without benefits. The bus ride was ten minutes and she could walk from her apartment in forty minutes.

With any free time, Nicole headed to the Los Angeles Public Library on Santa Monica Boulevard, just south of the West Los Angeles VA hospital. She searched the archives of all the Southern California newspapers for any clues or hints regarding kidney transplantations that might have occurred in the days and weeks after Tony's kidnapping. She found nothing.

Two months after arriving, Nicole set up a conference call with Rogers, Karson, and Lazzari.

"Nico, how you doing?" Karson asked first.

"Physically fine. Mentally in the toilet. I'm getting nowhere," she lamented. "Maybe I should just go to the press and say what I know and see what happens. They have to respond and come out of the woodwork."

Rogers responded, "Bad, awful, terrible idea."

In unison, Karson and Lazzari echoed, "Yep. Bad idea."

"Why? I don't see a way around it," Nicole said.

"Because we don't know who *they* are," Rogers semi-shouted. "They are very powerful, very rich, and I'm guessing could get very angry. Promise me you won't go Lone Ranger on us."

Nicole said, after a moment of silence, "I promise."

"You said 'I promise' before you ran off to wherever to meet the wine guy," Karson said.

"I promise that I won't do anything without discussing it. I swear."

"Nuff said, you guys," Rogers said. "Maybe you should try to find out more about the transplant programs in Southern California."

"Your doctor friend would have been helpful," Lazzari said.

"I'm not talking to him anymore, and don't ask me why or again. It's over. Got it?" Nicole said, not nicely.

"We're trying to help," Rogers said. "Don't bite anyone's head off. We'll talk again in two weeks. Same time, same day. Okay?"

"Oorah, Sarge," Nicole, Karson, and Lazzari said in unison.

Two days later the neurosurgery charge nurse, Niki Halper, called Nicole into her office at the beginning of the shift.

"The hospital is closing this ward because of staff illnesses with the flu," Halper said, "and moving our inpatients to Four Southwest. Anyway, the Transplantation unit has lost four daytime aides. Can you work days for a while until they get healthy?"

"Absolutely," Nicole responded, thinking quickly, *Good news.*

"Good. Go home now and get some sleep. You need to be on Eight North at seven a.m."

"Aye, aye."

"Always the Marine." Halper laughed. "You're doing good work, Nicole. I think you're smart and should consider going back to school for an LPN or RN certification at some point."

"Thanks. I haven't gotten that far in my thinking."

"Regardless, I hope you come back to Neuro."

"I guess we'll see," Nicole said. *I hope not.*

* * *

Nicole called Rogers and told him the change in wards.

"Maybe the break we need. Might learn something," he said. "Can you stay there?"

"I don't think so. It's just temporary."

"Work your ass off. Make them want you to stay."

"I'll try."

Nicole arrived early the next morning on Eight North and checked in with Patricia Green, RN, the day-shift head nurse.

"Thanks for making the change. You know this is only for a week or so, or less," Green said. "Once the regular staff is healthy, you'll return to your usual night shifts on Neuro. That understood?"

Nicole nodded. "Yes."

Nicole made it a point to arrive early every day and stay late. She returned early from mandatory breaks, never complained, took on any task, and helped other aides and nurses whenever she could.

A week later many of the regular staff had returned. Nicole approached Green at the end of her second-to-last shift.

"I'm really liking Transplant. So much more interesting than Neurosurgery. I'd like to stay here if possible?" she asked.

"I can't promise anything and I told you that when you joined us a week ago," Green said. "But, admittedly you've been great help and everyone enjoys working with you. I'll see if we can find you a spot."

The next day Nicole received a call from the Nursing office that she was to report back to Neurosurgery in forty-eight hours. After two day shifts on Neurosurgery, Nicole was reassigned permanently to the graveyard shift on Eight North—Transplantation.

Nicole called Allen Rogers the next day.

"So, big deal. You haven't learned anything," Rogers said. "Did you expect someone to come up to you and say, 'Hey, I've got your brother's kidney.'"

"Yeah. But I might learn something."

"I give up. So how are you doing?" Rogers asked.

"Pretty good. I'm lonely and miss my parents and brother and Paul."

"So you do miss your doctor friend?"

"Yeah, but I needed to let him go. He was putting himself in danger, and I couldn't let that happen."

"If it means anything, he's called me twice. I told him I didn't know exactly where you were, but from your emails you were apparently okay. He asked for your email address and I said I couldn't give him that."

"He was putting himself in danger of losing his license to practice," Nicole said.

"Whatever. Just know that he really cares for you. I told him that he could call me every so often and I'd tell him what I thought he could know."

"Fine. Just don't give him my phone number, address, or email. Got it?"

"Yeah, yeah."

"I'll call you in a week."

* * *

Nicole learned quickly that very little happened on the Transplantation floor from midnight to seven. She understood that if she were to glean any information about transplantation in Southern California, she'd need to be on daytime shift. Alas, the coveted 7:00 a.m. to 3:00 p.m. shifts were staffed with nurses, aides, and secretarial staff with at least ten years of seniority. The afternoon shift, 3:00 to 11:00 p.m., was the usual stepping-stone to the morning shift, but even that change would take years of seniority and still not be as valuable, in Nicole's mind, as the daytime hours.

The graveyard supervisor, Leah Formicone, thought Nicole would likely need to be at UCLA for six to eight years to achieve enough seniority to make any move on a permanent basis.

I don't have that much time.

Nicole told Rogers on their next call that she'd work so hard, if any openings on daytime opened they'd have to choose her. Rogers said, "That's not the way life always works. Trust me. But it can't hurt."

Nicole received kudos from the supervisors as she continued to work diligently, asked for no favors, and took on any task Formicone asked of her.

Four weeks later, Formicone approached Nicole at the end of her Monday shift telling her that one of the daytime aides would be on emergency leave for a family death and would be absent for at least four days. Formicone wondered whether Nicole would temporarily switch to daytime starting Wednesday. Nicole agreed.

Nicole checked in fifteen minutes early with the head nurse, who thanked her for switching on short notice. Nicole would be assigned to two RNs working post-transplant patients.

Day shift on the transplant service was another world. From her time on graveyard, Nicole knew the

196

hierarchy of the service. The chairman of the transplantation services was Dr. Ralph Michaels. Michaels kept his own staff separate from the rest of the service. Two nurses, Becky Brown and Judy Marks, had been with Michaels for years. Three senior nurse's aides were assigned to Michaels' service, and one of those aides was the one absent for the family emergency. The nursing supervisor moved another aide into that slot thinking that Nicole's lack of experience would not go well with Michaels' team.

People talked. Judy Marks, the most senior of nurses, had been on the transplant service for twenty years. Marks had little time for anyone—nurses, residents, and especially aides who didn't have experience.

Becky Brown was only a few years older than Nicole but had the reputation of being uber-approachable and having the answers to almost any question.

On her second day, Nicole entered the nursing lounge to get her bag lunch. Becky Brown and Judy Marks sat at a corner table talking. Neither senior nurse took any note of Nicole.

Nicole introduced herself. "Hi, I'm Nicole Marrone. I'm new here. I just moved from Seattle."

Marks eye-rolled, nodded to Brown, stood, and left the room.

"Did I do something wrong?" Nicole asked, standing in front of the refrigerator.

"Ignore Judy. She's having a bad day. Normally, she's worse," Brown said quickly, then laughed.

Nicole knew enough not to laugh.

"Sorry about that," Brown continued. "One of her patients is some kind of big-shot Hollywood-type producer and was giving Judy a hard time. I'm going to take over his care."

"Oh."

"Leah Formicone told us about you when one of our aides had to leave. She said you were really good and probably too smart to be a nurse's aide."

"Thanks, I guess. People have told me that before."

"Still, Judy thought it best that you rotate on the regular service."

"I understand."

"Leah also told me you were a Marine, served in Afghanistan, and saw some action."

"Yep." Nicole quickly stood at attention and said, "I mean, yes, sir."

"You're funny. If you have any questions, just ask me or one of the other nurses. Probably don't want to ask Judy on a bad day. This is a bad day and tomorrow will be too, if you get my drift."

"Got it."

"So there it is. Welcome to dayshift. I heard that you'll only be here a short time before returning to nights," Becky said.

The next morning, after bedding a post-op kidney transplant patient, Nicole heard loud and angry shouts from the hallway. She exited the room quickly and turned to the right to see a man, mid-forties, tall, slender, and unshaven, yelling at Becky and Judy, who were guarding the doorway to a patient room. The man made a forcible move to the door knob and was pushed back by Becky.

"You are not allowed in this room," Marks yelled. "Please step back or we will call security."

"Screw you," the man replied, looking at Marks, and then turned to Becky and said, "And screw you too, bitch. I've gotta talk to Moller. He owes me, big-time, and I'm not going to see him die without paying me back. So stand back."

Brown and Marks locked arms, blocking the door. Both looked right and left, searching for help as the man again tried to separate the two women.

Nicole sprinted toward the man and shouted, "Hey, you. Stop now."

Marks yelled to Nicole, "Get help and call security."

The man turned quickly to see Nicole rushing toward him and shouted back, "Fuck you." He then turned quickly back to the door, moving aggressively forward and cocking his left arm.

Nicole came quickly behind the man and slapped him hard on the right shoulder as she repeated, "Stop."

The man turned quickly back to Nicole, his left arm prepared to strike. She put her right leg behind the man's left leg, grabbed his right shoulder with her left hand as she jammed her right elbow high into the man's chest, then twisted and pulled the man over her shoulder, flipping him onto the hallway floor. Dazed, he rolled over, preparing to stand. Nicole then grabbed his right arm and pulled it hard behind his back as she put a knee into the back of his chest and pressed a fingernail into his neck.

"Make one move, asshole, and I'll use this scalpel to slice your neck open," she lied. "Don't move."

The man, face plastered to the floor, finally relaxed. Stunned, he was able to say, "Okay. Okay. That hurts my arm. Stop, please. I'm not moving."

Marks ran to the nursing station but returned seconds later. "Someone has already called security," she said.

Every nurse and aide had now converged around the melee, including two large male attendants.

"Okay, everyone, the excitement's over," Becky said, scanning the crowd. "Get back to your duties."

As the staff slowly dispersed, two armed security guards ran down the hallway, allowing Nicole to release her hold and stand up.

The lead guard turned to Nicole. "We'll be back to take a statement from you once we figure out what we're going to do. Might be an hour or so."

"Okay," Nicole said.

"Anyone else involved?" the guard asked.

"Nurse Brown and I were here at the beginning," Marks said. "This man tried to enter a patient's room without permission. When it got out of control, this nurse's aide subdued the man. Quite impressively, I might add."

The guard looked at Nicole and nodded in disbelief. "Right." He and the other guard then turned and escorted the man down the hallway to the elevator.

Marks faced the lingering gapers. "Everyone back to work. We're done here." She then turned back to Nicole and Becky. "Okay, you two, into the lounge now so we can write up reports. I've been through this before. They'll give us some forms, but we can attach a pre-written note. Let's get the stories straight before the real cops and lawyers show up."

Marks, carrying sheets of blank paper, followed Becky and Nicole into the nurse's lounge and slammed the door.

"We're going to sit down," Marks said, "and write down and remember the same story. I would not be the least surprised if this doesn't make the eleven o'clock news and lawyers are giving interviews on late night TV."

She then turned to Nicole. "You're new but I do remember you coming in here earlier to introduce yourself. Normally, I couldn't care less about a new aide. Is that how I made you feel?"

"Pretty much." Nicole nodded.

"Well, don't take it personally. I do that to everyone. But I have two things to say to you. First, I gave you an order to call security to get help. You disobeyed that order."

"Uh...yes."

"I'm glad you agree. Don't let it happen again. Second, I want to thank you for disobeying the order. Honestly, I was scared. What you did was quite impressive. I had no idea you would or could do what you just did. So, thanks."

Becky, now laughing, said, "Nicole was a decorated US Marine and saw action in Afghanistan. I learned that from Leah but one never knows how much is true." She turned to Nicole. "Every Marine can do that?"

"Pretty much," Nicole said. "We learn judo and some jujitsu in basic. Honestly, Nurse Marks, I didn't hear your order. I just saw the trouble and felt I needed to be there. The guy wasn't that bulked. The men I wrestled with in camp were much bigger."

"How'd you do against them?" Becky asked.

"I got my ass kicked over and over, except for some of the new smaller recruits. Then I did okay."

Marks added, "Good to have you close by today. Now let's get our stories down."

Nicole accomplished little that shift as each nurse, aide, secretary, and some of the residents came by to congratulate her.

At the end of the shift, Nicole went down to security to fill out the required adverse action forms and handed in her description of the events.

The next day, Marks approached Nicole. "Do you have any desire to move to daytime?"

"I'd love to but I've got no seniority. Nurse Formicone told me it would take years to even transfer to evenings."

"Normally that's true. But the nurse's aide on leave isn't going to be back for a while, and when Dr. Michaels heard about your exploits, he thought maybe you should be working beside Becky and me."

"I don't know what to say. Thanks."

"That's good. Welcome to Dr. Michaels' service. You'll start tomorrow. I'll take care of the other nurses and aides. I don't want anyone pissing and moaning behind our backs. You didn't ask for it; Michaels and I demanded it."

* * *

Nicole conference-called Rogers, Karson, and Lazzari a week later.

"Good and bad," she started. "First, I have to tell you what happened. You'd all be proud."

She then related the story of Nurses Brown and Marks, the takedown of the door intruder, and then her move to dayshift.

Lazzari asked, "Have you learned anything about your brother?"

"Nothing," Nicole said. "Not a thing. I'm thinking it's a lost cause. On the other hand, I really like my new job. I'm going to learn so much. In time I may go back to school and get a nursing degree."

Rogers added, "Good for you. By the way, your doctor buddy in Seattle has called me three times since our last call, pleading to find you. If you're going to stop looking for your brother's kidnappers, you might want to give him a call. He actually seems like a pretty good guy and obviously cares for you."

"I miss him but I can't put him in jeopardy. You can call him and say I'm okay," Nicole said, "and I promise that I'll get in touch with him when I feel certain that finding out about Tony's kidney is going nowhere."

* * *

Nicole came early and stayed late every day. She hung on every word from Becky and Marks, the residents and Dr. Michaels. What she didn't understand she read about in the library or on the Internet.

"Nicole, you're way too smart to be an aide," Becky said. "You pick up things way too fast. I really think you ought to consider going back to school and get a nursing degree."

Judy Marks, sitting next to Becky, chimed in, "Becky's right. You've been here for, what, three weeks and you're already picking up things that most of the nurse's aides and some of the nurses would miss. And by the way, I think you can call me Judy."

They both looked at Nicole, waiting for an answer.

"Two things," Nicole said. "First, I can't even start to thank you both for being so supportive and helpful. I'm loving it here on the service and working with you and Dr. Michaels. I'm learning so much. Second, I don't have enough money to stop working for even a month and go to school. Even if I did have any extra money, I'd probably send it to my mom and brother. They're just getting by up in Washington."

Two weeks later, Friday, as the dayshift ended, Nicole sat with Judy and Becky finishing charting.

"I've said it before," Nicole said, "and I'll say it again. I just love working around you two and Dr. Michaels. I feel like a human vacuum sucking up all sorts of information. Thanks so much."

"You're welcome," Judy said, as she exited the lounge. "See you Monday."

Becky waited for Judy to leave and said, "Nicole, I really like working with you too. I don't know much about your social life and it's probably none of my business, but do you have a boyfriend here in LA? Is that why you moved?"

"No. No boyfriend. Not for a long, long time," Nicole lied. "I spend most of my free time learning about transplantation on the web."

"Well, I'm having a small party tonight at our house," Becky said. "Just a bunch of friends. You want to come and meet some new people?"

"Sure," Nicole said. "Am I supposed to bring someone, like a date? Because I don't really have one."

"No. Just you. Dress casually and bring a bathing suit, or not." Becky slid a piece of paper with her address toward Nicole. "Seven p.m. It's cold at night, especially up on top of Mulholland, so bring a coat."

"You have a house. Your own?" Nicole asked.

"Yep."

"You've got a pool where you live?"

"Actually, we've got anything you'd ever want. You'll see."

"Oh," Nicole replied, not knowing exactly what Becky meant. "Is Judy coming?"

"Nope. Not her style," Becky said. "See you tonight."

"I don't have a car."

"Oh. Really?"

205

"But I can take a Uber," Nicole said immediately. "Don't worry, I'll be there."

"Great. Our place is on Mulholland west of Coldwater Canyon. There's a guarded gate."

"A guarded gate? What's that about?"

"You'll see. Have the driver let you off in front in the turnaround. There'll be two guards posted at the gatehouse, and your name will be on a list. One of the guards will drive you up to the house. If need be someone will drive you home afterwards."

"Uh. Thanks. I...I guess I'll see you tonight."

Becky left the lounge, and Nicole sat hard onto a chair. *I'm not sure about this, but somebody has some serious money and not from a nurse's salary.*

* * *

Nicole phoned Allen Rogers as soon as she got home to tell him of the invitation for that night.

"She's the nurse that's been so nice to you?" Allen asked.

"Yeah. She and another one, more senior."

"You think she's trying to set you up with some guy?"

"I don't know what to think. She did ask me if I had a boyfriend. I told her I didn't. Still, I don't think that's it, but I don't know why. She actively seeks me out to explain stuff, which is great. I think she still can't get over me barrel-rolling that guy in the hallway."

"I dunno. Maybe she's just nice and likes you," Allen said. "Although I don't know why anyone would like you."

206

"Thanks, Sarge. I needed that."

Nicole wore her nicest pair of jeans and a blouse she'd purchased at Marshalls two weeks earlier. Even though she had been in Southern California for months, she had no bathing suit. *It's cold at night. No one is going swimming.*

* * *

Nicole stood transfixed just outside Becky's gate after being dropped off. The night air was Pacific coast cool and without the ambient light from the city, the stars and half-moon dazzled the sky. Before approaching the gatehouse, she dialed Allen.

"You're not going to believe this," she whispered, although no one was within thirty feet. "I can barely see the top of the house from the gate. It's huge and has to be a click away. It looks like a goddamn castle."

"Hey, forget about it and have a good time. Call me later," Rogers said.

Nicole approached the gatehouse and was immediately confronted by two armed-to-the-teeth guards, one black male and one white female, although it took Nicole a moment to tell if the second guard was a woman.

"Miss Brown told us to expect you. You're Nicole, the Marine. Right?" the male guard asked, coming forward. "I'm Lucas."

"Yep."

"Where'd ya serve?" Lucas asked.

"Why ask?" Nicole said, with attitude. "You think I'm kidding?"

"Nah. I was there too. Second Battalion, Fourth Marines."

"Sorry about the attitude. I was with the First Battalion in the Sixth. Drove trucks."

"You were in Musa Qala, eh? Under Hughes?"

"Oorah."

"Good unit. You weren't that crazy who spun a MRAP into a hut?"

"That'd be me."

"Ballsy move. We all heard about it. Anyway, follow JoJo. She'll drive you up to the house. I'll let Miss Becky and Miss Claire know you're on the way up."

JoJo, the female guard, stood a head taller than Nicole and sixty pounds heavier. She exuded not a single ounce of feminism, accentuated by a close-cropped buzz cut. Nicole followed her to a golf cart ten yards away.

"Who's Claire?" Nicole asked as she settled into the cart.

JoJo responded with a grunt. "Follow me."

Nicole didn't ask again, assuming she'd find out soon enough.

The fifteen-minute ride to the mansion along a curving, mountainous, cobbled road made the property seem as big as Lopez Island. Nicole sat quietly in awe. *Who lives like this?*

Becky Brown was waiting at the massive front double doors as the golf cart pulled up. "Hey, Nicole. Thanks for coming." She kissed Nicole on each cheek, European style, then grabbed her hand. "Most everyone is here already. Hope you're hungry. Did you bring a bathing suit?"

"No. I didn't have one," Nicole said as they walked into the house.

"No big deal. Most won't use one."

Before Nicole could digest the comment, she gasped at the entry. The round foyer with a cupola was easily bigger than her parents' house, centered by a fifteen-foot copy of Michelangelo's *David*.

"Holy shit. Where am I? Whose place is this?"

"It's where I live. My partner actually owns it. On my salary I couldn't afford the door knobs," Becky said.

"Who's your partner? Bill Gates?"

"Claire Boothe."

"I don't know who that is. Should I?"

"Most people from California know. She's Bobby Boothe's daughter."

"That sounds familiar, like a baseball player, but I'm still in the dark."

"You'll have to read the newspapers more. Bobby Boothe is probably the richest person in California; he's governor of California, and most people think he'll be the Republican candidate for President in 2020."

"I do try to keep up. But I'm a Washingtonian. When I think of rich, I think Bill Gates, Paul Allen, and Jeff Bezos to start. And our governor is Jay Inslee."

"Good for you. I'm sorry. Didn't think of it that way," Becky said.

"How did you meet?" Nicole asked.

"We met at a beach party on Venice Beach ten years ago. Honestly, I had no idea who she was either. I guess I could have cut you a little slack. We had a ton in common and hit it off immediately. Within four months we knew we'd be partners for life."

"Oh," Nicole mumbled. *That kind of partner.*

Becky and Nicole cleared the foyer and walked down a long, wide hallway decorated with amazing art. Voices could be heard coming from the end of the hall.

"It smells like chlorine," Nicole said.

"It is," Becky said.

They turned the corner into a massive lounge-like room centered with an indoor twenty-five yard, four-lane swimming pool. In the far corner, a two-lane bowling alley sat unlit. Twenty people, all women, occupied the room and had gathered near a large table of hors d'oeuvres, cut vegetables and dips, and several bottles of wine.

All quieted quickly, turning toward Becky and Nicole. A woman, perhaps in her late thirties, walked quickly toward Nicole.

"So you're the hero of the transplant ward," she announced. "I'm Claire Boothe. Welcome to our house."

She gave Nicole a hug and stood back. "Thanks for saving my Becky's ass."

Claire then turned to the group and waved both hands to get everyone's attention.

Nicole quickly scanned the room—an eclectic group of women. She thought everyone was over thirty but less than fifty. Some were very feminine, some not, although none looked like JoJo from the guardhouse. All were stylishly dressed other than a few who wore terry cloth bathrobes that Nicole assumed covered bathing suits. Nicole tried to think of an all-women party that she had attended, other than wedding showers or bachelorette parties. She could think of none.

These women are all gay. What did Becky think?

"Everyone, this is Nicole Marrone, who works with my Becky at UCLA. She's my hero for helping Becky out of a scary jam. She's also a decorated U.S. Marine. After we've eaten and taken a swim, maybe we can get Nicole to tell us some of her exploits. Come and introduce yourselves."

Nicole stood transfixed and overwhelmed as the entire group surrounded her with welcomes and new names.

"I'm Marianne. Nice to meet you. Were you really a Marine?"

"Yep."

"I'm Ruth, Claire's oldest friend."

"I'm..."

Becky finally grabbed Nicole's hand after all the guests had introduced themselves. "Let's get something to eat and drink."

Nicole feasted on crab toast, grilled oysters, Abruzzo-style grape focaccia, and a garlicky sweet potato crostini. Each bite better than the previous.

A young Asian woman poured wine and brought out more dishes when the plates emptied. Nicole approached the server. "Hi. Did you make all this?"

"Yes. I'm Li Yong, Claire and Becky's cook," she replied in impeccable English with a distinct Asian accent.

I've never met anyone who has a cook.

Nicole shook her head. "I don't know that I belong here," she said. "This is way over my head. All this."

"If Becky invited you, you belong here," Li Yong said. "Don't worry. They're all really nice."

I don't belong here.

Nicole then turned to find the three women who had been wearing bathrobes dropping them on nearby lounge chairs and diving into the pool. All were naked. Moments later three others exited dressing rooms wearing only open robes and followed the others into the pool. Nicole stood statue-like, watching.

Claire came up from behind her. "You okay?"

"Uh. Yeah," Nicole stammered. "I didn't know, uh...what...the party was about."

Claire laughed. "You're straight. Right?"

"Yes. Definitely so."

"Becky assumed so. Becky and I aren't."

"Why was I invited?"

"Because she said you were special. You'll be fine. Half the women here are straight," Claire said. "They're just dear friends. That pretty lady, Marianne Charles, in the pool is the daughter of my dad's Chief of Staff. I've known her for years. She has three kids and a great husband, Fred, who handles most of my legal matters. Betsy Anderson, sitting in the lounge chair, is texting her kids' babysitter. She's an art historian, and her husband, Ron, does our taxes."

"Oh."

"We've all been friends for years and have these parties here every four to six weeks or so. Relax. No one cares if you're straight or gay or bi. Honest. No one here judges. And anything you hear here, stays here. Capish?"

"Absolutely. I guess I'm really in La La Land," Nicole mused. "Welcome to California, Nicole, you country hick."

Claire laughed. "Hardly."

"Where can I change?" Nicole asked.

"The dressing room behind us has lockers and robes."

Five minutes later Nicole dove into the pool. Three women swam up to her immediately to welcome her again.

"I wasn't really sure about the Marine thing," Marianne said. "But I guess that tattoo seals the deal. I can't wait to hear more about you."

Betsy, the accountant's wife, drove Nicole home just before midnight.

Best night ever.

At the next party, five weeks later, a few new women who weren't at the prior gathering came specifically to meet Nicole. The hors d'oeuvres, all new, were even better.

* * *

Nicole continued to work diligently, side-by-side with Judy and Becky, reading and learning as much as she could about transplantation and post-surgical patient management. In turn, with Dr. Michaels' permission, Nicole was given more patient responsibility. She drew blood, started IVs, and learned the intricacies of EKGs and heart rhythm abnormalities.

Three months later, Becky asked Nicole to meet in the nursing lounge.

"Please don't take what I'm going to say wrong. I don't want you to feel as if I, or Claire, think you are a charity case."

Nicole nodded hesitantly.

"Claire's dad, besides being richer than most countries, is incredibly well-connected, and Claire asked him if he could do a favor for her, for us," Becky said. "I'll get to the point. There's a nighttime and weekend RN program at Saint Mary's University here in Westwood. Might take a few years, but you'll come out with a bachelor's degree in nursing. Normally, it's pricey but they have full scholarships for exceptional candidates. Claire thinks, as do I, that you are exceptional. It's yours if you want it." Becky slid a large, thick informational folder with Saint Mary's University Nursing embossed on the front toward Nicole.

Nicole could barely control her emotions and started to cry. "Yes. Yes."

Becky stood and Nicole followed and put her arms around her.

"I can't thank you enough," she said between sobs. "I'd love to do it. I'll make you all proud. I swear. You and Claire and Judy are the best things that have ever happened to me."

In her conference call with Rogers, Karson, and Lazzari, Nicole could not stop talking about her luck in meeting Judy, Becky, and Claire.

"We're all happy for you," Karson said.

"You're going to stop looking for your brother's kidnappers?" Lazzari asked.

"For the time being," Nicole said. "Besides, I wasn't getting anywhere, and I'll be too busy to breathe for the next few years."

"On another note, your buddy, Dr. Roberts keeps calling," Rogers added.

"Let me start the nursing program and get my schedule straightened out; then I'll call him," Nicole said. "I do miss him. That said, he's in Seattle and I'm here now and not leaving. For anything or anybody."

Chapter 16

Nicole entered Room 808 at 2 p.m. to help walk a patient. As she stood facing the bed, the male patient, two days post-op, was having difficulty getting his feet onto the floor.

"I'll lower the bed, Mr. Travis. Hold on a second," Nicole said.

A male voice came from behind Nicole. "Can I help you?"

"Sure, thanks." She turned, expecting to find an orderly or resident.

"What do you need me to do?" Paul Roberts asked. *Auburn and blue.* He could feel his pulse quicken.

Nicole's head shook back and she gasped, "What are you doing? You're not supposed to be here."

Mr. Travis, obviously uncomfortable swaying at the edge of the bed, begged, "Nurse, aren't you going to help me?"

Nicole turned quickly to the tottering patient. "Yes. Yes, of course. I'm sorry. I was just surprised when the doctor offered to help."

Together, silently, Paul and Nicole helped Mr. Travis off the bed onto the floor, and Nicole escorted the wobbly man into the hallway.

As Nicole entered the hallway with Mr. Travis in tow, Paul said, "I've got to get back to the ICU to start rounds."

Nicole said, "We need to talk."

"You know my cell number," Paul replied. "Ball's in your court because I don't know yours."

* * *

Nicole called Allen Rogers at her next break. "Paul Roberts is here at UCLA. You didn't tell him where I was, did you?"

"No. And you shouldn't have to ask," Rogers barked back.

"Sorry. You're right. Now what do I do?"

"If he's stupid enough to get involved," Rogers said, "he may find some answers."

"Maybe. I don't think he came here for any reason other than to see me. I'll find out, I guess. But I'm not looking for answers right now. I don't have the time."

"Not likely he'll find anything, but you never know."

"I expect so."

"But whatever you do, don't let people know you two are a thing, in case it gets dicey."

"Dicey from what? And we're not a thing, at least yet."

"Trust me and tell Roberts the same thing."

"Okay, Sarge."

* * *

Nicole didn't see Paul again on the floor, so she called him at 5:00 p.m. as she finished her shift. He answered immediately.

"What are you doing here?" Nicole demanded. "I thought you understood that I didn't want to put you in jeopardy."

"And I said to you, 'Isn't that my decision?'" Paul responded.

"No, dammit. It was my decision. How did you get here? How did you find me?"

"No one told me. I found you in Walla Walla. Finding you here wasn't too difficult. First, unless you robbed a bank, I knew you'd need a job. Four weeks ago I started calling nursing offices in hospitals in Southern California. Call number six was to UCLA. I lied that I had found a nurse's stethoscope with the name 'N. Marrone' on it outside the hospital. I said that if the owner was working at UCLA, I'd bring it by the office and leave it. The secretary said you were. Ta da."

"You should have been a cop. You are persistent, that's for sure."

"Next, I found that UCLA has a resident elective rotation on transplantation. My chief, Dr. Muller, dumbfounded that I wanted to come, made a call and voilà, I drove down and I'm here for three months. Rented a small apartment on Sixth Street in Santa Monica near Colorado Boulevard."

"You don't even like transplantation. Why would you do that?" Nicole asked.

"That's what Dr. Muller said. Honestly, I miss my T-shirt."

"You are such a piece of work. I hate you."

"No, you don't," Paul said smugly.

"Okay, I don't. But as long as you're going to be here, I might as well tell you how little I've learned about my brother and how unbelievably lucky I've been with the people I've met."

"Uh oh. That doesn't sound good," Paul said. "Did you meet someone else?"

"No. I haven't met another guy, just some fantastic people. Can we meet for dinner?"

"Sure," Paul said. "We're expecting a kidney at nine-thirty tonight, but I'll be free in twenty minutes until nine. No taco dives this time."

"Okay. I'll find something in Westwood that I can walk to."

"Why don't you wait in the lobby and I'll drive you."

"It's okay. I'll walk into Westwood and try to find a place to eat. You've got my number now."

     * * *

The Westwood restaurants were all packed, so Nicole directed Paul to a small Northern Italian bistro on San Vicente, relatively close to her rented house. They were seated quickly in a half-empty restaurant.

Nicole remembered to wait for Paul to open the door for her. When she stepped onto the curb, he put his arms around her.

"I missed you so much," Paul said.

"I know. Sarge told me. I missed you too, but my mind wasn't where yours was when I left. I had to go," she said. "We have stuff to talk about. Things that have happened since I arrived. All quite surprising."

219

She kissed him softly on the lips, held the moment longer than just hello, and then pulled slowly away. "That's just to let you know there's no one else."

After Nicole ordered a glass of Malbec, Paul told the waiter that he had to go back to work. "Water will do fine." He then turned to Nicole. "Okay, let's hear the good, the bad, and the ugly."

Nicole explained about getting the apartment in West LA and applying for jobs at multiple hospitals before landing a midnight shift on neurosurgery at UCLA.

"Neuro. That's depressing."

"I needed a job and one close to where I was living. Besides, every day, I researched kidney transplant info from the web and local paper archives starting two years before Tony's kidnapping up to now. I learned absolutely nothing. Not a clue. After four months I realized I could go no further."

"Why didn't you call me? Maybe I could have helped."

"You did plenty and I don't need to repeat what you told me, quite clearly I might add, that if caught misusing data you could be prosecuted and possibly lose any chance of practicing medicine. I couldn't handle one more second of that responsibility. Not one. You don't have a dog in this fight."

"I would have liked it to be *our* fight," Paul said.

"Okay, then let's look at the whole picture of this mess," Nicole answered. "Upside to winning and downside to losing. Upside, at best you make a crazy girl, me, happy and maybe some bad guys go to jail. But whatever happens, it's not going to put Tony's kidney back or make him happy."

"Okay. I agree."

"Downside risks include you losing your license and, worse, someone tries to kill you, me, and my family."

"First, I came because I can't get a crazy girl, you, out of my mind. Second, do you really think your life would be in jeopardy?" Paul asked.

"Allen Rogers thinks so, and that's good enough for me."

"So, end of story. Then why not come back to Seattle?"

"Here's where being at the right spot at the right time helps. I've had the most amazing luck at work. So I started on neuro but had a chance to transfer to transplant when someone got sick, and then..."

Through the bread service, salads, entrées, and desserts, Nicole told Paul everything that had happened, particularly her newfound friendships with Judy Marks, Becky Brown, and Claire Boothe. She carefully omitted the details of the swim parties at Boothe's mansion. Nicole ended with the offer of the nursing degree, paid for by the governor of California, and the new friendships with an array of people inside and outside the hospital.

"You really flipped some guy in the hallway?" Paul smiled broadly. "You never cease to amaze. Glad I didn't piss you off that first night when you figured out that lady's drug reaction."

"The upshot of all this," Nicole explained, "is that I'm not leaving UCLA until I finish my nursing training. I've never been so excited about every day, and I have a ton of friends. The kind of people that wouldn't have talked to me in Seattle. At the same time I'm willing to put Tony and the kidney on the back burner. I know I was possessed about it while in Seattle. But not now. I've got too much to do."

"Well, I'm going to be here for three months. I won't stir up any hornet's nests, but I'd love to see you."

"Absolutely, but we probably shouldn't be seen together," Nicole said.

"Well, you haven't changed," Paul said. "Is UCLA going to fire you if they find out? Nobody knows me yet, so it's not likely anyone will ID us."

"But they know me and they will know you," Nicole said, "and I think it best not to look real friendly at work. When they find out you're from Seattle, everyone is going to ask if you knew me there. Say no."

"Whatever you say, Miss Queen of Transplant. By the way, you still owe me a lasagna dinner."

"You haven't changed a bit. I guess I missed you more than you or I knew. I was ready to call you because I'm in such a good place now," Nicole said.

"I'm happy for you. Really," Paul said, "I mean it."

"I'm off tomorrow," Nicole said. "How about I drive you back to the hospital and then I'll pick you up whenever you call and we'll go to your place."

"You expect me to concentrate tonight after that proposal?"

"No. I just want to make sure everything still works," she said with a sly smile.

Nicole picked Paul up at 3:00 a.m. in front of the hospital.

"How'd the transplant go?" she asked after exchanging seats.

"Great. You were right. Dr. Michaels is amazing."

"I may pick up your patient on Monday," Nicole said. Opening her jacket to reveal his Michigan T-shirt, she added, "Hey, you like?"

"Of course. Go Blue. I was kind of hoping for a raincoat and pizza."

"I did miss you," Nicole said. "Are you on call and what time do you have to be back tomorrow?"

"Rounds are at eight. Until I learn the protocols and routines, Michaels won't let me take night call. Maybe a week, then I'll be on every third night."

"Are you tired?"

"No. Michaels actually said to me, 'Dr. Roberts, you seem to be very happy at this late hour.' I lied and said, 'I feel so honored to be here.'"

They didn't fall asleep until 6:00 a.m., exhausted and sore. Paul rose an hour later and showered quickly. He scooped his Michigan T-shirt off the floor of the bedroom and inhaled its sweet scent, which was all the aphrodisiac he needed. He wore the tee under a dark collared shirt and tie. He then grabbed a bagel and left his apartment at seven thirty to make rounds, leaving Nicole asleep in his bed. The one-hour power nap wouldn't be enough sleep, but he only needed to make rounds and come back, hoping to find Nicole still in bed.

stab wound

He did.

Chapter 17

On Monday, during the second transplant of the morning, Dr. Michaels asked Paul if he had any desire to do some research during his three-month stint.

"It's up to you, Paul," Michaels said, "but you never know what might spark some interest. Transplant is like OB—never know when a baby's coming."

Paul knew from Dr. Muller in Seattle that Michaels expected him to say yes. "Of course I would. You have any suggestions?

"After we're done today you should head over to the Boothe Research Center across the plaza and look up Howard Resine. He's a PhD-MD researcher who's run our lab for the past twenty years. He has a bunch of stuff that he's working on and some stuff he hasn't started. Resine loves it when residents come up with anything fresh. So if you've got any ideas, bring them. But it's probably a good idea not to start something you can't finish while you're here."

"Got it."

From the time Michaels suggested doing research, Paul thought of possibilities to help Nicole find Tony's recipient. Possibilities that would open closed doors and locked boxes. He used the time wisely.

* * *

Paul entered the office of Howard Resine, M.D., Ph.D. and sat. Resine looked about fifty years old but his appearance suggested a throwback to the Haight-Ashbury sixties with large rimless glasses, balding, collarless shirt and a shoulder length ponytail. His

225

intense and serious gaze intimidated Paul. Resine would not suffer fools.

"So what do you think you'd like to study?" Resine asked Paul.

"Dr. Michaels suggested something I could finish during my three months here. I was thinking about studying the long-term outcomes in patients with the rarest compatibility factors versus those with the most common? Throw out everything in the middle," Paul suggested. "Has that been done?"

"Actually," Resine said, "not to my knowledge, but how will that help anyone?"

"If nothing else, the data might give us a better idea of their long-term results. It might be interesting. Besides, I can finish the data-crunching in Seattle if I don't finish here. Just need access to the charts, which are all electronically stored now."

"Maybe so. How are you going to break down the types? Have you thought about that?" Resine asked.

"I think, at first, we need to stick to Caucasians only. Just keeps it purer. We could always add Africans and Asians later. O is most common, and AB is least common. But I'd like to go further. HLA-A 02, 24, and 01, HLA-B 35, 44, and 51, DRB1 11, 13, and 07 are most common. HLA-A 23 and 33, HLA-B 42 and 39, DRB1 9, 10, and 14 are the rarest."

"You've done some homework, Dr. Roberts."

Paul hesitated a moment, then asked the most important question. "Also, I was thinking that the numbers from the rarer types from just UCLA may not be great enough to generate statistically significant results. If so, I'd like access to all of the Southern California data. If need be I could drive to the other facilities on my off time to do chart research."

"I don't know about all the Southern California access," Resine said. "I'll have to give it some thought and I'll need to ask the other transplant research teams in our area. Write up a brief proposal by Thursday. I'm impressed that you had an idea before walking in. Most three-monthers merely say to me 'anything you want.'"

Paul walked out of Resine's office and mumbled loudly to himself, "Beware of what you wish for."

Resine called Paul on Tuesday morning to green-light his proposal.

Three days later, Paul had computer access to all the historical transplant data in Southern California.

Now what do I do?

He called Allen Rogers. "Sergeant, this is Paul Roberts. I've got a problem."

"Lemme guess," Rogers said. "Your problem rhymes with Nicole."

"Funny," Paul said. "Here's the deal. For the next three months I will have access to all transplant patients, both recipients and donors, in Southern California from the past twenty years. That means there's a chance that I might be able to figure out Nicole's brother's recipient."

"Shit," Rogers moaned.

"Yeah. Shit. Nicole's in a good place now and seems not to even care about her brother and family's catastrophe. At least, she's not talking about it twenty-four/seven like she used to."

"Shit. I know where this is going."

"Yeah. I could tell her now, get her hopes up, but then later disappoint her that I've found nothing. I'd be re-opening a can of worms. Or she could tell me not to even look."

"But you'll likely never get another chance at the database, right?"

"Right," Paul said. "Or, I can see what I find first. If I find nothing, say nothing. Only you and I will know."

"I'm thinking that might be the best thing that could happen," Rogers said.

"The problem with that," Paul said, "is if I publish a paper and we're still together, she'll know I had access to the data."

"Shit."

"But if I come up with something, then present it, she'll be upset that I didn't tell her earlier that I was looking."

"You're right. She'll be pissed."

"I was hoping that I could say I'd talked to you if she goes ballistic. Maybe that'll save my ass."

"I don't know. Seems like the choices are bad and awful. But I'd say tell her now. The truth will set you free, as they say. That's honest and let her handle what she wants you to do."

"Shit," Paul said.

"Well, at least we're on the same wavelength. Good luck, cowboy," Rogers said. "Gotta go. We didn't have this conversation."

* * *

Nicole was asleep, curled on her side, fully clothed, on top of Paul's bed when he came home just before midnight. The room lights were on, and soft pop emitted from Nicole's iPhone.

He turned off the room lights but turned on the bathroom vanity light and left the door ajar. Enough to bathe the room gently. He slipped out of his surgical greens and put on an old cotton T-shirt.

Paul sat at the edge of the bed and brushed the hair from Nicole's face. He kissed her softly on the ear and then her eye and cheek. She merely scratched her ear and rolled away. Paul buried his nose in the middle of her tousled hair and inhaled deeply, twice.

"How lucky am I," he said softly.

Nicole turned back and fluttered her lids for a moment but kept them closed. "What time is it?"

"'Bout midnight."

"Have you eaten?"

"I'm okay. How about you?" he asked.

"I'm good." Nicole opened her eyes and put her arms around Paul's neck. "I was dreaming about you."

"I'll take that as a positive. Right."

She pulled him closer and brushed his lips. "You could," she said. "I was so tired that I didn't have enough energy to get undressed."

"You need a top to wear?"

"No. What are you wearing?"

"Nothing." Paul slid Nicole's socks off and started massaging her soles.

"I was on my feet all day. That feels so good. Don't stop."

"Never."

Eyes closed, Nicole unbuttoned her jeans and her blouse as Paul continued the foot massage until she signaled she wanted more by raising her pelvis off the bed. He slid her jeans and then underwear off and rolled her back and forth to remove her blouse. He then joined her under the covers and smothered her face and eyes and ears and lips with kisses.

"Where were you in the dream?" he asked.

"I only remember where *you* were," she said. "I kept pleading for you not to stop."

Paul's tongue traced a course between her breasts and continued down as she parted her legs. He moved between her legs until his tongue found its way home.

"That's it. That's where I was in the dream. That's it. Oh my God, that's it."

At 1:00 a.m., both spent, Paul nestled in the small of Nicole's neck. "I've got something to tell you," he said. "I don't think it's bad but I need you to know."

230

"I'm all ears for ten minutes; then I'll be dead to the world."

"Dr. Michaels suggested that I do some research while I'm here. More correctly, he strongly suggested it."

"That's good, I guess."

"No, but I met with a Dr. Resine who runs the research labs for the department, and we came up with a plan."

"Okay. Does this mean I'm going to see you even less?" Nicole asked.

"No. Not really. The research entails reviewing charts for patients who've had transplants. So while I'm here I will have some access to all the patients who've had a transplant or been a donor for the past twenty years. Better yet, I will have access to charts throughout Southern California."

Nicole propped herself up on her left elbow and turned to her left. "Really."

"I know you understand where this is leading, but I don't want you to get your hopes up. I have no idea what I might find. Remember that Tony's chart was missing in Washington. I would have to guess that the chart here might be just as gone. I guess I'm asking if you want me to look. I'll only have this access while I'm here at UCLA. I know you said that Tony's kidney wasn't a priority now because you've got so much to do and accomplish and..."

"Can you get in trouble? I mean put yourself in jeopardy like you did in Seattle?"

"I don't know. I hope not, but I don't..."

"But you'll tell me what you find? No matter what?" Nicole interrupted.

"Only if you want to hear," Paul said.

"Do it," Nicole said. "Do it."

* * *

Basing his data search back twenty years using specific tissue types, Paul selected out all of the recipients and donors with rarer blood types including those known to belong to Tony. For personal protection, all patients were listed as first and last initial, whether they were the donor D or recipient R, and finally with the date of the donation or transplant. Within seconds, Paul was looking at data from a range of dates of Tony's kidnapping, May 5-8, 2002. Twenty-two donor patients were listed from Southern California but none with Tony's initials, AM. He then opened each file and reviewed the specific tissue specific HLA typing, looking for a match with Tony. He found Tony in the seventh file. He had been listed at JD.D.050602-3.

"Figures. John Doe, I suppose," Paul mumbled to himself. Going further to access Tony's detailed chart, he ran into an "ACCESS DENIED – NEED PASSWORD TO UNBLOCK."

Searching recipients by a span of dates May 6 to May 8, Paul came up with twenty-two and opened each to view the HLA typing. He found JD.R.050702-3.

"Okay, Jane Doe. I get it," Paul told the screen. JD.R.050702-3's chart was also met with ACCESS DENIED – NEED PASSWORD TO UNBLOCK. He typed in the word PASSWORD, hoping that something stupid would work. ACCESS DENIED – NEED PASSWORD TO UNBLOCK.

Searching other donors and recipients, he ran into no other cases of ACCESS DENIED – NEED PASSWORD TO UNBLOCK.

The other charts, easily accessed, revealed names, dates, times, diagnoses, surgeons, hospitals, tissue preservatives, anti-rejection protocols, medications, follow-ups, renal function, complications, and all other pertinent data.

Paul created an Excel spreadsheet with enough data points that he believed would show Dr. Resine that his research was in earnest. Four days later, Paul sat with Resine with his laptop open.

"I'm making some headway, but I've run into one transplant donor and recipient with blocked access. They are from one of the tissue types that I have in my rare list. As it is, I can retrieve no data. Any idea why?"

"Do you really need it?" Resine asked.

"The research will be incomplete if we select out anyone from the database. You and I both know the statisticians will go crazy. If we publish and then someone finds out we dropped even one case, you know the naysayers will climb all over us."

"Don't know that I've ever seen this before," Resine said. "I wasn't running the lab then, but I can call Joe Lilly at Michigan. He was here before me."

* * *

Toni Lord, RN, a nurse on the transplant service, entered the nursing station as Becky Brown took a seat at a computer. "Guess who I saw with guess-who last week?"

Not taking her eyes off the screen, Becky said, "I give up. Maybe Elvis with Jimmy Hoffa."

"Funny. No. I saw your favorite nurse's aide with the new resident from Seattle Med."

Becky turned. "Okay. I'm listening. Her name is Nicole and she said she hadn't known Dr. Roberts from Seattle. I haven't seen them together here on the floor or anywhere in the hospital. But they certainly could have met."

"Whatever. Jerry and I were having our tenth anniversary dinner at Nick's in Manhattan Beach. They were across the room. Couldn't hear what they were talking about, but from the body language it wasn't a business meeting."

"Did they see you?"

"My back was to them but I don't think so," Lord said. "I can't be sure. I asked Jerry if either were looking our way and he said they weren't."

"Thanks for the info. Not sure what to do with it. It's a free country. I'll talk to Dr. Michaels and see if there's a conflict. Either way Dr. Roberts is out of here in ten weeks."

Ten minutes later, Becky closed the door to her office and called Dr. Michaels.

After hearing Becky's concerns, Michaels said, "From what we've seen, Nicole has a ton of promise and Paul Roberts seems like a pretty straight-up guy. He's a good doc and an excellent surgeon already. We're glad to have him. I've got him doing research with Dr. Resine. I'll ask Howard if he knows anything. I wouldn't make too much of it."

Michaels called Resine later that afternoon. "Just curious how the resident, Paul Roberts, from Seattle is doing in his research. He's very strong clinically and he's the kind of doctor we'd love to have on the faculty down the line."

"He's fine," Resine said. "He came up with an interesting project and is gathering data. I haven't gotten to see his data analysis skills or writing, but I doubt we'll be disappointed."

"That's good. Apparently, Roberts has been seeing one of the new aides on the floor. Has he said anything to you?"

"No and I wouldn't even think to ask."

"You're right. There'd be no reason for you to ask." Michaels said.

"We do have a little glitch in the data collection though," Resine said. "A donor and recipient's records from the database are not accessible, and it throws the statistical analysis off. Roberts was clearly upset when I suggested dropping the records from the analyses. I couldn't solve the problem and so I called Joe Lilly in Ann Arbor. He knew exactly what I was talking about and told me, and I quote, 'Tough shit' and 'Leave it alone.'"

"This wouldn't be a record from 2002, would it," Michaels asked.

"Actually it is. Do you know what this is about?"

"Leave it alone," Michaels said emphatically. "And don't ask me again."

Michaels was rarely short with Resine, so when he hung up abruptly, Resine sat back in his chair and shook his head. "What was that about?" he asked the telephone.

He swiveled in his chair to a file cabinet. Soon he was looking at a folder labeled "J. Lilly – Private" and then logged onto the web. Within seconds the Southern California Transplant registry was at his fingertips. He first went to JD.D.050602-3 and typed in the first of ten passwords listed in the Lilly file. ACCESS DENIED – NEED PASSWORD TO UNBLOCK. Password number six opened the file. Resine snickered at the password which he thought too simple and rather plebian.

Much to Resine's surprise the file was completely devoid of personal information and clinical material other than the tissue-typing data, that the donor was alive at the time of the kidney removal, the date and time the kidney was retrieved, and the tissue preservative used. All other fields were blank.

Isn't that strange.

Resine then opened the JD.R.050602-3 file. He searched every subfolder of the file. All were devoid of information until he opened 'Operative Notes.' He took one quick look and closed the file as soon as he saw the name and logged off the website.

No way Dr. Roberts gets to see this.

* * *

Paul received a text the next afternoon to return to Resine's office as soon as he could. He arrived twenty minutes later.

"I made three calls," Resine said. "First to Joe Lilly in Ann Arbor. He told me not to ask anyone about those two records but couldn't or wouldn't tell me why."

"Is that unusual?" Paul asked.

"Incredibly unusual. He wouldn't give me the password. So then I called the statisticians for Department of Surgery just to check on what they told you. They agreed that the 'n' value was low enough that one unknown outcome might question the validity of the study.

"I then called Lilly back, told him what the statisticians said, and he told me, 'Howard, you're not listening. Those files are not to be opened. Don't even think about asking Dr. Michaels about it either. He won't be happy.' He wasn't nice."

"So now what?" Paul asked.

"Good question," Resine said.

Paul nodded in quiet acceptance. *I was so close.*

"Do the analysis as if those two files didn't exist," Resine said. "Besides, to you those files *don't* exist."

As he stood to leave Paul couldn't help noticing a basket marked "TO FILE." It contained an irregular stack of papers and folders at the edge of Resine's desk. Just below the top of the stack, the edge of a yellow folder stuck out enough for Paul to read "J. Lilly – PRI..."

Maybe, just maybe.

"When do you want to meet again?" Paul asked Resine.

"Do you think you'll have some parameters and data sets in forty-eight hours?"

"I think so."

"I have a UCLA research council meeting on Thursday from three to five. Can you meet me here after five?"

"Sure. Assuming we don't have an emergency transplant, I should be out of the outpatient clinic by four, four thirty," Paul said.

"Good. Here at five on Thursday. I might be a little late. My secretary will be probably be gone, but have a seat."

* * *

That evening Nicole returned to Claire Boothe's house for the third time. The guards merely nodded hello, and JoJo took Nicole up to the house. She let herself in and walked back to the pool to find Li Yong putting out the food and wine. Becky and Claire were snuggled together reading their iPads on a double-wide lounge chair by the pool. A few guests were already munching on goodies.

"Hey," Nicole said.

"Hey, back," Becky said. "I've got to ask you something."

"Shoot." Nicole walked over and sat at the foot of the lounge chair.

"Do you remember when I asked if you knew Dr. Roberts from Seattle and you said no?" Becky asked. Claire put down her pad and listened.

"Yes," Nicole said. *Uh oh.*

"Well, Toni Lord saw you eating at a restaurant in Manhattan Beach. She said it didn't look like you were discussing transplantation."

Oh shit. "I'm sorry and I can explain," Nicole said. "In Seattle, nurse's aides were strictly forbidden from socializing with the doctors or even the nurses. It would be grounds for immediate dismissal. I wasn't absolutely sure of the policy at UCLA, so I wasn't being truthful."

"So you did know him?" Claire asked.

"Yes. Actually, he saved me big time," Nicole said. "It's an interesting story."

"Okay. Let's hear it."

"Well, Paul made a pass at me, more than a year ago at Seattle Med. I totally dismissed him and reminded him of the hospital rules. A few weeks later I helped him out trying to take a bus home one night. He asked me out again and I caved. I went out with him twice. Dinner and home and a promise not to call me again. I liked him but I needed the job. We didn't talk again for months. Sometime later another surgical resident groped me in the elevator. When the elevator door opened, I slapped him and started yelling. The long and short was that the jerk denied everything and I was fired that morning."

"So what's new in the world," Claire said.

"Knowing you, I'm surprised you didn't flip him and put a knee in his back," Becky added.

"Too many people around. Paul heard about the incident from a nurse and thought it unfair. He knew this guy had done some bad things to a nurse on the Urology floor a year earlier, so he secretly taped the resident admitting that he groped me and then presented the tape to the hospital attorney. I knew nothing about the tape or that Paul had done anything."

"He blackmailed the hospital guy?" Claire asked.

"Blackmail may be too strong a word, but let's say I got a nice check, a clean slate, and a job at another hospital. The administrator alluded to the fact that Paul was responsible, although he didn't mention him by name."

"I'm impressed," Becky said.

"It's better than that," Nicole said. "Paul didn't contact me to tell me what he'd done. I found him and said I needed to pay him back. Paul got angry with me, saying that he did the tape because the guy was an ass and not that he wanted anything from me. At that point in my life not too many people had done anything for me without wanting something in return. After that, I started seeing him."

"Wow. Roberts seems like a real stand-up guy," Becky said.

"So you did pay him back?" Claire said, smiling.

"Yes. I suppose so," Nicole said.

"Why did you leave Seattle then?"

"Personal family stuff that had suffocated me for a decade. I needed to get away. Paul wasn't happy about it. I knew he would be upset, so I didn't even give him my contact info, but he tracked me down. I've told him I won't come back to Seattle in the near future. I'm too happy here, and that has mostly to do with you two."

"Well, he seems pretty nice, and Dr. Michaels thinks he's really good," Becky said.

"Yeah. He is. He doesn't deserve how I treated him. Anyway, while he's here I'm going to see him. If that's okay?"

"Fine by me," Becky said. "I just wouldn't make it public at the hospital."

"Thank you. Maybe the four of us could go out one night for dinner. My treat," Nicole said.

"That would be our pleasure," Claire said.

Nicole stood and gave both Becky and Claire a hug and kiss on the cheek. "I am so lucky to have met you two. So damn lucky."

* * *

Nicole returned to Paul's apartment at eleven thirty.

"Did you have a good time?" Paul was sitting on the couch, reading the latest issue of *Transplantation.*

Nicole flopped onto the couch into Paul's lap.

"The best. Such interesting people. Everyone has a story. I can't tell you how lucky I've been meeting Becky and Claire and their friends."

"That's good. I'm happy for you."

"Oh. I guess one of the nurses IDed us at that restaurant in Manhattan Beach and told Becky."

"Really. Are you okay with that? Was she okay with that?"

"I apologized. I told them about the policy at Seattle Med and that I wasn't certain how UCLA Nursing would act. Apparently, it's okay. I told Becky and Claire everything about us. The whole story about us meeting on the ward, then at the bus stop and then telling you, lovingly I might add, to get lost. I told them about Dr. Hendriks and the elevator and what you did for me."

"I assume you didn't tell them about Tony?"

"No."

"Did you tell them about the pizza delivery?"

"I might have omitted some of those details. But, we're cool. They know you're leaving in a couple of months and I'm staying here in LA. You'd really like Claire. I suggested we all go out to dinner, the four of us. They said they'd love to."

"I know Becky and I'd love to meet Claire," Paul said.

"Someplace quiet so we can talk, I suppose. Becky did tell me that Claire usually goes out with a bodyguard. Her dad demands it."

"Aren't you bodyguard enough?"

"Funny. No, I'm not," Nicole said. "But funny." She stood up and turned toward the bedroom. "It's late but I've got to take a shower and wash the chlorine out of my hair."

"Me too," Paul said, jumping off the couch.

* * *

Paul finished the Transplantation Clinic at 4:25 on Thursday. He left the charts to be dictated later and ran

242

to the Boothe Building and the Transplant Research Department office.

At 4:50 Paul walked into the Research Department's outer office to find Resine's secretary straightening up to leave.

"I've got a scheduled meeting with Dr. Resine at five," Paul said.

"Yes, it's on his schedule. Have a seat and he'll be here. Sometimes the council meetings go late, but he knows about the meeting and will be here by five thirty for sure," the secretary said as she exited.

I'll never get another chance.

Paul sat for a moment and checked the hallway. The secretary entered a down elevator and disappeared. Paul turned and re-entered the department office and walked immediately into Resine's private office.

He knew that four-drawer file cabinets lined two walls of Resine's office, and if Lilly's file had been replaced he wouldn't likely find it for days, let alone in five minutes.

Resine's desk was cluttered and the TO FILE basket was filled to chin level. Three yellow folders stuck out in the pile of manila and vanilla paper.

Paul carefully lifted the entire pile up to the first yellow folder and placed it on the floor.

DEPARTMENT SALARIES

The clock read 4:59.

He picked up the second stack down to the next folder.

401K – RESINE

The clock read 5:01.

He placed the second stack on the floor next to the first stack and picked up the remaining pile down to the third yellow folder

J. Lilly – Private

The folder contained a single sheet of paper with twenty-five lines of text. Paul took out his mobile phone and took a picture of the paper and another backup photo. He quickly put the two files on the floor back in place and exited to the department office and sat.

The wall clock read 5:07.

Paul opened his briefcase and extracted the data sheets to show Resine. His hands shook so badly that he couldn't concentrate on numbers, so he put the papers back in the briefcase and shut it. He spent the next five minutes trying to control his breathing.

At 5:15, Paul Resine walked into the department office and said, "Let's talk."

Ten minutes into the discussion of the first data sheets, Resine said, "You might want to consider laying off the coffee in the afternoon. You're wired tight as a drum."

"Yeah. You're probably right," Paul answered. *You'll never know.*

Paul returned to the clinic and spent the next hour dictating the charts from the afternoon. Before looking at the pictures taken from the Resine/Lilly file, he called Nicole and found her at his apartment. He wanted to make sure she'd be home that evening but had no intention of telling her what he'd done, what he'd found, and what he might be able to reveal. *Not yet.*

"What time will you be home?" Nicole asked.

"I don't think too late. Maybe forty-five minutes or an hour," Paul said. "I've just got to do a little more work."

"I was just walking out the door to go shopping," Nicole said. "Anything you want?"

"No. Just you."

"You're corny. I'll get us something interesting to eat. Back by eight thirty."

Paul thought it interesting that she didn't ask about the database.

As soon as Nicole hung up, Paul logged onto the Southern California Transplant data network. He immediately went to Tony's file, JD.D.050602-3, and received the same message: ACCESS DENIED – NEED PASSWORD TO UNBLOCK. Using the photograph of the paper, he saw a list of passwords and started typing them in.

PASSWORD INCORRECT came up five times. The sixth password made Paul laugh. GOBLUE02.

Figures. He and I must have drunk the same Kool-Aid everyone at the University of Michigan drinks.

The password opened Tony's file.

Last name: Doe

First name: John

Date kidney retrieved: 05/02/2002

Time kidney retrieved: 16:45

Facility: ---

Surgeon: ---

Preservative: Sachs Solution

Donor: Live

ABO: AB

HLA-A: star 02:110:03:02N

HLA-B: star 01-109-03-02J

HLA-DP..........

Before closing the file Paul saw a three-bar menu sign on the top right of the file. A simple click gave him exactly what he thought he'd find.

NO ADDITIONAL DATA AT THIS TIME.

"Shit. Shit," Paul yelled to the screen. He knew the data was Tony's from the tissue typing, but the file didn't give a name or anything that would point to Anthony Marrone.

He checked the notes from Tony's contact information on his phone. All the dates and typing were identical to Tony's.

Paul closed the file and went to Jane Doe's file, JD.R.050702-3.

ACCESS DENIED – NEED PASSWORD TO UNBLOCK

Paul mumbled, "Here we go. Let's try the same password," and he typed in GOBLUE02.

Last name: Doe

First name: Jane

Date kidney received: 05/02/2002

Time kidney received: 22:45

Date of transplant: 05/03/2002

Time of transplant: 02:30

Facility: ---

Surgeon: ---

ABO: AB

HLA-A: star 02:110:03:02N

HLA-B: star 01-109-03-02H

HLA-DP..........

"Shit," Paul yelled at the screen. "I know all this. Damn. Damn." He then hit the menu bar and a file menu appeared.

"Hmmmm."

1. Clinical information
2. Contacts
3. Operative Notes

Paul clicked on Clinical Information. The screen read "No Data."
"Shit."

Then he clicked on Contacts. The screen again read "No Data."

"Shit."

Then the third option, Operative Notes.

The computer screen went blank other than a cursor at the top right and a twirling hourglass.

"Oh."

Five seconds later a typical operative note appeared on the screen.

UCLA -- Department of Surgery

Date: 03 May 2002

Name: B..........

Paul looked hard at the sheet. Blinked twice and relooked at the patient's name. "Holy shit. Oh my God!" He hit the PRINT button, then immediately logged off the database and shut down the computer. He folded the two page Op Note and stuffed it in his pocket. "Holy goddamn shit," he said over and over as he exited UCLA and headed to his car.

* * *

Don Gordon's cell phone made the most annoying siren sound as he was about to get into his car to pick up a pizza and beer. Gordon was the systems manager for the Southern California Transplant Database and had held his position for thirty years. He worked for and with every transplant program south of Fresno and down to the Mexican border. He had written the programs to maintain the database for not only Southern California but the National Tissue Registries as well. He had programmed certain triggers to be set off if a data breach had occurred. The trigger would automatically text his phone and set off a siren response. Gordon knew the files had been opened two days earlier by Dr. Resine but thought little of it. As head of the Southern California Registry, Resine was supposed to have access to everything.

Gordon immediately returned to his home office and examined the file activity expecting another entry by Resine. The entry had been made by someone Gordon did not know from UCLA. Two files had been opened that should have never been opened. He had no interest in the file contents. Not his bag. He opened a private note section in each file that only he could access.

His first call was to Howard Resine at UCLA, who knew exactly the files in question. And he knew exactly who had opened the files before Gordon told him.

"Paul Roberts, M.D."

"I know, I know," Resine said. "He's a visiting resident from Seattle Med and will be out of here in three months. I am extremely disappointed. He's doing some research for Dr. Michaels and me. I specifically told him not to open those files. Honestly, I don't know how he did it. I'll take it from here. Dr. Michaels is going to be pissed off beyond belief."

Resine hung up and called Ralph Michaels. Resine had guessed correctly. Michaels did not take the news well.

Don Gordon made a second call, off protocol, to a unknown number associated with no names. He had never called this number before to his recollection.

The phone rang three times and went to voicemail as expected. Gordon spoke slowly per the instructions on the notes, "This is Don Gordon." He then hung up and waited.

Four minutes later his cell phone rang.

"Mr. Gordon?"

"Yes."

"The password?"

"Lopez. Capital L-small o-p-e-z."

"What happened?"

"Both files were opened tonight," Gordon said. "I'm not sure how the guy got the password. He was logged in for less than thirty seconds."

"You have the name?"

"Paul Roberts, M.D., a rotating resident at UCLA."

"Do you know anything else about him?"

"He has been doing a research project for Howard Resine and Dr. Michaels at UCLA. I know he's doing a short-term rotation for three months and then will be gone and have no further access to the database."

"Can you find out any more about him?" the unnamed man said.

"I can try. I know he's from Seattle Med."

"Interesting. I'm not too worried, but see if you can find anything else about him."

"My notes say that if a breach occurs and I notify you, I get something. Is that still in effect?" Gordon asked.

"Yes. You will receive an untraceable money order for three thousand dollars within three days. Keep this to yourself. Thank you."

* * *

Paul entered his apartment to find it empty. He looked at his phone. Ten after eight. *She'll be home soon.*

At 8:22 Nicole came into the apartment with two bags of groceries. "I'm here and I'm starving. Let's eat."

Paul exited the bedroom and approached the kitchen.

"Are you okay?" Nicole asked. "You look sick."

"Oh, God. Where do I start?"

"Something bad happen at the hospital?"

"You could say that," he said.

"Did someone die? Did you do something? Damn, what's up?"

"No one died, no one was hurt, but it couldn't be worse..."

A heavy knock on the door interrupted him.

"Who could that be?" Paul asked.

"Got me. Maybe someone needs a cup of sugar."

"Okay. I'll get it," Paul said. "Hold on."

He opened the door to find three large men. The two men on the sides stood like bookends with both hands, hidden, together at their sides.

"Are you Paul Roberts?" the man in the middle said.

"Yes."

"I'm Special Agent Ricardo Puerto of the FBI," Puerto said, holding up a brass badge.

"What?" Paul said.

Without letting Paul examine the badge, Puerto pushed Paul into the room forcibly and spun him around. The other two men, armed with revolvers, entered quickly, split in opposite directions, and scanned the apartment.

"You are under arrest for a violation of Public Law 104-191, which is a felony," Puerto continued, "the HIPAA law. By law you will be placed in handcuffs and taken to Federal Court. You have the right to remain silent. Anything you say can and will be used against you in a court of law. You have the right to an attorney. If you cannot afford..."

Nicole screamed, "What the hell is going on?" as she rapidly approached the door.

The armed bookends turned simultaneously. "Back off," one man yelled. "and keep your hands up where we can see them."

Nicole stopped. "Paul. What's going on? Why is this happening?"

"Oh, God. Nicole. I'm sorry. Today. The database," he cried as Puerto was applying handcuffs. "Ouch. That's too tight."

"What database," Nicole yelled. "What are you talking about?"

"Anything you say may be evidence," Puerto said.

"The transplant database."

"I will remind you not to speak any more," Puerto yelled. He then turned Paul around, put the flat of his palm at the back of Paul's head and forced him out the apartment door.

Nicole ran into the hallway. "Talk to me, Paul," she yelled. She tried to run abreast of him but was blocked by one of the bookends walking backward.

Paul turned his head as much as he could with Puerto forcing him forward. "Claire Boothe received Tony's kidney."

"Back off, ma'am," the bookends spit back at Nicole.

"What. What are you talking about?" Nicole cried as Paul moved down the hallway.

The elevator opened and Puerto forced Paul through the door.

"Claire Boothe got Tony's kidney on May 2nd, 2002," Paul yelled. "I got into the..."

The elevator door slammed shut.

"What?" Nicole yelled at the closed elevator door. "How could that be? Oh my God no."

Nicole ran into the apartment and called Allen Rogers. The call went to voicemail.

"Think, Nicole, think," she said to herself.

She dialed Becky Brown.

"Becky, this is Nicole."

"How could you do this, Nicole?" Becky barked back. "Claire and I trusted you. And because of you, Dr. Michaels and I trusted Paul. I can't talk to you now, or ever. I feel so betrayed."

"You have to listen," Nicole pleaded. "Paul wasn't looking for Claire. I swear on my life and my mother's life. He didn't know what he was looking for. I didn't even know Claire had had a kidney transplant."

"I don't believe you," Becky yelled. The line disconnected.

Nicole called Becky again, but the call went to voicemail. She tried again and her number was blocked.

"Oh shit." She tried Allen Rogers and again went to voicemail.

Nicole thought for a moment, then dialed Marianne Charles, Becky and Claire's friend whose husband did legal work for Claire.

"Marianne. It's me, Nicole."

"Am I supposed to be talking to you? I think not," Marianne stated with authority.

"I swear we weren't looking to do anything to Claire or Becky," Nicole said. "On my life, I swear. I need to speak to your husband, alone. Better yet I need to meet him for

254

a few minutes to prevent something terrible from happening. Please believe me."

"Hold on."

"This is Fred Charles. You're Becky's acquaintance that was a Marine?" Charles asked.

"Yes. We need to meet now. Something terrible has happened and I need to speak to someone who can contact the family. I don't know where they took Paul Roberts, but I need to make sure you know what he might say. It's absolutely crucial. I don't want to do it over the phone. You need to believe me."

"Okay. I'll meet you at the bar at the Luxe Hotel, northwest corner of Sunset and Sepulveda in fifteen minutes," Charles said.

* * *

Nicole found Paul's keys on the bedroom dresser, ran to the garage, and drove to the Luxe Hotel. She arrived, found a booth, and waited. Fred Charles arrived five minutes later.

She jumped up to meet Charles, whom she'd never seen before.

"Thanks for coming," she said nervously. "Thank you."

"Have a seat, miss," Charles said.

Both slid into opposite sides of the booth.

"Do you know where they took Paul?"

"To jail," Charles said. "He will be booked into the LA County Jail, downtown. He'll be allowed to make one call, probably to a lawyer or to you to get him a lawyer. He will spend tonight in jail no matter what and will come in front of a judge for a plea around ten a.m."

"You can't be his lawyer?" Nicole asked.

"No. I represent the Boothes. Besides, you can't afford me."

"Can you recommend a lawyer for Paul?"

"Yes. He'll need a good one. I have a friend from Hastings Law School, Mark Edwards who does criminal work." Charles wrote on the back of a business card.

"Paul is not a criminal," Nicole yelled, garnering the attention of everyone at the bar.

"That remains to be seen. Here's his number," Charles said. "You've got to calm down."

"How can I be calm? My life just got turned over," Nicole cried. "This is all a terrible mistake, but worse things might happen if the Boothes and Dr. Michaels don't understand."

"Dr. Roberts illegally and willfully broke into Claire Boothe's private medical record. And he had been specifically warned not to do so. That was a significant breach of medical ethics. Given that her father is the governor of California and a possible presidential candidate, any judge will treat illegal release of personal data harshly. I only hope that you aren't involved as well," Charles stated firmly.

"I am involved but I had no idea that Paul would find Claire's record. But there's more than that. So much more that you're not understanding."

"Tell me. I'm listening, but remember, I am not your lawyer and whatever you say may be evidence against you. I represent the Boothes and only the Boothes. Do you understand?"

"Yes. And I don't care. I don't want Paul or Claire or Claire's dad hurt. I swear. But what I'm about to tell you is the absolute truth."

"Okay. Go ahead, I'm listening."

Nicole spoke quickly but with confidence. She took twenty minutes to explain the entire saga of Tony's kidnapping and how it destroyed her family. Then she told of meeting Paul, then Paul meeting Tony, and Paul's presumption that Tony's kidney was used for transplantation.

"At that point, Paul and I were dead-ended. We had no idea to whom the kidney went."

"Stop. What the hell does this have to do with Claire or Bobby Boothe?" Charles said, angrily.

"On May 3rd, 2002, Claire Boothe received my brother Tony's kidney. And I can prove it."

"You're joking."

"I'm not joking."

"You better have some solid evidence."

"I do. Rock solid. But given what I know to be true, I think you need to hear what Dr. Michaels and Governor Boothe have to say. I assume that one or both of them will deny everything or say it's absurd. Trust me that I can prove everything I'm talking about."

"This is crazy."

257

"Yes. But I think it better that we have a discussion with Dr. Roberts, Dr. Michaels, the governor and me before any of this gets out to the media."

"Is that a threat, miss?"

"I sincerely hope not. It's just the truth. I need to find out how and why this happened to my brother. I'm not going to stand by and watch Paul Roberts hung out to dry. He was just trying to help me find out who took Tony's kidney. We had no idea it would be Claire. I swear that on my mother's life. Plus I have a friend who's an MP. He thinks some really bad people were in on this. If it gets out, my friend thinks some people might get hurt, including my family."

"Your friend, the MP, knows about this?" Charles asked.

"Yes and two other Marines that served with me. They know pretty much everything," Nicole lied, knowing that her Marine friends didn't know about Claire receiving Tony's kidney.

"You're not afraid they'll go to the media?"

"Not a chance. Not without me saying so. We trust each other with our lives. They'll do whatever they need to do to help me."

"I need to make some calls," Charles said. "This is not going to go well for you or Dr. Roberts if there are any untruths with what you've told me. You, I guess, don't have much to lose. Dr. Roberts' career, however, could be in serious jeopardy."

"I understand."

"Give me your cell number, go home, and I'll call you."

"Tonight? I hope so."

"I'll call you."

"Maybe we could meet at the jail?" Nicole asked.

"Not likely the governor is going to meet anyone at the jail. And it's even unlikelier that LA County is going to let him go before his plea in front of a judge."

"Like I said, I don't think the media needs to hear about this. For some reason I think the governor will figure some way of talking to Paul and me, with Dr. Michaels tonight," Nicole said.

"I'll call you. Go home and wait. You could use the time to call a lawyer for Dr. Roberts in the meantime," Charles said.

* * *

Nicole was back in Paul's apartment by nine thirty. She called Allen Rogers first. He agreed with everything she had done. Rogers said getting a lawyer was absolutely necessary. Nicole then called Mark Edwards's office. The message gave an after-hours phone number, which Nicole dialed. That call went immediately to voicemail. Nicole left a message for Mr. Edwards to call her immediately.

Fred Charles called Nicole at 10:15 p.m. "The governor is at a Republican fund-raiser in Honolulu. He will be available to FaceTime at 11:15 tonight. It's three hours earlier in Hawaii."

"Good," Nicole said.

"Not good. Dr. Michaels is madder than you can even imagine and said your claim is 'totally fully of shit.' Those were his exact words. But he said he'd go with me downtown to face Dr. Roberts. This may not go well for you and especially for your friend."

"I'll be there," Nicole said.

"Did you get hold of Mr. Edwards? Dr. Roberts will need an attorney."

"No, but I left a message for him to call me. I'm waiting. I don't need or want him to hear what we have to say, yet. I'm not sure there will be an arraignment," Nicole said.

"Don't count on that," Charles said.

"Fine. I will see you at the LA County Jail in forty minutes."

* * *

Chapter 18

Fred Charles had to pull more than a few strings to arrange what seemed to be an unusual request. Governor Boothe would be Facetimed into the interview from his hotel suite in Hawaii.

Charles and Dr. Michaels sat across from Nicole in an interview room at the LA County Jail awaiting Paul.

Nothing was said. If icicles were hanging from the ceiling they wouldn't have been as cold as the atmosphere in the room.

Charles had made certain that no recordings of the meeting would take place, and the room next door with the two-way mirror was empty.

A jailer escorted Paul Roberts into the room. Paul wore a bright orange top and pants with the words "LOS ANGELES COUNTY JAIL" in broad letters imprinted on the front and back of the shirt. Other than the color, the outfit looked like surgical scrubs, or "greens." His legs and hands were shackled by jail protocol.

Charles told the jailer to uncuff Paul's hands. "I take full responsibility for the detainee," he said. He then asked the jailer to leave and stay outside. Paul, a look of defeat etched on his face, sat next to Nicole. She squeezed his hand for a moment. Michaels could only glare rays of hate toward Paul.

As Charles was trying to get the governor onto a live feed, Paul leaned over to Nicole and whispered, "How did you arrange this?"

"Necessity is the mother of invention," Nicole whispered back. "I talked to Allen Rogers, and he said that before anything hits the media, we have to explain what happened. We have to be truthful one hundred percent."

Paul nodded assent.

"I don't think this meeting will last more than a few minutes," Charles announced to the room as the jailer exited and shut the door. "I've told Dr. Michaels and the governor, when we get him online, to say nothing. I will do all the talking." Michaels nodded. Charles then opened his computer, and within a minute, Governor Boothe was in the room on a wall screen.

"Bobby, you there?" he asked.

"I'm here and I'm not happy. What bullshit," Boothe said.

Nicole shook her head. *No way this goes less than an hour.*

Michaels glared at Paul but continued his silence.

Charles sat opposite Paul and Nicole. "Okay, Miss Marrone and Dr. Roberts, the floor is yours. Remember that you have three witnesses to what you will be saying, and anything said can be used against you. You have waived your right to an attorney for this meeting. Is that correct?"

"Yes," Nicole and Paul said simultaneously.

"Go ahead and tell me how this happened," Charles said.

Nicole then related in more detail the kidnapping of Tony on May 2, 2002, and what the Marrones were told by Dr. McNeil and the hospital staff over the subsequent days. She then explained a bit about her father's bankruptcy and the effects on her family.

"About a year and a half ago," Nicole continued, "I met Dr. Roberts at Seattle Med, and we started seeing each other about six months after that. Paul met Tony about that time. Tony had complained for years that his scar ached, and Paul offered to look at it. That's what started all this."

"Ten seconds after seeing the position of Tony's scar," Paul said, "I knew something was amiss. The scar was a posterior subcostal flank incision, inappropriate for an exploration of a deep abdominal or flank stab wound. I will assume that only Dr. Michaels here in the room can corroborate that statement."

All in the room turned to Michaels, who nodded tacit agreement but said nothing.

"When Nicole found that the hospital had no record of Tony being there I was pretty sure something was wrong. I thought then that Nicole's brother's kidney might have been illegally taken for transplantation........"

Paul spoke for fifteen minutes, leaving nothing out, including the illegal database searches in Seattle and the payout to the data manager.

"......finally, I stole the passcodes from Dr. Resine's desk and found Claire Booth as the recipient of Tony's kidney on May 3rd, 2002."

The room was death silent, save the breathing of three men and a woman.

Paul broke the silence, saying only, "And here we are."

Nicole spoke up. "I've known Claire for only a few months. Until tonight, I had no idea that she had even received a kidney transplant nor did Paul."

The room was again silent.

"Can't be," Michaels finally said. "I have to review these records. I just don't believe it."

"I swear on my children's lives that this is the first I've heard of this," Boothe said. "We were told that the donor had been a head injury from the St. Louis area and that the family did not want to know where the kidney was going, nor did they want the recipient to know the donor. As Claire got sicker and sicker, we just thanked God that she had a kidney after looking for eighteen months. We thought God had intervened."

"Actually, that's what I recollect as well," Michaels said. "I didn't know the governor before Claire's transplant."

"I have something to add," Nicole said. "And this will be the reason that I demanded the meeting. My friend, a sergeant in the Marine Corps, is now an MP. He has said from the beginning that some very powerful people had to be involved to kidnap a child, have the kidney removed and transported, erase un-erasable databases, and remove hospital charts. His fear was that if information got out about Tony's kidney, these powerful people may not want anyone with knowledge of what happened to talk. He thought that people could die. That might include my family, the recipient's family, Dr. Roberts, the kidnappers, the entire team of doctors at the hospital in

Washington State, and the entire team of doctors wherever the transplant was done."

"I still find this hard to believe, but it won't be hard to check," Michaels said. "Paul, how many laws did you break in finding all this out?"

"A few, I admit," Paul said, "but at no time did I have any idea that the recipient would be Claire Boothe. But as Nicole has said, if we had gone immediately to the police, an investigator or the media, people's lives might be in jeopardy."

"Well, I think I know where this is going," Charles said. "Paul will remain in jail until Dr. Michaels has reviewed the facts presented here. I will have the arraignment postponed until that time."

He turned to the screen and said, "Bobby, you and I are going to have a long talk later tonight. We need to get to the bottom of this quickly. I'm going to call you from home in an hour."

"Okay, Fred," Boothe said. "This is surreal."

"Talk to no one. Is that perfectly clear?"

"Yeah, yeah."

"No one," Charles repeated, then pushed a key on his laptop and the monitor went black.

"Does Paul really have to stay in jail?" Nicole asked.

"Unfortunately, yes," Charles said, "until we've verified what you have told us. As I told the governor, I shouldn't need to tell any of you not to speak one word of this to anyone, including family and friends. No one."

265

Charles then went to the door and had the jail guard re-enter.

Nicole stood quickly and gave Paul a hug. "Everything is going to work out," she said. "Hang in there. It's not like I didn't tell you not to get mixed up in this with me."

"Thanks," Paul said. "I'm still in a fog about how quickly this happened. I didn't know who to..."

The jail guard interrupted Paul. "Time to go, buddy. You must be one special dude to have this going on. Move." He re-cuffed Paul's hands and escorted him out the door back to his cell.

Michaels came up to Nicole, who turned around to face him.

"I have to admit your story and facts sound credible," he said. "I came here tonight thinking you and Dr. Roberts were the two most conniving and deceitful people I'd ever been fooled by. I guess we'll see."

"How long will it take to check out their story?" Charles asked as he closed his briefcase.

"It's late," Michaels said. "I'll make some calls first thing in the morning and have Howard Resine help. Won't take more than an hour."

Charles turned to Nicole. "I'd go back to your apartment, get some sleep, and I'll call you by nine a.m. Here's my cell number. If you and Paul are on the level, I'll have the charges dropped and he'll be out of jail by noon."

"Do I need protection?" Nicole asked.

"Not if everyone keeps their mouths shut."

Chapter 19

As soon as Nicole got into Paul's car to drive back to Santa Monica, she called Allen Rogers and carefully recapitulated the entire meeting.

"How's the doc doing?" Rogers asked.

"Not well," Nicole said. "I don't think he's used to this kind of stress. He's certainly out of his comfort zone."

"How you doing?"

"Okay, I guess. I think Boothe and Michaels believed us. I hope so. I guess we'll have to wait for Michaels to confirm everything. I couldn't tell from the lawyer reactions."

"Think. Anything else they said that was important?"

"Actually, there was," Nicole said. "Dr. Michaels said he didn't know the Boothes until the day of the transplant. I guess that suggests Michaels wasn't part of this."

"Probably, but don't take anything for granted. Boothe is still the most likely person to be covering something up. He had motive, enough money and traction to make all this happen."

"Yeah. The lawyer alluded to that at the end of the meeting. He was going to call Boothe as soon as he got home. Michaels drove in with him, and I suspect he doesn't want Michaels hearing what the governor knows."

"Go home. Lock the doors and windows and close the shades. Park your car in an open area if possible."

"A little paranoid, aren't you?" Nicole asked.

"No. You have to listen. There are some really powerful people behind this. The governor is going to call someone other than the lawyer for advice. Be alert and watch your six."

"Oorah," Nicole said.

"Do you have room in your apartment for me to stay if I come up?" Rogers asked.

"We'll make room. You'd do that for me?"

"I was already packed and have told my CO that I might need a few days for emergency leave."

Nicole gave Rogers the address to Paul's apartment and said she'd leave a key above the light fixture to the right of the door.

* * *

"Bobby, are you alone?" Charles asked.

"Yeah. As far as I know my cell phone is secure. Beverly's in the other room sleeping."

"Did you tell her anything?"

"Of course I did. She's my wife and Claire's mother. Why wouldn't I? Besides, she just thinks this is a joke," Boothe barked back.

"You can't be telling anyone else yet. Trust me. And that goes for Beverly too," Charles said sternly.

"I'm getting ready to announce my run for the presidency in fourteen days. We've got to contain this false news."

268

"Until we know for sure, this is not false news. Those two kids had a compelling story with facts and dates."

"I had nothing to do with any kidnappings. Neither did my wife, dammit. I need to get my campaign team together to handle any fallout if this gets out."

"Don't tell anyone. Nobody," Charles demanded. "If I were a cop, you two would be the only ones I'd be looking at. You and Beverly had motive and money and could have made this happen. Or you told somebody to make it happen, which makes you just as guilty. If you tell anyone who might have involvement, they'll do everything they can to cover this up."

"Yeah. Okay."

"Bobby. You two have to think back to the time you started looking for a kidney for Claire. Who might have gained something? Family, business, politics? Anyone who needed to see this happen, with the wherewithal to make it happen without you knowing? Think."

"Nobody comes to mind."

"Has to be, unless you or Beverly are lying. That's how the cops are going to look at it."

"Hasn't the statute of limitations run out, even if we find someone?" Boothe asked.

"No. The boy was a minor and the crime wasn't discovered until a year ago. Makes no difference. Even if it's no longer a punishable crime but comes out, you wouldn't be elected dogcatcher in Siberia. Call me back with a list of anyone who might be involved, even remotely," Charles said.

"Anything else I can do?"

"Yes. I need to get the police records on the kidnapping. Who do you know in the AG's office in Sacramento that can obtain police files quickly? Can't be more than one police department on Lopez 'fucking' Island."

"Carl Harris. He's the assistant AG now. He'll do it for me. I'll call him and have him call you."

"Don't tell him why, if you can," Charles said.

* * *

Bobby Boothe called his friend Carl Harris in Sacramento at home. Harris said he would obtain the records first thing in the morning and get them to Fred Charles. Boothe then walked into his bedroom portion of their Honolulu suite to find his wife reading.

"Bev, we have to talk," he said.

"Not about that cock and bull story from that nurse's aide," Beverly Boothe said. "You know it's a lie and someone is trying to blackmail us."

"Actually, the story, while farfetched, was backed up by dates and facts. Ralph Michaels and Fred both think that it's plausible."

"How could that be?" Beverly asked. "You didn't know about this before, did you?"

"No. I swear. The first I heard about this was tonight," Boothe said. "Fred wants us to think and try to remember anyone before Claire's transplant who would have benefitted and would have done something so outrageous, so terrible."

"That's almost impossible. That's everyone. Everyone on your campaign staff and all the loyal supporters and large donors over the years. It could be anyone."

"Most, if not all, knew about Claire's kidney problems, but few knew how we really felt about it," Boothe said.

"It's a time in my life I don't want to think about," Beverly said. "I remember the kidney doctors saying that they probably wouldn't find a match before Claire's kidneys failed."

"Fred said we can't talk to anyone about this. If it's true and gets out, my candidacy is sunk."

"Oh, God, Bobby. This is terrible. I don't believe it's true for one second. It's like the Democrats timed this perfectly so you can't run."

"Maybe I should call Tommy and see if he has any ideas."

"You think he'll talk to you? What has it been, four, five years since you fired him?"

"I trusted Bobby with everything, with my life. Shit, he ran all my campaigns. He did everything we asked him and more. He and Joan were our best friends. Why he had to embezzle from the California Republican Caucus, I'll never know. He had only to ask me for money."

"Well, he did embezzle. He's lucky he didn't go to jail even after making restitution. Your testimony probably saved him."

"Yeah," Boothe muttered.

"I actually miss Joan. She was closer to me than my two sisters."

"Maybe for old time's sake I should get his advice and see if he has any ideas. What do you think?" Boothe asked.

"Can't hurt. If he doesn't have any answers, we're no worse off. He'll just say you're being paranoid and dismiss the whole thing," Beverly responded.

"Fred said not to talk to anyone. He said it more than once."

"That's crazy. Call Tommy."

* * *

Bobby Boothe rarely made mistakes and he exuded confidence. Confidence oozed from every pore in his body. He was the personification of George Washington standing on the bow of a rowboat crossing the turbulent Delaware River on his way to Trenton. Rock solid and steady. And he didn't get to be one of the wealthiest men on the planet and governor of California by misjudging the people around him.

Thomas Clark, or Tommy, had served as Boothe's chief of staff, right hand man, and best friend for thirty years. Their wives were friends and confidants. Their kids grew up together. Every important decision Boothe made had been bounced off Tommy first.

That was true until four years earlier when Tommy got greedy, put his hand in the proverbial till and got caught. When Tommy pleaded guilty, it was Tommy who advised Boothe, correctly, to keep his distance if he ever wanted to run for president. Since then, Tommy and

Boothe had not communicated, in any way. Boothe missed him badly.

Boothe had toyed with the idea of bringing Tommy back once he formally announced his candidacy, using Tommy's advice but with no official title. He did not share these thoughts with anyone, including his wife.

Nicole and Paul's declarations, which seemed so credible, caught Boothe totally off guard. With his scheduled announcement of candidacy for president about to happen, he had reason to be worried. He needed sage advice for an incredibly difficult situation. He needed and badly wanted Tommy's input.

Fifteen minutes later, Boothe walked back into his bedroom. Beverly Booth lay in bed reading. She knew her husband better than anyone and she didn't like the way he carried himself before slumping down in lounge chair across from the bed.

"That bad? So what did he say?" Beverly asked.

"I told him only that someone had contacted me about the possibility that Claire's kidney was illegally obtained and did he have any idea where that might have come from."

"You didn't give him any names?"

"No, none. He didn't act surprised, which was curious. But he said we were crazy to worry about it just like you said he would. He said someone coming out of the woodwork just as I'm about to run for president is a Hollywood plot and they're trying to blackmail me. He said that if I pay them one red cent, they'll come back for more later."

"I'd agree with him," Beverly said.

"He then said he'd take care of it for me. It was the old Tommy."

"What did you say?"

"I said I'd talk to Fred Charles, and that didn't go well. Like I had thrown a light switch from on to off. He said he wouldn't do a thing for us if I went to Fred. Remember it was Fred who found out about Tommy's embezzlement."

"So what did you say then?"

"I told him I'd have to think about it because Fred was already involved," Boothe said. "But then he said, 'God damn it, Bobby, give me the names of these creeps. I'll fix this.'"

"Did you?"

"No. The way he said it was kind of scary. I told him I didn't know their names. Only Fred did and he wouldn't tell me. He then said, 'Fuck it. Call me back when you know,' and hung up."

"Are you going to tell Fred you talked to him?"

"No," Boothe said. "I think I screwed up. I'll wait and see."

"Now that I think about it, Joan was my rock during those months before Claire got a kidney when we thought she might die," Beverly said.

"I know. So?"

"I told her that if Claire died, you and I had agreed that you would pull out of the race for governor. I told her that we had not said that to anyone, including Tommy, and not to tell anyone."

* * *

Don Gordon called the unnamed man again.

"What did you learn?"

"He apparently has been dating a new nurse's aide who had come down from Washington."

"Do you know her name?" Tommy said.

"Nicole Marrone."

"Marrone?"

"Yeah, Marrone."

"Shit. That figures. Thanks."

* * *

Ralph Michaels called Fred Charles at nine the next morning.

"Everything Paul Roberts told us was true," Michaels said. "I even talked to the systems guy at the national tissue registry and he admitted reluctantly that he'd helped Paul and restored two deleted files, Anthony Marrone and Claire Boothe. Paul's description of Claire's file and Marrone's file in the California database are just as he said. The odds of Claire's transplanted kidney not being Anthony Marrone's kidney are infinitesimally small."

"Plus I got the files on the kidnapping from the Lopez PD," Charles said. "Nicole's description was right on. They had no clues and the case was listed as dead. I talked to the detective, Jack Tacher, who handled the case in 2002. He said it was the most unusual case he'd ever had. No clues. No motives. The police had no reason

275

to think that the kidney was used for a transplant, so they didn't look."

"So what now?" Michaels asked.

"I'll call Nicole and then the DA and cancel the charges on Dr. Roberts. Since it was your office that started this, fax me a statement from you saying it was all a mistake."

"No problem."

"We'll meet at my office at two p.m. You, Nicole, Roberts, and I'll get the governor live from Honolulu."

Charles hung up and called Governor Boothe.

"Bobbie. Fred here."

"What have we learned?" Boothe said.

"Everything they said is true. Every fact," Charles said.

"I can't believe this is happening."

"We're going to have a conference in my office at two p.m. Pacific Time or eleven a.m. in Hawaii. You need to be free."

"I'll cancel my meetings from ten forty-five to two, Hawaii time."

"Have you or Beverly come up with any thoughts about who might be behind this?" Charles asked.

"No. Neither of us could believe it was true. It just made no sense to us. I think I should call Tommy," Boothe said, hoping that Fred would agree. "He was running my campaign in '02 and might know something."

"Bobby, Tom Clark is a crook. He's the last guy I'd call."

Boothe did not respond.

"Don't call him," Charles repeated.

"I'll be back in LA tomorrow night," Boothe said. "At some point, I've got to get my people involved in this mess. I can't announce next week like we planned. This would suck all the air out of the room."

"Then hold off announcing. There is simply no Plan B. Talk to you at eleven," Charles said. "Keep thinking about who might have done this."

* * *

Charles called the U.S. Attorney General's LA office after faxing Michael's declaration that Paul Roberts had been falsely accused.

He then called Nicole and told her that all of her and Paul's statements had checked out and that Paul would be freed in the next hour.

"You need to pick him up and head back to your apartment. You are not to talk to anyone," Charles said.

"Like it or not," Nicole said, "I've already talked with my Marine friend, who is an military police sergeant and knows everything. He's given Paul and me great advice from the beginning, and I'm going to keep him in the loop. You might consider bringing him along. He's smart."

"Maybe. I am going to need any and all names you can think of that have to do with your brother's kidnapping and surgery. We're going to meet again at my office at two p.m."

"Fine. But just so you know, I'm thinking that the governor is still responsible. Do Paul and I need protection?"

"If I were you, I'd probably agree. But I've known Bobby and Beverly for thirty years. They are both deeply religious and were prepared for the worst as Claire got sicker. I don't see them behind this. Could I be wrong? Sure. I just don't think so."

"You didn't answer my question. Do we need protection?" Nicole asked. "Sarge thinks we do and he's coming up to LA today."

"I don't know and I wouldn't even know where to start. See you at two," Charles said.

* * *

Paul and Nicole parked their car in the lot under Charles's law firm on the thirty-seventh floor of an office building in Century City.

They didn't see a man in a dark corner away from the entrance watching every car that entered the lot and taking photos of the license plates.

Hand in hand, Nicole and Paul entered the Harvey Gordon & Charles LLP law firm and were escorted to a conference room.

Fred Charles entered a few minutes later.

"Dr. Roberts, you doing okay?" he asked after taking a seat.

"Better now. Thank you for getting me released," Paul said.

"You have the names?" Charles said, turning to Nicole.

"Yes," Nicole said.

"Let's go over them one by one."

Nicole then listed her parents, Henry and Susan Marrone, and Dr. Charles McNeil and his wife. She remembered vaguely a nurse at Everett General named Pam or Pat Chase or something similar. She listed a detective on the Lopez Police Department, Jack Tacher. She didn't know the names of the anesthesiologist who came to visit the next morning or the hospital administrator who had an argument with her father. Lastly, a woman named Thelma at Everett General who had unsuccessfully looked for Tony's records.

Ralph Michaels entered the conference room and sat.

"Paul. Right or wrong, you broke the law going into those files," he said.

"Yes," Paul said, nodding.

"Let's see how this all plays out before I make a final judgment on you," Michaels said.

Paul nodded. He grabbed Nicole's wrist and made a soft "shh" sound to stop her from responding to Michaels.

Charles opened up a live feed from Honolulu until Bobby Boothe was online.

The list from Nicole and Paul was reviewed. Michaels vaguely remembered the name of Charles McNeil and the fact that he had quit medicine and opened a winery.

"At the transplant meetings, some of the surgeons were jealous as hell of McNeil after his winery became uber-successful," Michaels said, "like he was smarter than everyone."

"It's not likely he kidnapped Tony," Paul said. "Others must have been involved. Nicole and her Marine friends have talked about this endlessly. McNeil was certainly involved, but the mastermind was a pro."

"Plus, my Marine friend said McNeil may have been dealt with by a middleman with an alias," Nicole added.

"Still, I think we need to contact McNeil," Charles said. "He's the only viable lead."

"Wait. This is why we need a professional cop. Someone we can trust," Paul said. "If McNeil tells anyone that we're snooping around, his life and all the people on the list are potentially put in harm's way. Plus McNeil is almost certainly going to deny everything. I would."

"Any suggestions, Governor?" Charles asked.

"I don't know," Boothe said. "I can't afford to let this get out. I'd have to think about it."

"I'd choose the FBI," Charles said. "The kidney was transported over state lines, which makes this a federal case. Furthermore..."

"Oh my God," Nicole shouted, looking at her iPhone. "Oh my God."

"What's up?" Paul asked as the conference room quieted.

"I just googled Reversement Vintners to get a phone number for McNeil," Nicole said. "There's a breaking story posted by the *Seattle Times* from Walla Walla—Dr. Charles McNeil, owner of Reversement Vintners, shot and killed his wife and then took his own life. They were discovered today at six a.m. by the housekeeper."

"This is way too coincidental," Charles shouted. "Has anyone in this room told anyone anything? I need to know now."

The room was silent.

"Bobby, did you or Beverly say something?" Charles asked.

After an uncomfortable moment of silence, Boothe said, "Okay. I'm sorry. I talked to Tommy last night. I guess I just wasn't thinking. Tommy said it was a hoax and he'd take care of it. I didn't give him any names. He doesn't know about Claire's friend or the doctor."

"I pleaded with you not to tell anyone," Charles said.

"There's more. After I talked to Tommy, Bev remembered a conversation from before my run for governor with Tommy's wife, Joan. You know the four of us were very close at that time. Bev said she told Joan that she wouldn't allow me to run for office if Claire died or needed dialysis. Bev told Joan that I felt the same way. Beverly never told me of that conversation until now. My guess, in hindsight, is that Joan told Tommy. Tommy would have done anything to make sure that I ran. His whole professional life to that point depended on it."

"Bobby, that still doesn't explain how he did this," Charles said.

"Before Tommy joined my staff, he practiced criminal law for four years, which means he probably knew some bad people," Boothe said.

"There's your motive," Charles said. "I wish you hadn't talked to that scumbag."

"I made a mistake," Boothe said. "Neither of us believed the story."

"Christ. My parents and Tony are on Lopez. They need to get off the island!" Nicole cried. "Their lives are in danger."

"You have reason to be concerned, and I don't think you have time to wait for formal protection," Charles said. "Call them and have them book themselves into a hotel out of town."

"I'll take care of the costs," Boothe said. "Just have them leave."

Nicole looked at wall clock as she dialed her mother. "Mom. Listen carefully, I'm okay. I want you to know that I'm okay," she said.

"What are you talking about? Are you in trouble of some kind?" Susan Marrone asked.

"I have to explain later. Trust me. Are Dad and Tony around?"

"Dad's here working out back. He's leaving tomorrow morning to drive a load down to Bend. Tony's working at Jake's as a busboy. He'll be home tonight at ten."

"Please listen. You need to get off Lopez now. All of you. All of you are in danger," Nicole pleaded.

"What are you talking about? Is this a joke? I can't leave just like that."

"This is serious, Mom. I don't have time to explain it."

"Where would we go, even if we did leave?"

"You need to check yourself into a hotel in Seattle until we find someplace safe. I'll make a reservation for you and call you on the road," Nicole implored.

"We can't afford that, and Dad would lose his job. We need the money. Tony would get fired too."

"Mom. If you've ever trusted anyone, trust me now. I have friends and we'll take care of the money. You have to leave. Take only your medications and a change of clothes for you, Dad, and Tony. If you leave now you can catch the twelve fifty-five to Anacortes. You can't wait until four. Please listen to me. I will explain later. Please."

"I need to talk to your father," Susan said.

"Mom, you don't have time to talk about this. Please believe me. Get Dad, pack light, get Tony, and get off Lopez. Keep your phone charged so I can call you."

"You're scaring the shit out of me."

"Good. Then maybe you'll believe me. I'll explain later. Go now," Nicole pleaded again.

"Okay, already. I'll call you from the road."

"Mom, I love you," Nicole said and disconnected.

"Will they leave?" Charles asked.

"I hope so. My dad will argue but he'll lose to my mom."

"I'll call John Carlson," Boothe said after listening to the call. "He runs the Four Seasons in Seattle and will take care of them. I use Century Security for protection when I'm home. David Hart runs it. I'll call him and let them know they've got to protect all of you."

Nicole's phone vibrated. She looked down at the text message.

"Uh oh," Nicole said. "One of my roommates texted me. She says I have to call her. I haven't been there for a while." Nicole dialed quickly. "Hey, Sydney. What's up?"

"Some guy knocked on the door asking where you were."

"What did he look like?"

"Not nice or happy. He definitely wasn't selling anything."

"What did you tell him?" Nicole asked.

"I said you were out of town, and he answered back, 'No, she's not. Someone saw her in Santa Monica this morning.'"

"I told him that he knew more than I did and he turned and left," Sydney said. "It was creepy. Are you in trouble?"

"No," Nicole lied, "but if anyone asks again, just say I'm out of town."

Boothe came back to the monitor. "I told the story in a nutshell to the California AG. He's going to see if he can get the FBI involved and then get a judge to allow a wiretap on Tommy. We'll know in an hour."

* * *

Henry and Susan left the house fifteen minutes later to drive to pick up Tony. They made the 12:55 ferry to Anacortes with only minutes to spare and headed directly to Seattle. Nicole called them forty minutes later telling them to check in at the Four Seasons Hotel on Union and First Avenue. The room and parking would be taken care of by Bobby Boothe.

284

The 3:00 p.m. ferry from Anacortes to Lopez unloaded on time. Exiting the ferry, a black Escalade with license plates dirty enough to be unreadable headed south on Ferry Road toward Center Road. After two wrong turns, the Escalade turned down Dusty Road and backed into the same turnout to Fadder's shed that had been used a decade earlier when Tony had been kidnapped. Two men exited the Escalade, surveyed the area carefully, and then walked slowly toward the Marrone home. They returned thirty minutes later to wait. No one had been home. They stayed in the car until six the following morning, and then departed to catch the 6:40 ferry off the island.

* * *

"Paul and Ralph, I think you will all need protection for a while," Charles said. "I will too. I don't think Tom Clark knows about Paul being involved."

"He probably does know Paul's in on this," Michaels said. "Whoever told Howard Resine that someone illegally opened Claire's file probably told someone else, unless it was Howard himself. How else would McNeil have been eliminated? I'll have some housecleaning to do when this all ends."

Charles nodded agreement and added, "Tom Clark certainly knows about me and has scores to settle and knows Ralph is a close friend of the governor. I'm guessing he thinks you found out what happened. He must know something about Nicole or will soon enough. Until we get this straight, you may all want to check into a hotel and stay away from your houses."

"Really. Is that necessary?" Michaels said.

"You'd have to ask Dr. McNeil that, but of course, he's dead," Charles said. "Sorry for the gutter humor. Do any of you carry a firearm?"

Michaels and Paul said "No" simultaneously.

"I have a handgun but I'm not registered to carry in California," Nicole said.

"Ever used it?" Michaels asked.

"Yes. It's the same type as my service sidearm, a Glock nine-millimeter. Maybe better."

Michaels blinked hard.

Boothe said, "Nicole, I'll take care of getting you registered. Consider it done. I'll be back in a few minutes. I've got the attorney general of California on the line."

"Governor, before you take the other call, did you explain to Claire what's going on here?" Charles asked.

"No. Only that it was a mistake," Boothe said. "I will explain everything in due time."

"Trouble is Tom Clark doesn't know what Claire and even Becky might know. You may want to increase security for them too," Charles said. "Maybe they can stay at your apartment downtown."

"I agree with you, Fred, but hold on," Boothe said. "I've got to handle this call from the AG."

Once Boothe left the screen, Nicole said, "My Marine friend was driving up this morning from San Diego. I trust him. I expect him at Paul's apartment about now."

* * *

Allen Rogers arrived at Paul's apartment just before 3:00 p.m. He found the key as promised over the hallway light. He let himself in and threw his suitcase into the small, second bedroom closet.

Rogers then received a text from Nicole:

> *I'm guessing ur in Santa Monica. Got a call from roommate. She says somebody was looking for me. I'm guessing they'll be looking at Paul's next. If so watch your six.*

Rogers:

> *I'm here. All quiet. Where's your Glock?*

Nicole:

> *In my purse. You armed?*

Rogers:

> *Always. I'll go out and check perimeter. When u come back, park outside or take Uber. Garage not safe.*

Nicole:

> *I'll text you when heading back.*

Rogers:

> *OK.*

Rogers put his revolver under his coat and headed out. He scanned the periphery of Paul's apartment looking for places where someone could watch comings and goings. The front of the inside third-floor unit had no outside visual sightlines, but the back had a porch and large sliding glass door that opened into the main bedroom. One hundred ten yards to the west was a four-story parking structure with a flat roof and perfect sightlines. He turned on all the lights in the bedroom, draped a red towel over the guardrail on the porch, then exited the apartment building and walked to the parking garage and climbed to the top. Rust-red access doors to the roof stood in opposite corners of the garage. Each had clearly posted signs – NO ACCESS TO ROOF. One door had a sturdy padlock while the other had a mere passage lock with a cheap strike plate. Using a credit card, Rogers opened the door in seconds, climbed the stairs onto the roof, walked to the east edge, and looked west. The red towel marked the apartment.

If I wanted a clean shot, this is where I'd be.

Rogers walked back to the apartment, removed the towel from the porch, and drew the curtains. He then texted Nicole.

We're going to need at least one more set of eyes. Wish Karso or Lazee were here.

Nicole:

Me 2. Century Security will provide cover. 310-422-8772. Ask for David Hart. Boothe will have talked to him.

Rogers:

OK. These guys probably have eyes on you from following the lawyer. Let me know when ur on way back.

Nicole:

OK.

Fifteen minutes later, two armed guards from Century Security were heading toward Santa Monica and met Rogers in the parking lot. One, Otis, had been in the US Army, the other, Brad, a policeman from New Jersey. The security team brought walkie-talkie ear buds.

Rogers laid out his security plan. He'd return to the apartment to watch Nicole and Paul. Otis would stay on the parking garage's fourth floor, and Brad would stay on the street across from the apartment building's entrance and underground parking.

Once in place, Rogers and the guards confirmed communications and waited. Rogers' phone vibrated an incoming text just after 4:00 p.m.

Nicole:

On way w/ Paul. Ur right. Guy in corner watching.

Rogers:

I'm in apt. 2 guards outside with me. Text when parking.

Nicole:

K.

Fifteen minutes later, Otis reported two men on the garage fourth floor. One man jimmied the access door lock and stood to the side watching the garage. The second man, carrying a long duffel bag, closed the door and ascended the stairs. Rogers peered through the drapes in the darkened bedroom until he saw the man on the roof scanning Paul's building with binoculars, counting the porches from right to left until settling on Paul's porch.

Rogers radioed, "I'll replace Brad in front. Brad to assist Otis. I'll call the Santa Monica PD and get a SWAT team here. Don't even think about going up on the top floor of the garage."

Rogers then called 911 and quickly told the receiving officer about a shooter on the roof deck and a guard at the access door. He told them to come quietly, stay clear of Fifth Avenue, and come from the west from Fourth.

Nicole:

Turning onto 5th.

Rogers:

All clear in front. Park and come up.

Nicole:

K.

Rogers scanned the building front. Parked cars and pedestrians were everywhere. He rechecked the underground lot and waited for Nicole and Paul, then entered and parked. Rogers, back to Paul's parking spot, watched the underground parking entrance. No one had followed Paul's car into the lot, but Rogers assumed that eyes were on the street telling the men in the parking roof that Paul and Nicole had returned.

Nicole jumped out of the car and bear-hugged Rogers from the back as he watched the entrance.

"All clear here. Let's get out of the garage," Rogers said.

The three entered the stairwell and ascended to Paul's floor. Rogers exited the stairwell and led Paul and Nicole into the apartment.

Once in the unit, Rogers locked the door.

"Don't go into your bedroom," Rogers said. "There's a shooter on the roof across the street. I've got two guards in place and more coming."

"Nice to meet you finally," Paul said. "Thanks for coming."

"Nice to meet you too," Rogers said. "For a doc, you're not too bright getting involved with Marrone."

"Thanks, Sarge," Nicole said. "Then I'm not too bright getting involved with the likes of you."

"Okay, you two. I get it," Paul said. "Anyway, thanks for being here. I know it makes Nicole happy. Not too many people she trusts around here right now."

"What's the plan?" Nicole said.

"I want to keep those idiots on the roof there until the SWAT team arrives. They can't see in the bedroom with the drapes closed and the lights off. I'm going to partially open the drapes and get out of the bedroom. We'll turn the light on and off slowly and let him wait."

Rogers entered the dark bedroom and, staying close to the walls, inched around to the sliding door and opened the curtains about two feet. He then inched back to the bedroom door and turned on the lights, and turned them off five minutes later.

Five minutes later, Otis radioed Rogers that the SWAT squad had arrived and closed off the garage.

Otis radioed back ten minutes later that the door guard and shooter were in cuffs and the police captain would be up to Paul's apartment to interview Rogers in about thirty minutes.

As they waited for the police, Otis radioed again. "Hey, Sarge. These guys were serious. The sniper had a Heckler and Koch MSG90 rifle with a Hensoldt telescopic sight. Gotta cost twenty-five k."

"That figures," Rogers said. "You guys can come around to the building front and keep eyes out. Doubt we'll have any more trouble. I'm guessing they had eyes out front and know about the guys on the roof. Doubt they'll do anything here now."

Nicole gave Rogers a big hug and kiss on the cheek. "Thanks for being here," she said.

"Does that mean we're even," Rogers said, smiling.

"No. Never. I always want you to owe me," Nicole said. She hugged Rogers again.

"Okay, you two. Tell me everything that's happened. This ain't gonna end yet," Rogers said.

For the next twenty minutes, Nicole and Paul told as much as they could.

Rogers thought for a moment. "Unless this advisor guy for Boothe has his own army, it's likely he's got some powerful connections in the underworld that are doing his work. The underworld guy could be anyone, but we'll call him Mr. Big. Now that we've got a couple of Mr. Big's guys, they know we're on to him. I'm guessing this advisor's ass is new-mown grass with Mr. Big. He's likely more afraid of the advisor than he is of us. They're not going to let him talk, which means they're probably not going to let him live. If I were this asshole, I'd be out of the country, now and forever, or go to the Feds and ask for protection. My guess is, if he's got money stashed away in the Cayman Islands or Switzerland, he'll leave. If he stays, at the least, he'll be up on accessory charges for Nicole's brother's kidney and the deaths of McNeil and his wife."

"I just called Fred Charles and let him know about the guys on the roof," Nicole said anxiously. "We're both concerned about Claire Boothe. The governor didn't want to tell her what this is all about yet. She could be in trouble and not know it."

"Is he going to call the Gov?" Paul asked.

"Boothe is on an airplane heading back from Hawaii. Won't be in until later tonight," Nicole said. "Charles thinks I should go over there just to be with her. He'll get hold of Century Security too. You and Sarge can come after you're done talking to the local PD."

* * *

After the Santa Monica police team arrived, Nicole called Claire Boothe.

"Hey, you mind if I come over?"

"What's going on?" Claire asked. "Fred said you might be coming over and to say yes. This has been the strangest twenty-four hours. First, Dr.

Michaels calls and tells Becky you're in a boatload of trouble and not to speak to you. Then he called this morning to say it's a big mistake and it had to do with my dad. I didn't even know that you'd ever met my father. What the hell is happening?"

"It's a long story. Is Becky there?" Nicole asked.

"No. She's at work but called to say that Dr. Michaels cancelled all his work and wouldn't say why. She's just sitting around doing nothing."

"I think you better call her and have her come home. She really needs to come back," Nicole said.

"Why? Is something still wrong?"

"Yes. But I think I need to be there with you and Becky needs to be there too. I'm going to head over now." Nicole hung up and said, "I'm going."

"You didn't tell her we were coming later," Paul said.

"Yeah. That'd just scare her more. I'll explain when I get there."

* * *

Nicole arrived at Claire's mansion thirty minutes later.

Lucas and JoJo were both at the gate when Nicole got out of Paul's car.

"Hey, Miss Marrone," Lucas said.

"Hey. Did Claire tell you I was coming?"

294

"Yeah. Nice wheels," JoJo added.

"It's my boyfriend's car. Too nice for the likes of me. Listen up, you two. You need to know that there's some shit going down that Claire and Becky don't know about. So just be extra careful and eyes on everything," Nicole said.

"What's up?" Lucas asked.

"Long, long story that I can't tell you about until Claire knows first. Just be extra careful."

"Oorah," Lucas said as Nicole drove away up the driveway.

Nicole entered the house, said hello to Li Yong at the door and walked back to the pool area to find Claire sitting on a chaise reading a novel. Nicole drew up a rattan chair and sat next to her.

"Hi," Claire said. "You want to explain everything to me?"

"I'd love to but this whole situation is so whacky that I think Becky needs to be here and perhaps your mom and dad. It's that crazy," Nicole said.

"Do you even know my dad?"

"I've never met the governor in person, but I did talk to him a bit for the first time last night and today on a live feed from Hawaii. He seemed nice, if that matters."

"He is nice. What the hell is going on? This whole thing mystifies me. Becky had not a clue

what was going on either. Can't you tell me?"
Claire asked.

"No. I can't but I'm here. Let's wait."

"And why exactly did you need to be here?
That's a mystery too." Claire sat up, facing Nicole.

"All I can say is that something very strange
and very illegal happened, and it involves you, me,
your dad, and my friend Paul Roberts, a transplant
fellow at UCLA."

"Is Becky involved in this? I'd guess not
because she doesn't seem to know any more than I
do."

"You're right. Becky is not involved. But since
she's your partner, she might be in harm's way,"
Nicole said.

"Harm's way? How? What did I do or what do I
know that would put me in harm's way?"

"Actually," Nicole said, "you did nothing and
know nothing, at this point. But..."

"Aha, the *but*," Claire said.

"The people who would want to hurt you and
Becky don't know that you don't know anything."

"Okay, I'm frustrated. Becky will be home in
half an hour and my dad's supposed to touch
down at seven p.m. So I guess we'll wait," Claire
said. "Can Li Yong get you something to eat?"

"It's okay," Nicole said. "I can wait for Becky,
but I don't know that we can talk about this..."

"Hold on," Claire interrupted, as her cell phone vibrated and the screen lit up. "FRONT GATE." She pushed one button on the screen and put the phone to her ear.

"Uh. Really. That's strange but this has been a very strange day. Okay, sure. Send him up." Claire disconnected. "What a day. My dad's longtime campaign manager was at the gate and says he has to talk to me. He was like an uncle and his wife an aunt to me until a few years ago when he and my dad parted ways."

Nicole sat up straight. "You mean Tom Clark is here?"

"For someone who doesn't know much about my dad, how do you know the name of his old campaign manager?" Claire asked.

"Because he just happens to be the one that worries your dad, Fred Charles, and me. You shouldn't have let him up," Nicole said.

"No. He's fine. We were so close and I know him. He's not a dangerous person. Trust me," Claire said. "I'm going to go to the door to greet him. Li Yong won't know who he his."

"I'm not comfortable with this."

"Well, he's already on his way up, and you're being silly."

"You have to do me a favor then before you let him in," Nicole said. "It's absolutely essential."

"What's that?"

"Don't use my real name. I suspect he knows me by name but not by my look. Call me Mary Brown. Marrone means brown in Italian. Please."

"Okay, okay. Mary Brown it is. You're such a worry wart." Claire then stood, slipped on a pair of flip-flops, squeezed Nicole's shoulder, and walked out of the pool area to the front door.

Nicole moved quickly to her purse, which was sitting on a nearby table, and extracted her nine-millimeter Glock and a full magazine of six 124-gram Speer Gold Dot shells. Eyes only on the entrance to the pool area, she pulled the gun slide back, shoved the magazine in place, and released the slide with her right thumb. The gun was cocked and loaded. She knew the Glock's safe-action trigger would prevent her from firing an unwanted round. She quickly grabbed a beach towel from a pile near Claire's chaise, wrapped herself in the towel, and sat at the table. The gun sat in her lap.

Nicole heard voices and multiple footsteps coming down the hallway to the pool area.

More footsteps than expected? More than one person?

Claire turned the corner first, followed by a nattily dressed, smallish man in his late fifties, handsome, clean-shaven, dark hair parted neatly on the side, and piercing brown eyes. His right hand was slender, almost effete, while his left hand rested in the pocket of a five-thousand-dollar Italian wool suit. Nicole assumed correctly that this would be Tom Clark. He smiled broadly and confidently as he entered the room.

Following Clark, a larger man walked in. He had a two-day shave and wore an ill-fitting suit looking like it had been taken from a rack at Goodwill. The man quickly scanned the room, including a quick turnaround to see if someone had followed him in. Without being asked, he stood at the corner of the entrance, erect, with his hands folded in front of him. He was fifteen feet from Nicole, off to her right.

"Uncle Tom, this is...uh, Mary. Mary Brown. She's a nurse at UCLA and works with Becky," Claire said.

Clark nodded hello.

Claire looked intently at Nicole. "What's with the blanket? You cold?"

"Yeah," Nicole said. "I just felt chilled. Maybe I'm catching something. Do you mind if I don't stand?"

"No problem. Do you want some tea?"

"No. I'm fine."

"This is my pseudo-uncle, Tom Clark. I've known him my whole life," Claire said.

"Nice to meet you, Mr. Clark," Nicole said.

"Nice to meet you too, Mary," Clark said. He then turned to Claire. "I've got something personal to talk about. Do you think we can be alone?"

"Mary is a very close friend and confidant. Whatever you ask me, I'll just tell her when you leave. She might as well stay."

"Have it your way then," Clark said, not nicely.

Claire resumed her position on the chaise and Clark took the seat that Nicole had vacated.

"I'm sorry it's been so long since we've seen each other," Clark said.

"Me too. A shame," Claire said. "What's up?"

"I need a favor."

"Okay."

"Do you still have your own plane at the Santa Monica airfield?" Clark asked.

"Yes. Of course," Claire said.

"I need to get to Nicaragua by tonight for a business deal. There are no commercial flights available, and I'm happy to pay all the expenses. It would be a great favor to me. Can you help me out?"

"You know it's my dad's old plane that was too small once he got elected Governor. He made me promise that I would never loan it out. I don't want him getting upset with me. I'd have to ask him," Claire said.

"That won't do. I need to go now to get there tonight. Not to mention the fact that Bobby and I aren't seeing eye-to-eye right now. He'll probably say no just because it's me."

"I don't know about this," Claire said.

"Your dad doesn't need to know you've helped me," Clark said. "Aunt Joan was planning to come with me for some vacation time. I just need the ride there, and the plane can turn around and head back without me. I thought Joan and I would head to the beaches in Costa Rica afterwards. Please. It's important."

"I'm sorry. I just can't do it. I don't like sneaking behind my dad's back," Claire said. "I have to say no."

Clark sat for a moment gritting his teeth and shaking his head. "Please, Claire. I've never asked you for a favor before," he said.

"I can't do it," Claire said. "If you need money for a regular flight for you and Aunt Joan, I'm happy to loan you the money."

"It's not the money. I need to go today. Not tomorrow. You owe me, dammit."

Nicole's mind wandered to another day. *The motor pool walkie-talkie erupting, "Marrone, Marrone. We're in trouble. Marrone."*

"I'm sorry, the answer's no. And I don't owe you anything," Claire said.

"Yeah, you do. You owe me your life. Without me, you wouldn't be sitting here so nice and easy."

"I don't know what you're talking about, and I don't appreciate your tone."

"You'd be dead now if it weren't for me. Even your dad doesn't know about it. If it gets out, Bobby will never get elected to anything."

"I have no idea what you're talking about. The answer is still no," Claire said.

Nicole blinked. *I know what he's talking about. Tony's kidney.*

Clark gripped the rattan chair's arm hard enough to snap a few strands of weaving. He stood, looked back at the man standing in the corner of the room and then back to Claire. "I'm afraid then, I'll have to make you do it," he demanded loudly.

"You can't make me do anything I don't want to do," Claire said. "What's gotten into you?"

"I'm desperate and I'm in trouble and I have to get out of the country today. Your plane is my only way out of the US. I can't go to the airport!"

Nicole blinked as Clark's tone set off a trigger. *We were set up. Six of us in a small hut...third of a click... We're surrounded... We're almost out of ammo.*

"I can't help you and certainly not when you're acting like this," Claire said. "I want you to leave my house."

"I'm not going until you say yes. If I have to use force, I will," Clark said.

Nicole quickly moved her head toward the man at the door. His hands had moved to the lapels just outside of his ill-fitting suit.

Li Yong walked into the room past the man at the door. "I heard noises all the way into the kitchen. Is something wrong?"

"Yes. This man used to be a close friend but is now threatening me, I'd like you to show him out," Claire said.

"I'm not leaving," Clark yelled again.

Li Yong looked to Nicole wrapped in the beach towel. "Nicole, are you okay?"

Nicole's eyes widened as she shook her head violently *no* toward Li Yong.

"Nicole. What's wrong? Can I get you something?" Li Yong asked again.

"Li Yong, you can leave," Claire said.

Clark's head swiveled quickly to Li Yong. "No, I want you to stay. You said her name was Nicole. I thought this lady's name was Mary?"

"No, it's Nicole..." Li Yong started.

"Li Yong, be quiet," Claire demanded.

Clark's head turned quickly, looking at a frightened Li Yong and Nicole, wrapped in a blanket and turning her head back and forth between the man at the door and Clark.

"Nicole, huh," Clark screamed. "Now I get it. You're not Mary at all. You're here to fuck me. You think you've figured it all out, do you?"

"What are you talking about?" Claire asked. "This is crazy."

"What I'm talking about is that you're alive, your dad is about to be President, and this nosy cunt is trying to fuck us all," Clark spewed. "Her brother is fine, I checked. Still stupid. And you're alive because of it."

"What are you talking about?" Claire pleaded. "Whose brother? You're not making any sense."

Nicole's right index finger slid firmly over the trigger, feeling the play of the Glock safe-action mechanism.

"I'm going to kill two birds with one stone. Makes it easy," Clark said calmly. "Either you call and get me on your plane, or I kill your friend, your cook, and take you with me."

"I'll do nothing of the sort, and you're not going to harm anyone. Nicole was right. I shouldn't have let you up here." Claire was now standing. She pointed a finger at Clark. "Get out of here and take that goon at the door with you. I'll never give you a ride."

Clark turned to the man at the door. As calmly as one would order a side of fries, he said, "Kill her now," pointing at Nicole. "It's all her fault."

We need backup now or we're dead. Marrone, do you...

The man started walking rapidly toward Nicole. With the first step his right hand entered his jacket. With his second step his hand grabbed something under his coat. With his third step his hand cleared the coat lapel with a pistol and silencer. At the same moment, Li Yong and Claire screamed and Nicole brought her Glock above the table edge. With his fourth step the man's eyes widened as his gun pointed toward Nicole.

304

stab wound

Pop. Pop. Pop.

Chapter 20

The screaming lasted for minutes.

"Oh God," Claire yelled. "Oh my God. Oh my God."

Blood covered the floor and the walls near the entrance to the room.

Li Yong lay on the floor, passed out. Claire continued to scream, "Oh my God."

Nicole stood and faced Clark. She didn't need to look at the man on the floor in a pool of blood. The first bullet had entered his skull just above the left eye. The second grazed his scalp, and the third entered the top of the pool entrance's transom. Nicole didn't care about bullets two and three.

The man's gun lay beside him, equidistant between Nicole and Clark. Clark took one step toward it.

"I'd stop if I were you," Nicole said. "Nothing, and I mean nothing, would make me happier than you trying to pick up that gun. If you could only know how much grief you caused my family. Back off."

Clark looked at the gun, the dead man, Claire, and then Nicole. "Kill me if you want," he said as he turned and ran out the door.

Nicole followed Clark, who exited the house and drove away without looking back. She ran back to the pool to find Claire sitting on the ground trying to revive Li Yong.

Nicole put the gun under her waistband and faced Claire. "Call Lucas and JoJo," she said, "and tell them there was a shooting and not to let Clark leave until the police come. He may be armed, so they need to be careful."

Claire, visibly shaking, handed Nicole her cell phone and said, "Press four one star dial, I can't do it."

Nicole picked up her phone from the table and called Lucas at the gate to warn him and then the Los Angeles police to report a shooting.

She then joined Claire on the floor, trying to console Li Yong, who had awakened to find herself covered in blood. While Nicole wiped blood from the cook's face and glasses, Claire had her in a loving and rocking hug. Claire's phone vibrated and lit up once again with "FRONT GATE." Claire handed the phone to Nicole.

"Miss Boothe, it's me, it's me, Lucas. Something terrible has happened. Something..."

"Lucas, stop. It's me, Nicole, Miss Boothe is busy. What's happened?"

"Both JoJo and me we was armed when that man come barreling down the driveway," Lucas said in staccato fashion. "He stopped at the gate 'cause it's closed and yelled, 'Let me out.' I told him we were told not to let him leave until the police arrive. He started to reach into his glove compartment and I yelled for him to stop. He rolled up his window, and JoJo and me, we backed away with our guns pointed at the car. I didn't know what this asshole was going to do. He put his seat back almost flat and then the next thing I hear is a gunshot. I look over at JoJo and she's okay and heard it too. We walked over to the car, and he just shot himself in the head. There be blood everywhere."

* * *

When the Los Angeles Police left Claire Boothe's mansion at 2:00 a.m., Nicole called her mother in Seattle at the Four Seasons Hotel.

"I know it's the middle of the night, but everything is okay now. You and Dad can go home in the morning," Nicole said.

"I haven't been sleeping. We've been worried sick about you again. What happened? Why were we in danger?" Susan Marrone asked, seemingly lucid despite the late hour.

"It's a long, complicated story and one that I can't tell you over the phone. I have a close friend here in Los Angeles whose dad is the ex-governor of California. I was mistaken for someone trying to hurt him," Nicole lied. "That put our family in danger, but it was all a mistake. You're safe, that I'm sure of. As I think about it, maybe it's better if you stayed in the hotel for a couple of days and use room service. The hotel bill will be taken care of, every penny. I'll call you later this afternoon to make sure you're okay."

"I need to know what happened, Nicole. I'm your mother," Susan pleaded.

"I promise I'll be up to Lopez in a week to spend time with you and Dad and Tony and try to explain of all this. Maybe Paul Roberts, you know the doctor from Seattle Med that was my friend, will come too. Until then, don't worry. I'll call you tomorrow and give you a better idea of when I'm coming. Bye, Mom. I love you and Dad."

* * *

Thirty-six hours later, Nicole, Paul, Fred Charles, Becky, Claire, Bobby and Beverly Boothe sat in Claire's living room trying to make sense of the past three days. Allen Rogers had already gone back to Camp Pendleton. By this time, all seven knew the entire saga of the Marrone family.

"Where do we go from here?" Becky asked. "Hopefully we can go back to our normal lives."

"I don't think anyone in this room has a normal life," Charles snickered, "but I see what you're getting at."

"Honestly, I'd like to get back to Seattle," Paul said. "That's, of course, if Dr. Michaels will let me."

"He'll understand," Governor Boothe said. "He told me that he's already talked to your chief, Dr. Muller, and everything is fine."

"Either place, people are going to be pestering me for the story," Paul said. "Too bad there's no rotation I could do in Mongolia or Timbuktu."

"Nicole, what do your parents know?" Charles asked.

"Nothing yet. I talked to them right after the police left and then five or six hours later. I told them they could go home in a couple of days and not to worry. I'm going to head up there day after

309

tomorrow and make sure things are explained and settled before coming back to work and nursing school."

"They must have questions," Paul said.

"I told them it's all a big mistake," Nicole said. "I lied that some political crazies who knew the governor confused me for someone else. I don't even know if my parents know about Clark's suicide or the McNeils."

"They don't know yet about me getting your brother's kidney?" Claire asked.

"No, and I don't know when or how I'm going to tell them. It will come out, but I think I need to be there when that happens. Maybe Paul too."

"I'd come if that would help," Governor Boothe said.

"Me too," Beverly and Claire Boothe said simultaneously.

"Not yet," Nicole said. "They'd be overwhelmed."

"How are they going to take it, you think?" Beverly asked.

"God, I wish I knew," Nicole said.

"Bobby, are you going to announce for president next week as planned?" Charles asked.

"I've told my staff to hold off for a week. A lot depends on Nicole and her family, I guess," the governor said.

"Really," Nicole said, "I'm not that important."

"Actually, you're not, but your brother and the story are," the governor said. "We don't know how the media is going to spin it, how my competitors are going to spin it, and how the public is going to accept it. How your family reacts will be huge."

"You did nothing wrong," Nicole said. "Claire and I heard Tom Clark say that specifically. He had nothing to gain by lying to us at that time."

"Yeah, but doing nothing wrong doesn't sell ad space on cable news," Beverly said.

"I am wealthy, running for president, and your brother was helpless. That's enough for a media heyday."

"I'd campaign like hell for you," Nicole said. "It'd be hard to say the family wanted blood when my mother and I are standing next to you smiling and waving. Let's see how my parents do. Tony won't care."

"I am going to hold off until I hear from you," the governor said. "I'd take the high road and tell them absolutely everything. You can never go wrong or have to backtrack off the truth."

Later that night, Beverly Boothe confronted Bobby. "You know you can't make restitution to Nicole's family. It'll look like you bought them off."

"You're right," Boothe said. "I was thinking how we could make things right for them. They suffered greatly."

311

"Later, Bobby, later. When the election is over, we can make it right."

* * *

Nicole and Paul flew into Seattle two nights later. The July sun had yet to set and massive Mt. Ranier, all 15,000 feet and snow capped, stood guard over the Emerald city.

"Still takes my breath away," Nicole said as they Ubered to Paul's condo. They left early the next morning for Lopez Island.

"Sooner or later you'll need to decide what exactly you're going to tell your parents?" Paul asked.

"Yeah. I think I'll tell them everything."

They walked into the Marrones' small three-room cottage on Lopez Island three hours later.

The Marrones had purchased the cottage when Nicole was in Afghanistan. The home had been a summer getaway for a wealthy family from Portland, Oregon. When the younger generation wanted nothing to do with Lopez Island, the seldom seen cottage fell apart. After three years and no offers or showings, the family was desperate to sell – to anyone.

Henry had finally put two nickels together from driving long haul trucks and made a low ball offer which was accepted. When his credit check at the three different banks failed because of the earlier bankruptcy, the deal collapsed. Two months later and no offers or showings in the horizon, the family contacted the Marrones

312

privately and offered to finance the sale without a bank. The Marrones accepted and moved back to Lopez. Nicole had forewarned Paul that the home needed work badly

"Mom, Dad," Nicole said, "this is Dr. Paul Roberts. Paul, my mom, Susan, and my dad, Henry. You know Tony."

"So nice to meet you finally, Paul. Tony spoke so highly of you," Susan said.

"Amazing what a Big Mac and fries will do," Paul said.

"Ooh," Tony said, "you shouldn't have said that."

"Amen. You must know we would never let the kids eat fast food," Henry said. "But forgiven."

"Why don't you two get unpacked first. Tony's moved out of his room," Susan said.

Twenty minutes later, Nicole and Paul returned to the small central living area-kitchen.

"Let's sit and talk," Susan said.

"Yes. It's going to take a while to get this all out," Nicole said.

Nicole and Paul talked for almost three hours and then repeated the story in parts over the next three days.

* * *

"Governor, this is Nicole Marrone."

"Yes, Nicole. How are you doing?"

"Fine. I've been at home with my family for four days, and I'll be heading back to Los Angeles tomorrow."

"Claire has asked if I talked to you," Boothe said. "I told her you'd call when you were ready."

"I'm ready now, Governor. Go ahead and announce," Nicole said. "The Marrone family will not be a problem. They were mystified about the whole thing, but at the end of the day, my mom says all of us, including Tony, are doing well. I've told them how Tony's kidney possibly saved Claire's life and how wonderful she has been to me, even before we knew about her transplant. I think that was the most important thing to my mom."

* * *

Nicole and Paul drove back to Seattle and stayed the night in Paul's apartment.

"You're going again," Paul lamented, lying next to Nicole, looking up at the ceiling. "You know how I feel, but you don't know how I do when you're not here. It's brutal."

"I know, I know," Nicole said, "but I want to finish the nursing program at St. Mary's. It'll take two years, and I'll regret every moment of my life if I don't finish."

Paul continued staring at the ceiling, looking as if he might cry.

Nicole rolled toward him and kissed his eyes and nose. "Some time ago you said you loved me. I knew you meant it. I responded that I loved you too, but both of us knew I was just using words."

Paul nodded tacit agreement.

"Tell me you love me again," Nicole said.

"You know how I feel," Paul said.

"Tell me anyway."

"Okay. I love you."

"I know and I love you too. I will never find another man who puts me first every time over himself. I talked to my mom for hours the last two nights on Lopez. She watched you looking at me and could see that you're hopelessly in love. She asked if I loved you and I said I think so."

"Well, that's pretty definite," Paul said.

"My mom agreed with you and told me that she was disappointed in me and 'think so' isn't good enough for you, her, or me. So she asked me again, 'Do you love him?'"

Paul waited.

"I said that I would never know anyone else I would want to spend the rest of my life with but you."

"Really. You mean that?" Paul asked, now looking at Nicole.

"Mom said she knew I'd been burned so many times by bad relationships but that I need to take a leap of faith. She promised me that I could search the ends of the earth and never discover someone as nice to me as you, someone who would love me as much. She promised me that if I did take that leap, I would be the happiest person in the world."

"What are you saying?"

"I'm saying that I love you and I want to be with you forever."

"Really?"

"Really. Finish at Seattle Med and find a job in Los Angeles for two years. After I've got my RN, I'll go anywhere in world with you, and that includes Mongolia or Timbuktu."

"Will you marry me?" Paul asked.

"Of course," Nicole said, straddling Paul and holding his arms against the headboard, then laughed. "I thought you'd never ask."

Epilogue

Robert "Bobby" Gary Boothe was elected President of the United States with 56 percent of the popular votes and a two-to-one majority of the Electoral College.

Dr. and Mrs. Paul Roberts, Henry, Susan, and Tony Marrone sat just behind Claire Boothe and Becky Brown at the inauguration.

Two months later Claire Boothe and Henry Marrone became partners in an Italian restaurant, Henry's, on Lopez Island. On the restaurant's opening night, July Fourth, the guest list included the President, a Republican, First Lady, the governor of Washington State, a Democrat, both Washington senators, and all the members of the San Juan County Council. The next open reservation for a table at Henry's would be three months later.

As soon as Nicole finished her RN degree at St. Mary's, Paul left his urology position at Kaiser Permanente in Los Angeles and took a job as an assistant professor of urology at the University of Michigan.

The number and variety of "Go Blue" T-shirts available in the local Ann Arbor stores overwhelmed Nicole. She bought ten, five for her and five for Paul.

Walking back to their apartment off Main Street in Ann Arbor, something unusual caught Nicole's eye.

"What's this?" Paul asked that evening, looking at an unopened box on the living room sofa. "A catapult kit? Fifty-five easy pieces? Who's this for?"

39315559R10189

Made in the USA
Middletown, DE
17 March 2019